# Living Memories

## Jerome and Rosella Goddard

Livingston Press
The University of West Alabama

isbn 13: 978-1-60489-117-1, trade paper

Library of Congress Control Number 2013930866

Typesetting and page layout: Joe Taylor
Proofreading: Warren Enriquez, Carmon Hamilton, Alesha McNeese,
Melissa Lafond, Creed Robbins, Morgan Jowers, Emma Kay McClung
Cover design and layout: Laura C. McKee
Cover art: Charlie Busler

# Living Memories

*To our sons and daughter-in-laws,*

*Jeremy and Lindsey*

*Joseph and Lauren*

# Chapter One

*C*ould a *man* experience a *woman's* memory? Dr. Gregory Poindexter wondered this as he sat in a university laboratory one afternoon watching a video consisting of a complex pattern of flashing lights and colors. He was about to find out. Dr. Poindexter stared at the screen trying to absorb the pattern of dancing lines and colors on the video player. They weren't ordinary squiggly lines and light flashes, somewhat similar to a television barely receiving a signal. These were derived from medical, brain-scan firing patterns. Soon the researcher slipped into a dream-like state and was enveloped in a thousand sensations; he was re-living the memory. Someone else's memory. Yellow iridescent light swirled in his periphery, but the center of his field of view remained clear. The memory was clear and realistic, though in some ways like looking through a viewfinder, except that emotions accompanied it. Intense emotions such as fear, anxiety, even panic, all from a female point of view. Very strange:

*It was a day early in March, which had started out seasonally warm, but now was radically different, as if the weather had suddenly turned schizophrenic. Wind barreled down the natural corridor, whipping the river into an angry frenzy. A cold front must have been coming through. Dark clouds hung low overhead as the girl and her boyfriend crossed the choppy mile-wide river in a small fishing boat. Ice-cold water sprayed into her face each time they hit a large wave and soon lapped at her ankles in the bottom of the boat. A sense of panic seized her when the wind began to howl out of the northwest which was, unfortunately, perfectly in line with the direction of the river. She was experienced enough with the Tennessee River to know this meant trouble. Big trouble. The girl watched her boyfriend wrestle the boat against the wind and waves, tossing them back and forth, making it almost impossible to head toward shore. They wouldn't make it. She was sure of that.*

*Waves, growing ever larger in size, slammed them from the left, causing that side of the boat to be temporarily airborne each time. She screamed and held on to the sides of the boat as it rocked violently. The boy gripped the steering wheel like a cat hanging on the side of a tree. His face went white and large veins became visible along his arms and neck. She knew that if they capsized in the frigid waters of the Tennessee River during a ferocious storm like this, they might not be able to swim to shore.*

*The girl gave a death-scream as a monster wave sent the boat flipping through the air, slinging its occupants headfirst into the icy river water.*

Inside the lab, Dr. Poindexter grabbed his head trying to ease the intensity of the memory. He grabbed at the air as if holding on to the sides of the boat, then fell to the floor, flailing wildly, unable to stop the sensation of sinking in the icy waters. He kicked his feet and waved his arms, desperately trying to swim upward, even though there wasn't a drop of water inside the room where he was. Chairs, tables, and lab supplies flew in all directions as a result of his frenetic movements.

Then, as if someone had hit the "play" button again, the memory repeated in the young researcher's mind, this time with fresher feeling and intensity. He jumped up, trying to shake it off. Going through this once was enough. He didn't want to experience it again. But, sure enough, after two minutes, Gregory was again in the floor flailing wildly, unable to stop the feeling of being sucked deeper and deeper into the frigid water.

For the next twenty minutes, the memory replayed itself in his head, each time with new vigor and intensity. The feelings were strong and oppressive, almost as if they had a malevolent personality. In every instance, he ended up falling to the floor, flailing wildly, unable to stop the feeling of drowning.

Finally, like a huge storm moving ever so slowly across the countryside, the tragic memory retreated deep into Dr. Poindexter's subconscious. He sat back up in the chair thinking about what had happened, his body now bruised and aching from the violent movements.

This was serious business all right. He had just re-lived a memory. And one that wasn't even his. He thought of the obvious implications. What would happen if someone figured out a way to readily transfer memories from one person to another? Maybe even make that person thinks it was his or her own memory. Or, on the other hand, move therapeutically "happy" memories to a depressed person.

He suddenly remembered he was still at work. Maybe he shouldn't have tried the experiment while others were in the building, and especially his boss, Dr. Mathis, who was across the hall in her office. He hoped she hadn't heard all the flopping and thrashing around on the floor. Had he moaned, groaned, or even screamed?

Dr. Poindexter jumped up to run to the bathroom. That would give him an excuse to see if anybody had noticed the unusual sounds coming from his office.

\*\*\*\*\*

Across the hall, Dr. Seetha Mathis was ready to get home to her daughter. It had been a hellacious day of fifteen patients at the Sleep and Memory Clinic and her regularly scheduled university classes.

About four forty-five, she made her way toward her assistant's office in the lab to ask him to lock up.

When she opened the door, he burst out, wild-eyed, crashing into her. Their heads bounced off each other's as Seetha was knocked aside.

"Oh, I'm so sorry . . ." she said, grabbing her head.

Dr. Poindexter seemed nervous. "Oh, uh, I've got to go to the restroom. Didn't mean to run you over." With that, he turned to go down the hall.

"Dex," Seetha hollered after him, still rubbing her forehead. "I'm leaving. Can you lock up?"

"Sure."

Seetha momentarily remained in the doorway. For some odd reason, her thoughts went to a day long ago when she had been in a storm with her boyfriend. Her stomach clenched with fear thinking about it. She could literally see glimpses of the raging water, and had to blink her eyes several times to clear the terrible images.

She rubbed her head again and turned to go. What had made her remember that? She hadn't thought of that incident in years. Maybe bumping heads with her assistant somehow unleashed the memory from its hiding place.

How odd, she thought. How very odd.

# Chapter Two

"*I* can't believe it." Hope Williams buried her head in her hands. "He can't be dead. I just talked to him three nights ago."

Detective Jonathon Theodore Fox examined the college coed carefully, analyzing her body language. He was skilled at discerning if someone was lying. Murders were rare in this small town of Oxford, Mississippi, the home of the University of Mississippi and previously the quaint home place of William Faulkner and John Grisham. He was already fairly sure that Miss Williams had nothing to do with the grisly murder of her ex-boyfriend. The petite brunette weighed no more than a hundred pounds and couldn't possibly have beaten the crap out of a six-foot-one athlete. The detective looked again, noting that he could almost encircle her waist with one hand.

"Are you sure it was him, Mr. Fox?"

"Yes, it was definitely him, and you can just call me 'Fox.'" He didn't want her or anybody else struggling with his long and cumbersome name.

She nodded.

"I know it's late, but I need to ask a few more questions," Fox continued. "What exactly was the nature of your relationship?"

Hope looked up, tears running down her porcelain-like cheeks. "He was my boyfriend for a year and a half. We broke up a long time ago."

"You just said you talked to him three nights ago." Fox tried to show a poker player's face.

"Yes. But we weren't back together. We were just talking."

"Did he initiate the call the other night?"

"Yes."

"So, *he* was trying to get back with *you*."

Hope looked uncomfortable. "Well, uh, yes."

Fox lightened up a little. He could tighten the screws later if need be. "Where are you from, Miss?"

"Baton Rouge. I went to LSU for two years, then transferred."

"Quite a combination — LSU and Ole Miss. They hate each other." Then he popped off impulsively, "Any other deceased boyfriends I need to know about?"

At that moment, every bit of color drained out of Hope William's face.

"Well, yes, actually."

*****

Seetha Mathis, a thirty-five year-old, half-Indian, half-Caucasian professor of physiology at the University of Mississippi, paced the floor in her upscale apartment on the edge of Turkey-Run Lake development about three miles west of Oxford. As usual, she couldn't sleep. The thoughts were there again. Memories of her ex-husband. Strong, evil, oppressive. She swore sometimes she could smell them when they emerged from hiding deep inside her brain.

"What is it about me that attracts terrible men?" she mumbled, after remembering for the millionth time how intensely evil her husband had been. "Or is it me who turns them into monsters?"

By now, Seetha had trampled the carpet in her den floor into several clearly defined paths resembling a huge spider web. She stopped dead still in mid-stride when she heard something from the upstairs bedroom.

Samantha. Was she awake? Seetha slipped up the stairs to check on her thirteen-year-old daughter who had gone to bed earlier. She found Sam sound asleep. All seemed well. Seetha paused before returning downstairs and thought about her beautiful child. Samantha was everything to her now since the divorce and Rodney's imprisonment three years ago. Good riddance. His drunken tirades had tormented them both for a decade. Not only that, but he had refused to sign the divorce papers for a long time, saying crazy stuff like, "If I can't have you; nobody else will."

But it hadn't been his obsessiveness and violent streak that sent him to jail; he had always been clever enough to avoid that. Instead, it was a money-laundering scheme at the bank where he had worked. Nonetheless, significant damage had been done. To this day, the thought of physical contact with a man unnerved her and interfered with the development of any loving-romantic relationships.

As for her daughter, Seetha had hoped the damage done to Samantha by Rodney was temporary. After all, she and Sam were both safe now that he was gone, weren't they? Apparently not, as lately Seetha had been seeing disturbing changes in Sam's behavior that signaled deep scarring. For one thing, Sam constantly looked at herself in the mirror with disgust and commented about being overweight. And Seetha had recently noticed what appeared to be cuts and scratches on her arms. Were they self-inflicted? Sam had denied it upon questioning, but Seetha knew if they appeared again she might have to take her daughter to a therapist.

Seetha went back downstairs and searched for her digital recorder, recalling how she too had demons resulting from her upbringing. Her own dad had been a hard-nosed college physics professor who for years treated Seetha like an army recruit, hollering at her, demeaning her, and harshly criticizing her. Looking back, she could see that he had probably meant well, in some twisted way, trying to help her become an academic like him. But hindsight didn't help much now; the damage was done.

Sweat broke out on her forehead as a vivid memory sparked to life in her mind, playing like an endless recording. "You're fat, Seetha. And lazy. You'll never amount to anything if you don't get more discipline in your life." The words were as clear and sharp, if not clearer, as they were twenty-five years ago. They certainly were louder now in her head than when originally spoken. She suddenly desperately wanted to run to a closet or hide under her bed.

Seetha clutched the digital recorder close to her chest, and went to the bedroom where she plugged it into an I-pod docking station. The recorder would help her through this event. Being a sleep researcher at Ole Miss had its advantages. She was able to use some of the equipment from the lab for her own personal experiments. Thank goodness for Dex, she thought. Gregory Poindexter was her Ph.D. post-doctoral researcher working on memory and sleep disorders who had helped her construct the device which played uplifting, soothing messages during her rapid eye movement, or REM, sleep periods. She had found that the messages helped ease tormenting thoughts and memories.

Seetha peeled back the aluminum foil protecting a 25 mg dose of prednisone and swallowed the pill before climbing in bed. She thought about the way she came to know that playing the device while also taking steroids seemed to overwrite deeply inscribed traumatic memories. Serendipity, she thought, as she hooked up the earphones and set the alarm so the device would come on in ninety minutes, right in the middle of her first REM period.

Seetha reached for a scientific journal on the nightstand. Maybe she could read a little before falling asleep. The article she had been reading was marked with a sticky note protruding from the journal. With a title like, "New Ways of Looking at Memory Function: Certain

Traumatic Memories Function like Viruses, Replicating Themselves," she hoped there would be some answers in it for her.

She rolled up a pillow, stuffed it behind her neck, and read on: *"The more we re-visit traumatic memories, the more deeply they become entrenched in our neural pathways. Emotions may enhance this process by activation of stress hormones. Apparently, traumatic memories create a feedback loop in which each episode of remembering and reliving produces a stress hormone response, especially adrenergic hormones which strengthen the memory itself, causing it to grow ever more vivid."*

Seetha stopped momentarily to let that sink in. "Amen on the fact that emotions enhance the whole process," she said, skipping to the next section.

*"People who have suffered traumatic experiences often say the memories escape from hiding and break loose inside them at various times. Perhaps it is a temporary dysfunction of the brain immune system, which allows undesirable memories to repeat unchecked. Extremely positive or negative emotional memories sometimes exert themselves by urges and feelings to repeat the experience anew. Memories may become dissociated from conscious awareness and voluntary control leading to behavioral reenactments."*

Seetha sat up in bed, raking a hand through her long coal black hair. There it was — right in front of her in black and white — the fact that both negative and positive memories could also exert themselves upon a person.

"I can't believe it." She stood and paced the floor again, her mind racing. "That's why my treatment works. It implants *positive* memories into areas of my brain where the traumatic memories are located, then that lets *them* work their healing magic."

After a minute, she tossed the journal on her nightstand and lay back down in bed. *Of course*, she thought. That's why, one time, after listening to an uplifting story about growing beautiful varieties of day lilies during one of her "treatments," the next day she felt distinct urges to walk into the yard and smell the flowers.

Seetha reached to turn off the lamp. Her hands were trembling. The steroids were starting to make her jittery.

Good. She knew that somehow the drug heightened her nervousness, enlivening areas of her brain where the traumatic memories were deeply embedded. Where ensembles of neurons served as the physical representation of her memories. And she knew that enlivening them somehow made them easier to overwrite or supplant.

She placed the earphones into both ears and closed her eyes.

*Jerome & Rosella Goddard*

## Chapter Three

The next morning Seetha awoke with painful slowness. She moved her head from side to side. Her pillow was gone, over the side of the bed. She reached to scratch her nose and became entangled in the wires from her earphones. Everything seemed wrong, her mind a mass of confusion, self-loathing, and mental fog. Her eyes flew open. She hoped nothing was wrong with her mind. She had enough troubles already without going crazy.

She tried to clear the fog. *I'm Seetha Mathis; thirty-five years old, divorced and with one daughter. I live in Oxford, Mississippi, where I'm a professor in the biology department at the University of Mississippi.*

She sat up. *I work and I must go get dressed now.*

Forty-five minutes later at breakfast, her daughter Samantha seemed to be in a good mood, something Seetha hadn't seen in months. For once in a long time, she ate at the table instead of grabbing it off her plate and running off to her room with the excuse of "Gotta hurry. I'm late." Seetha glanced over at her daughter with pride. She was growing up—taller than most kids her age, slightly overweight, and with beautiful brunette hair like that of her father. Today she was dressed in jeans, a yellow pullover shirt, and tennis shoes.

"Mom, can we get a dog?" she asked between bites of cereal.

Seetha paused before answering, not wanting to be too quick to shoot down the idea as it might squelch Sam's temporary happiness. "I don't know, honey. Why do you ask?"

"I think I want one. Mainly to be my friend. You know, dogs love you no matter what."

That statement worried Seetha. *Does she think I don't?*

"I guess I'd be open to the idea of getting a dog, but we'd have to make a lot of arrangements for it. For example, who would care for the thing while we're away during the day?"

Samantha huffed, but kept eating, then picked up the milk to pour more into her cereal and glanced at the label. She frowned. "Yuck, Mom, this is two-percent fat! I thought it was skim milk." She placed the carton at arm's length as if it were poison.

"I have both skim and two-percent milk in the fridge, dear. All you had to do was look at the label."

Sam scowled and wiped her mouth with a napkin. "I don't want that filth touching my lips ever again. Do you understand?"

With that, she got up and stomped off to her room.

The old Sam was back.

Seetha arrived at the Ole Miss Sleep and Memory Clinic about eight-thirty that morning. Her post-doc, Dex, was already there, making out the weekly schedule. He didn't say a word, but shot her a disapproving look for being late. She smiled toward him anyway. What did he know about being a single mom, trying to raise a kid whose emotions bounced around like a ping-pong ball in a Chinese tournament? She made her way to her office to put up her purse, don her white lab coat, and check her e-mails. Unfortunately, their receptionist was out that day, meaning double-duty for her and Dex.

Four pink slips containing phone messages greeted her as she pulled her chair back from the desk. Seetha sighed, picked them up, and sat down to check her e-mail. She knew she could get more things done around the lab if people didn't keep calling with silly questions like how to make their ten-year-old son go to sleep on time on a school night. That wasn't what the sleep lab was all about.

*Jerome & Rosella Goddard*

Seetha went back outside her office and plopped down by Dex at the lab bench. He was furiously scribbling notes in a research notebook.

"What we got today?"

"Mostly sleep apneas," he said flatly. "Can't people just get a CPAP machine or have surgery for that, instead of bothering us?"

Seetha tried not to get flustered. Dex could make even the best optimist want to jump off a bridge. "But they help pay the bills. Besides, they genuinely need help. That's why we're here."

"I'd rather do research than treat people."

"I'm sure you would. Is Frances in yet?" Seetha knew they could do nothing clinical without Nurse Frances, who operated under a set of standing orders given by their medical consultant, who was a physician.

"Yep. Down the hall somewhere."

"Tonya's out today, so we've got to cover the phone and take appointments. Okay?"

Dex grunted, then continued writing notes.

Seetha examined her thirty-year-old post-doc closely. The guy was brilliant, but clearly overworked, with hair — what little there was of it — disheveled, glasses askew, and facial stubble clearly visible. He was pudgy, often slouched in posture, and rarely smiled or said anything positive. No wonder he was a loner with a malfunctioning social life. Surprisingly, he had a "girlfriend" named Heather McHann, a gymnast actually, but gossip around the department said he was gay because he didn't show much interest in her. If there ever was an "asexual" person, it was Dex. All he ever did was study and do research. His success was evident by his undergraduate and graduate grade-point-averages, stellar GRE test scores, and numbers of scientific papers published so far. But he had been struggling recently, even somewhat emotionally unstable. Seetha had heard that he was in debt up to his eyeballs, and the research project she had assigned him was so bogged down that it looked like he might have to change the protocols to get meaningful data. She had a hard time understanding what he was doing with his time. Changing research protocols involving animal and human subjects was nightmarish to say the least since it required animal use permits from the Institutional Animal Use and Care Committee and Institutional Review Board approvals at every level. No experiments could be done without appropriate oversight from those two committees. Compounding the situation was that condescending attitude and difficult personality of his. Besides, Seetha had been so preoccupied with her own emotional issues, and now all this stuff with Sam, that she had neglected Dex. She made a mental note to try to be a better supervisor and mentor.

Seetha looked around the room. She really *should* be happy. She was director of an above-average science lab, and not many people at her age and stage in life had an entire lab with several staff members at their disposal. She recalled how she had been thrilled when Dr. Don Jackson, head of the department, offered her the opportunity to apply for grant funding to build the lab. It was some kind of National Institutes of Health grant in partnership with the Ole Miss Medical Center in Jackson. The arrangement allowed for a medical doctor to be assigned as "medical consultant" for the lab, but actually Seetha was in charge. The medical consultant was only there to cover the liability of doing research and treatment on humans.

The lab was built onto the back of the biology department. In fact, it was right next to the animal research lab on the south side of the building, which made it easy for certain experiments to be done because sometimes animal experiments were needed to corroborate their studies. The lab was about as big as an average sized house, with a big open room lined with white benches and several smaller rooms lining the walls — two offices and six rooms for the sleep disorder experiments. Out front was a very comfortable reception area, with beautiful cherry wood chairs, a coffee table, and a gorgeous ceramic tile floor. Poised by the doors were huge indoor potted plants, more like trees, giving the reception area a very warm and homely atmosphere.

Seetha had noticed recently that the leaves on one of the plants drooped sadly. She wasn't used to that. "Dex, what's wrong with that plant in the reception area? Hasn't that guy from Environmental Services been here lately to tend to the plants? We want to be a welcoming place to our patients."

"You mean Vincent Bonamo or the other guy?" Dex placed the lab notebook back on the shelf. "There's two of them that service the potted plants for the Biology Department."

"I guess Bonamo is the one I've seen around. Little guy . . . dark hair, scruffy."

Dex shifted, as if uncomfortable. "I'll make a note to tell him about the ailing plant tonight," he said flatly.

*Tonight?* Seetha knew she'd messed up. "Uh, do you know Bonamo?"

Dex walked to the large white-board showing the day's scheduled appointments and experiments. He erased a name in the ten-thirty slot and wrote in a new one.

"We're roommates."

Seetha squirmed. She had figured Dex might be gay. "Oh, sorry. I didn't mean anything negative about my comments. I'm sure he's a nice guy."

"No, actually," Dex walked to one of the pieces of electronic equipment without making eye contact with her, "he's not a nice guy. Crappy roommate. I wouldn't wish him on my worst enemy."

Seetha was bewildered and decided to drop the subject before she got herself in any deeper.

Someone tapped on the door of the big room and Duke Livermore, another professor in the biology department, stuck his head inside and waved meekly.

"Come on in, Duke," Seetha said, relieved to have a break from the awkward conversation, "so glad you've come by."

Duke walked in, seemingly sensing the tension between the two, patted her on the shoulder, and greeted Dex. "Hey buddy! How're you?"

She recoiled at his touch, but reminded herself that he meant nothing by it. Duke was a genuinely nice guy who seemed to call everybody "buddy," male or female, and whether he knew them or not. Dex kept his eyes trained on the paperwork before him, mumbling something about being busy lately.

"What brings you over here?" she asked.

"Just wondering if you might be interested in doing something for us. We have this thing called the philosophy club. You may have heard about it. Jeremy Allen and I started it a while back and it meets about once a month to talk about all sorts of philosophical things. Some of the graduate students and a few faculty members come each time to talk about the great unanswerables of life, and I was wondering if you might do a short presentation on your research here. And maybe entertain questions."

"I guess I could do it, but I'm not much of a philosopher. But we might talk about the sleep disorder research being conducted here."

"It doesn't have to be all that philosophical, just interesting and curious," Duke said. "Oh, I can give you an example. Something from your own discipline like, 'what's the relationship between memories and emotions?' That would be a good question for discussion."

Seetha perked up. Duke was a herpetologist. "How'd a snake man come up with that?"

"Oh, I know a little about everything, mostly from Liz, my wife, who has a master's degree in philosophy and religion. We talk about things like that a lot but never seem to resolve anything—"

Dex interrupted. "Emotions are attached to memories, but memories are not emotions, Doctor Livermore. Surely you're aware of the research . . ." He stopped mid-sentence and went back to working.

Seetha looked from Dex to Duke, fearing Duke might be offended by all the negativity.

He smiled, apparently unfazed by Dex's comments. "Dex, that analysis is exactly why we need you there. We could certainly flesh out that answer a little more when we meet."

Seetha tried to convey an apology for Dex with her eyes. "When is the meeting?"

"Next Wednesday, the 23rd, at three o'clock."

"Okay, one or both of us will give the talk." She stared at Dex who never looked up, then glanced back at Duke. She was fed up with the guy's rudeness. "You can count on us both of us coming, Duke."

\* \* \* \* \*

The first patient in the sleep disorder clinic knocked on the door at nine-o'clock. Seetha extended a hand and invited her in. "Hi, nice to meet you. I'm Dr. Seetha Mathis."

"Anna-Dalia Smith," she replied. The woman looked to be at least seventy-five and waddled like a duck as she walked into the room. Her hair, swirled high above her head in a beehive, reminded Seetha of women in scenes she'd seen in old movies. Seetha guided her to a small table on the side, gave her a questionnaire to complete, and told her that Robbie Obergon, their student worker, would retrieve it in a few minutes. Seetha took a seat at the receptionist desk trying to find the appropriate insurance papers for the woman to sign. She picked up the phone and asked Robbie to help her with Anna-Dalia's in-processing.

Seetha had hired Robbie last semester. He was a geekie little guy with a four-point grade average who had always seemed overly eager to help Seetha around the lab. In fact, he had offered to work for her for free, saying he wanted to convince her that the sleep disorder work was "simply fascinating." The only thing negative about Robbie was his commonly displayed facial expression, which reminded Seetha of a tormented clown's face — large toothy smile; troubled eyes.

Just then, Nurse Frances, a black woman almost as wide as she was tall, threw open the door to the lab and blew in like a tropical storm, loud and boisterous.

"Good morning!" she slammed the door behind her with her foot so hard it made pictures on the wall turn sideways. "Where's everybody at up in here?"

Even though Frances was a talented nurse and an invaluable asset to the clinic, Seetha was sometimes irritated by her antics. Seetha tried to shush her by nodding sharply toward the patient at the table who was by now staring at Nurse Frances with wide eyes.

"Oh, well 'scuse me. Didn't know we done had us a patient." She nodded and smiled, displaying a beautiful set of big white teeth. "How do you do, ma'am?"

"Well, tolerable, I guess. . . ."

"Don't pay me no mind. Just go ahead on and fill out that paper work. We'll get right to you in a minute."

With that, she walked into her office and closed the door.

Robbie walked in, his ever-present smile vividly displayed.

"Here," Seetha said, handing him the insurance papers. "See that she fills this out, as well as the questionnaire. Then, bring her on back."

"Yes ma'am."

After Anna-Dalia had completed the questionnaire and insurance paperwork, Robbie ushered her into an office where Seetha and Dex went over her questionnaire answers. Afterwards, Frances would hook the woman up to a variety of electronic gadgets for a few preliminary clinical tests.

"Now, Anna-Dalia," Seetha began, reviewing the woman's answers. "We need to clarify a few things before we can get started."

"Oh, please just call me A.D.," she said, her cheeks reddening. "I'm not comfortable using my whole name."

"Okay, A.D., may I ask specifically why you wanted an evaluation at the sleep disorders clinic?"

"I can't sleep at night. I mean, I sleep, but it's not restful. I think I'm half awake and half asleep. Sometimes, if I'm lucky, I'll drift on off into a light sleep for awhile, but never for very long."

"What about your eyes?" Dex snapped. "Do your eyes move around? Do you twitch a lot? Do you—"

"Now, how would I know if my eyes twitch, young man?" she interrupted. "I'm the one asleep."

"I apologize for the confusion, A.D.," Seetha said. "I think Dr. Poindexter was only trying to determine what stages of sleep you're getting to each night. There are distinct stages that people go through in the night, and one of them — REM sleep — is characterized by rapid eye movements and a particular breathing pattern. We suspect that you aren't getting to this 'deep sleep' phase."

"I don't know anything about sleep stages; I just know I can't sleep well at night. That's why I came for help."

"Yes, ma'am, and that's what we're here for." Seetha rested her hand on A.D.'s shoulder for a minute, trying to comfort her. She then continued going over the woman's answers to the questionnaire, looking for clues as to her sleep disorder. Sometimes, the problem was as simple as drinking too much caffeine or napping during the day.

"I think I could go to sleep at night if I could forget about what happened last spring," A.D. added, seemingly from nowhere.

Seetha thumbed through the questionnaire. "But you didn't say anything about that in here."

"I didn't know it was all that important."

"What happened last spring?"

"The tornadoes. That big tornado outbreak last April. My house was destroyed and two of my life-long friends in the neighborhood were killed."

All of a sudden Dex seemed keenly interested in the patient. "So, is it a traumatic memory that's bothering you? How often does it recur, and does it increase in intensity each time?"

The woman gave him a blank look. "Well, yes, I guess. I'm not sure how many times it occurs. I've really never tried to count—"

"It's okay, A.D.," Seetha interrupted. "This new information just means we need to ask you a few more questions to see if you are simply having a sleep problem or perhaps something more serious."

"Serious! Like what?"

"Well, post-traumatic stress disorder or something like that."

"Oh, I don't think I have anything like that. That sounds bad."

"How would you know you don't have it? Maybe you do." Dex eased into her face, eyes wild and exuding excitement.

"Dex, could you go get me a copy of that traumatic memory analysis form?" Seetha said, thinking quickly. "They're in a folder in that filing cabinet by Tonya's desk."

He made a face, but turned to go.

Seetha wasn't about to fill out a traumatic memory form on this lady. Not yet, anyway. She just needed to get Dex away from the patient. She continued talking with A.D. a minute or two, and then Frances came and escorted her to one of the exam rooms. The whole way, Seetha could hear Frances chattering about how beautiful A.D.'s beehive hairdo was.

Dex returned with the form. "Where'd she go?"

"Frances has her." She crossed her legs. "Let's talk about this case for a minute."

Robbie darted in. His voice was dramatic. "Want me to help Miss Frances? I've been working hard to understand how all the equipment in there works."

That worried Seetha a little. When was Robbie playing around with the laboratory equipment? The kid needed to be reeled in sometimes. "No, Robbie, please stick to the tasks I assign you to do. Understand?"

The clown smile reversed into a frown. "Yes, ma'am." With that, he spun around and left.

Seetha faced Dex again. "Anything in A.D.'s paperwork jump out at you?"

"Not in the paperwork itself, Dr. Mathis." He shook his head. "But that traumatic memory is something I'd like to try to help her with."

Seetha thought that strange. Dex usually didn't care about the clinical aspects of their work. He was a pure academic researcher. She rose to leave. The next patient would be coming before long.

"If you work with this patient, Dex, I want you to make sure you coordinate everything with either me or Frances."

He hesitated a long time. "Okay, sure."

That worried Seetha. What was the guy up to?

Dex's demeanor suddenly changed and he grinned. "Dr. Mathis, can I update you on the experiments? You know, the animal ones . . . and also that one I did with you."

She sat back down. Dex was so smart that she'd learned a long time ago to pay attention when he wanted to talk. Especially this time since it concerned work she had allowed him to do on her, which she now regretted. Dex had asked permission to evaluate her brain function during recall of certain traumatic memories. She had been so tormented by the memories that she had allowed it. Besides, he *had* given her a memory-healing device and methods which seemed to work. Pessimism aside, she certainly respected his ability to do insightful research.

"Sure, Dex, give me an update."

"There've been several papers in the science journals lately confirming that the hippocampus in the brain is extremely important in memory function."

She nodded. "I've read most of them, I think."

"Yes, I'm sure you have. Anyway, they're saying now that the hippocampus generates neuron-firing sequences during memory recall which, as you know, can be monitored with certain devices. Well, actually 'firing patterns' of the hippocampus or the frontal lobe. These firing patterns are somehow involved in recalling past memories." He looked off before continuing. "The hippocampus may not be necessary for traumatic memory recall."

He picked up a notepad, drew a human head, and pointed with the pencil near the outside of the skull. "Have you ever heard of people who are paralyzed learning to move a computer cursor simply by thinking about it?"

Seetha had a hard time following his rambling and didn't know where he was going with the conversation. "Yes, but that has nothing to do with *memory*. That's when they hook up a whole bunch of sensors on a patient's head trying to detect electroencephalographic signals and somehow get the person to concentrate enough to move a cursor on a computer screen."

Dex seemed lost in thought. "Maybe memories can be transferred through the air like that."

Seetha had heard enough. "Don't be silly, Dex. There's no evidence for any such thing. Dreams and memories are etched on our neural networks *inside* our heads."

"Okay, maybe you're right on that one, Dr. Mathis. I'll have to think about it more."

He pitched the notepad aside. "But back to the neuron firing sequences—" He stopped mid-sentence and straightened his back as if someone poked him. Then he looked over his shoulder as if checking for eavesdroppers. "I think they can be copied and translated into patterns of lights and color that can trick the human brain into recording a memory."

Seetha sat up on the edge of her chair. This was even weirder than memories flying through the air.

"You mean memories copied and comprehended by *another* brain? That's quite a bold claim."

"Yes. You may recall from reading the scientific papers that specific firing patterns in a person's brain start a second or two before a person reports recalling a memory. I recorded just such a pattern when I evaluated you during your traumatic memory recall. Then I used a light pulse translator algorithm I devised to change that pattern into something another human brain can understand. My computer program converts brain firing patterns into dynamic spatio-temporal cues that cause that memory to be recorded in *another person's* brain."

She looked toward the door to make sure Frances wasn't within earshot. She didn't have a clue what a "light pulse translator algorithm" was, but she did know research was supposed to have boundaries. "We shouldn't have done that, Dex. We shouldn't conduct experiments that aren't in the approved protocol."

"You didn't seem to mind then. . . ."

Seetha blushed. "I guess I just had a weak moment. You have no idea how strong the memories can be."

"No matter," he said flatly, apparently not wanting to waste any more time on that subject. "What I'm trying to tell you is . . . well, I think we can copy those exact firing patterns and then—"

Seetha stood up, shaking her head. This was scary. "It sounds to me as if you're saying that we can transfer specific memories from one person to another. That's not possible because memories are stored in the brain in a different spot than the hippocampus. The hippocampus might be the clearinghouse for memories, but it doesn't store them."

Then she realized what was *really* going on. She looked him hard in the eyes. "You said you wanted to update me on the *animal* studies. Are you pursuing this theory with the animals?" She paused for what seemed like an eternity. "We *absolutely* cannot be conducting experiments without appropriate animal-use approval and Institutional Review Board approval."

Dex's face reddened. "No, not yet, anyway. No experiments are being conducted except those we've been approved for." He stood up and nervously straightened his lab coat. It was as if he suddenly decided to clam up. "I need to go across the hall for a minute before the next patient comes."

Seetha watched him walk out of the room. "What a mess," she muttered. "It's like he's got a split personality." Dex was lying, and oddly, she suddenly felt guilty. On one hand, she was angry and terrified that Dex might be pursuing over-the-edge memory research, but on the other hand, she was secretly interested, if not thrilled. If he could somehow transfer or move traumatic memories, then maybe he could figure out a way to *remove* them!

# *Chapter Four*

*S*eetha's one-o'clock Human Physiology class was a welcome break from the non-stop flow of sleep disorder patients. Teaching didn't seem to be her forte, but she tried her best to train and mentor the next generation of biologists. After all, she understood from childhood the importance of university teaching. Her father had made sure of that.

She arrived in the classroom five minutes early to sort handouts. A smattering of students was already there, chatting, but not Robbie Obergon who always made a point to be first to arrive and last to leave the class. He sat statue-like on the front row, smiling widely. At times, the young man made Seetha feel creepy, but usually not. He seemed to be a good kid. Besides, he was a scrawny little thing with barely a muscle showing.

Perhaps she'd created a monster by hiring him as a student worker and staying after class occasionally to help him with homework questions, because now he seemed overly interested in her. She hoped not.

"Good afternoon," Seetha said, careful not to direct her comments to any particular student. This was to be another day in good ol' human phys class. "Class, we're ready to get started."

"Absolutely," said Robbie, his eyes glued to Seetha as she walked. "This is the highlight of my week."

Ignoring his comment, Seetha spread out the stacks of paper on her desk and began to arrange them for distribution. Several more students entered the classroom and took seats. When one student walked by the desk, his backpack raked across the stacks of papers, sending them flying to the floor.

When she stooped to pick them up, someone brushed against her hip. She jerked back. It was Robbie gathering up the scattered papers.

"Here, let me help you with that, sweetheart."

"Excuse me? Did you just call me *sweetheart*?" Seetha said firmly, careful not to let others hear her. That had been an entirely inappropriate remark.

Robbie blushed and looked side to side, then nervously resumed grabbing papers on the floor, as if trying to think of a way out of his comment. He held one up and pointed to a table of data on the front page. "Uh, oh, I mean 'chart.'" He fumbled for words. ". . . uh . . . stack of charts. *Not* 'sweetheart.' "

Seetha drilled him with her eyes. That was a lie, but she didn't know how far to push the issue, especially in front of the other students. She tried to rationalize his comments.

*Maybe it's normal for a small percentage of students to get crushes on their college professors. I need to maintain a healthy distance from this guy. He'll get the message.*

About three-thirty in the afternoon, Seetha called Samantha at home to make sure she had arrived from school safely. "Hello, dear. How was school today?"

"Oh, hi, Mom. Okay, I guess. I'll be glad when summer break begins. I'm sick of school." Then after a pause, with clear agitation in her voice she continued, "I'm tired of all the crap that goes on up there."

Seetha worried about what that meant. What kind of crap was she referring to? She knew from prior experience not to pursue things like that too much over the phone. That wouldn't work. Even face-to-face discussions with her seldom accomplished anything. "Yeah, summer break'll be great, sweetheart. We could . . . " Seetha searched for the right words to say . . . "hang out together."

Seetha clearly heard an "aggh" sound on the other end. She paused. This wasn't going too well. "So, it sounds like something is bothering you. Want to talk about it?"

A pronounced silence ensued, then an irritated, high-pitched, response. "Mom, please don't analyze me. You always put me under a microscope. My day was fine. I'm fine. Okay?"

"Sure, sweetheart, I'm just concerned about you, and interested in your day at school."

"Are you working late tonight?" Sam changed the subject.

"No, I should be there no later than six. I've got to run by the grocery store on my way home. Anything special you want me to fix for dinner tonight? You name it."

"No, Mom. Can't you tell I'm not hungry? I'll just eat a piece of fruit."

"Now Sam, we've discussed this before. You need to eat more than that."

The high-pitched voice returned. "Sure, Mom, and gain weight and have to face the kids at school. You're not there. You don't know what it's like."

Silence, this time on both ends of the line.

"Okay then, sweetheart. Keep the doors locked and don't let anybody in. I'll try to pick you up something special at the grocery store."

"Don't bother." Samantha hung up on her.

Seetha sat back in her chair and blew out a long breath. She had to get that girl into counseling as soon as possible.

After work, Seetha stopped by the Kroger store on her way home. She considered it the best grocery in Oxford, not that there were many to choose from in the tiny town. The parking lot was full so she parked way out in left field. Since daylight savings time had not yet begun, darkness was steadily encroaching upon the landscape. Young oak trees lining the parking lot danced in the cool March wind. Seetha walked briskly, weaving between parked cars. For some strange reason, fear suddenly gripped her. She tried to shake it off. *This is ridiculous. There's hardly any crime in Oxford.* Still, she couldn't help glancing behind her. A few people were walking to and from their cars. Nothing out of the ordinary.

Or so it seemed. What appeared to be a man dressed in a dark parka suddenly ducked behind a car!

Seetha's heart raced as she looked intently in that direction, trying to see him emerge again among the cars, but she couldn't because darkness was steadily deepening. Who was that? And why would he be so intent on avoiding her?

After about a minute, her better sense took over. *This is crazy! Probably just somebody bending over to pick up something.*

Once inside, the bright lights of the store soothed Seetha's fears and soon she was able to concentrate on her grocery-buying task. Seeing the store shelves brimming full of every food imaginable sparked pangs of fear and regret about Sam. Her beloved child definitely seemed to be developing an eating disorder, to say the least.

*Where did I go wrong? Maybe I should have left Rodney sooner before the damage was done.*

She picked up several items, went through the self-check-out stand, and headed across the parking lot toward her car. By now, it was totally dark except for the lights of the parking lot. Seetha's pace quickened as she recalled the earlier incident. When she got to her car, a dark lump-like figure appeared next to the dumpster at the edge of the parking lot not fifty feet away. Was it a human crouched beside the dumpster watching her?

*No way*, she tried to convince herself. Maybe it was just some boxes stacked there.

When she started the car and swung her headlights by the dumpster, there were no boxes or anything else stacked there. The mysterious lump was gone. She shoved aside the obvious, chalking it up to nerves. Maybe there was some other explanation. She needed to get home to Sam.

Turning out of the Kroger parking lot toward Highway 7, Seetha and the cars behind her had to pass under the bright lights of the gasoline island. She couldn't help noticing a brown or black car following closely behind her with what appeared to be a dark male figure behind the wheel. She tried to convince herself that a variety of people entered and exited the parking lot all the time. Why should she be so worried about *one* car? Involuntarily, her mind flashed back to times when Rodney tormented her, both verbally and physically. His presence always loomed large over her, like Goliath over David.

The car followed her down to the Highway 6 bypass, which was a four-lane highway, where it turned with her, headed West. All of a sudden, the car shot up close to her rear bumper at high speed, then falling back, only to repeat the action again.

Seetha's heart raced. What should she do? She reached for her cell phone to call 911, but before she could dial the number, the dark car shot up behind her again, almost hitting her this time. She jerked the steering wheel, sending the cell phone into the passenger side floorboard. Seetha screamed and grabbed the steering wheel even more tightly. This man was crazy. Not only had he apparently been stalking her; now it looked like he was trying to hurt her! She hoped to God it wasn't Rodney. Surely he didn't get an early release from prison.

Thinking quickly, Seetha got in the left lane and acted as if she were going to try to outrun him. She knew the next exit, about a mile away, led into town. This would be do-able, but tricky. As the exit approached, she gave no indication that she intended to suddenly swerve right, across the other lane, onto the exit ramp. Maybe the guy would be caught off-guard and not able to make the turn. She looked straight ahead and maintained her speed. The car was only about twenty yards behind her. When she got even with the exit, at just the right moment she shot off to the right, tires squealing from the sharp turn, heading into town toward City Hall. She figured she would drive to the Oxford police station, but beyond that, she didn't know what would happen. If the guy followed and wanted to kill her, he might do it before she got inside.

Seetha looked in her rear-view mirror. The guy had clearly missed the exit, so she slowed down to a safer speed on the city street. Then she spotted movement in the mirror back at the exit.

A brown car was backing up the on-ramp. He wasn't gone after all!

Soon his lights were visible again, rapidly coming her way. Seetha reached the police department where she whipped in the parking lot and stopped the vehicle right beside the front door. Her heart pounded; she was too scared to look in the mirror, so she ducked down below the line of sight. Was he still back there? Was he coming? Would he gun her down when she opened the door?

Seetha mustered all the nerve she had and peeped her head back over the seat. The dark car was nowhere in sight.

Someone rapped on the window! Seetha screamed and threw herself into the floorboard, grabbing frantically for her phone. "Oh, my God . . . help me! Don't touch me. Please don't touch me." But there was no place for her to hide.

The car door opened slowly.

"Ma'am? Ma'am?" The policeman asked. "What's wrong? Are you all right?"

*Chapter Five*

Detective Fox, a tall, fifty-ish man with salt and pepper hair, sat at his desk poring over the file about the murder of Hope Williams' boyfriend. Even though he was a detective, his face was weathered, as if he'd spent one too many years on the street. Other than those few wrinkles, he was a handsome man, with soft eyes and a well-toned body. His office was quite plain, but he had tried to make it inviting, with the wall behind him lined with pictures, certificates, and wooden plaques detailing awards he had won as a cop, including some for marksmanship. The other walls were splattered with artwork, letters, and photographs of his sister's three children.

Fox was bewildered. The Ole Miss coed had told him that more than one of her ex-boyfriends had died mysteriously, a fact he had verified with the Baton Rouge police department. Apparently, the girl had had five boyfriends since high school. Three of them had since died — two in suspicious "accidents" and one, the most recent, was flat-out murdered in Oxford. He considered the options. One, the girl was a black widow, killing her ex-lovers for whatever reason. Fox knew that looks could be deceiving. Even though Miss Williams appeared to be sweet and innocent, she could actually be the devil himself, or more precisely, herself. Second, maybe one of the previous boyfriends was insanely jealous, trying to prevent anyone else from dating her. He would definitely need to check on that possibility. And third, maybe the deaths were entirely coincidental with nothing linking them.

Fox closed the file. He would systematically investigate these options, interview her again, and who knew, maybe there were other scenarios he hadn't considered.

A knock came from the door. Patrolman Steve Ogilvie stuck his head in. "Detective Fox, can you help us a minute? There's a woman out here who says someone was following her from Kroger, even trying to bump her car. She's pretty upset."

Fox stood up. "Sure." He pitched Hope William's file on his desk. What was going on? Crime was usually *very* rare in the small college community where he lived. Lately, it seemed commonplace.

In the lobby he found an obviously distraught thirty-something female. He extended a hand, and she shook it, but he could tell she was trembling. He made mental notes: definitely scared, if not terrified. "Hi, I'm Detective John Fox. What's your name?"

"Seetha Mathis . . . uh, I'm a professor at the university."

"Okay, so Patrolman Ogilvie says you think someone was following you."

"Yes." She seemed to be trying her best to steady her breathing. "A man chased me in my car from the Kroger parking lot. He even tried to crash into me. And I had seen him earlier hiding in the parking lot—"

"Whoa." Fox raised his hands. He looked at Patrolman Ogilvie, who shrugged his shoulders. "Please try to calm down and not get ahead of yourself." He glanced behind him toward his door. "Come on, let's have a seat in my office. We can talk about it there."

Within minutes, Fox could tell that Seetha Mathis' story seemed legitimate and predictable. University professor; abusive husband; divorced; somebody stalking her. Duh.

Perhaps this case wouldn't be as difficult as he thought. Finding out whether or not Rodney Mathis had been released from prison would be easy enough to ascertain. Fox asked his assistant, Amber, to call or e-mail the federal facility where Mathis was imprisoned, for an update on his status. Then he tried to develop a profile on the suspect.

"Sounds like it could indeed be your ex-husband, Ms. Mathis." Fox folded his hands on the desk in front of him. "If we find out he's been released from custody, I'll help you get a restraining order immediately." He gave her a warm look. "There's no need for you to feel unsafe in your own town."

He turned a fresh new page in his notebook on his desk. "Could you tell me more about your ex-husband? It'll help me know what he is and isn't capable of." Fox took in megabytes of information as he looked her over — probably smart, successful professor at the university. Maybe a little unsure of herself. He couldn't help noticing how strikingly attractive she was. Tall; slightly overweight; curvy. Her long dark hair and deeply tanned skin made her look more like a full-figured model than a professor.

"Well," she began, then hesitated, "let's just say he wasn't a very kind man to me or our daughter." She looked down. "He was verbally abusive."

"Physically violent?"

Silence.

Fox leaned forward. "I understand this must have been a terrible chapter in your life, Ms. Mathis. My sister's been in a similar situation lately, and I've seen first-hand how cruel certain men can be toward women. If you don't feel comfortable talking about it now—"

"No, it's okay. I'm fine." She smiled and swiped the hair out of her eyes. "It just scared me being chased by somebody I thought might be him. Thank you for understanding."

Fox nodded. Looking at this woman suddenly stirred emotions in him about love and marriage that he'd just as soon leave buried.

He tried hard to focus on the interview.

The next morning Seetha was nervous. Dr. Don Jackson, the biology department head, had asked to meet with her at nine-o'clock. Although she had interacted with the guy a few times in the past without any problem, he had a reputation for being gruff and opinionated, even rude. He was especially mean-spirited toward the female faculty. She hoped that wasn't going to be the case this time.

His secretary, Shawanda, ushered her in. Dr. Jackson was seated behind his massive, empty desk reading *The Chronicle of Higher Education.* The scene reminded her of a funeral director sitting statue-like in a gaudy office.

"Seetha," he said, putting down the publication and sitting up straight. "So you're here." He frowned. "I'll try to make this brief. Maybe we can clear up this matter right away and let you get back to work."

A worried look crossed her face. "Yes, sir."

"I'm going to lay the cards on the table," he said. "Something's going on in the sleep unit, and it concerns the animals."

Her heart sank. "What, sir?"

"Central Purchasing tells me there was a recent purchase of zebra finches, picked up by your post-doc, and held in your lab, supposedly for Lindsey Southward." Jackson sat back and sighed. "Professor Southward tells me she had nothing to do with it. Didn't even want the birds."

Seetha was becoming increasingly uncomfortable. The man's tone and actions were similar to those of her father and stirred in her a strong compulsion to submit. She fought the urge, took a deep breath, and tried her best to meet Dr. Jackson's concerned gaze. "Yes, it's true. We did get some finches, but Dex assured me that he was only holding them temporarily for Dr. Southward."

"Have you ever noticed anything unusual or unethical about Dr. Poindexter's work?"

"No, sir." That wasn't exactly true, but close.

"Have any log books or animal-use forms been swapped or doctored?"

"Absolutely not."

"If we were to march over to the animal facility right now, would we find anything unusual or out of place?"

"Absolutely not."

Seetha watched him carefully, waiting for the other shoe to fall.

But it didn't. Just a long, icy silence.

"As far as I'm concerned," Jackson said, pushing back from his desk and coming to his feet. "This meeting is over. Now, I want you to go back to work and do your job . . . which includes properly supervising the scientists who work in your unit."

"But, sir," Seetha said, her voice rising. "I don't agree. Dex wouldn't order the finches unless Dr. Southward authorized him to do so. Maybe it's just a misunderstanding."

"Stop this," Jackson said, throwing up his hands. "This is escalating into something bigger than it really is."

Time suddenly seemed suspended. Just how deep did this unethical research of Dex's go? Had he totally ignored her warnings? Perhaps he intended to drag her down with him. She felt distraught and alone to think he had purposely betrayed her. She blinked. Her mind was wandering. What a difference there was in Detective Fox's office last night and this one. She remembered how warm, inviting, and safe Fox's office had felt, so unlike this one where she felt vulnerable and afraid.

"Do your job, young lady," Jackson's loud voice interrupted her thoughts. He loomed large over her. "Understand?"

In that instant, Seetha was no longer a thirty-five year-old research professor who lived in an upscale area of town. Somehow, this brief meeting with Don Jackson had projected her back through time and space, back to a place that was both long ago and never far away. She was once again an overweight, underachieving teen under the iron fist of her father.

# Chapter Six

*D*ex stopped by DeeVo's gas and convenience store on his way home from work. The gas station part of the complex was located out in the parking lot of the store. Some guy in a shiny new Jaguar had just finished getting gas and pulled out in front of him. Dex could have sworn the man smirked as he drove by.

Dex winced. He had always wanted a car like that.

"No way that's going to happen anytime soon with all my bills piling up," he muttered.

When he parked in front of one of the pumps and made his way to the glass-enclosed pay booth, he noticed how the attendant station wasn't much bigger than a phone booth, and was made almost entirely of glass. Probably bulletproof, he guessed. Cases of soft drinks were stacked head high around the pay booth like a rampart, as well as two candy vending machines.

Dex fished in his pockets for his last twenty-dollar bill to present to the clerk through the drawer. He recalled how lately the months seemed to outlast his paychecks. The retractable drawer at the pay booth was a complex, weird-looking, gadget which appeared to be designed to prevent someone from sticking their hands inside the pay booth. He looked up while the thin Asian guy took his money. The top of the booth had a large AC vent where an 18-inch air duct entered for heating and cooling of the booth. *This place isn't entirely theft-proof. A tiny person could squirm through that hole where the ductwork enters. Maybe even while the cash drawer is still unlocked when the clerk is outside checking the pumps before closing.*

He rubbed his chin. Now that was an idea!

Five minutes later, Dex whipped into his apartment parking lot. Soon as he walked in the door, he saw his girlfriend, Heather, coming straight at him. She must have come to the apartment looking for him. Her thin, gymnast body swayed with perfect symmetry with each approaching step.

She kissed him, but it was a cold, hard kiss. "You and I need to talk." She wagged her bony finger in his face.

"Why? What is it this time?"

"Come outside." She walked past him. "I don't want that creep Bonamo listening to what I have to say."

Once on the patio, Heather vented her frustration loudly like an erupting volcano. She covered everything from how Dex seemed to be neglecting her lately, to the untidiness of his apartment, and finally to his roommate, Vince Bonamo.

"He's a slob, I tell you, and it's rubbing off on you," she said loudly. "And, I don't like the way he looks at me when I walk near him. He's evil, I tell you. Evil."

"I know, but you know I've got to have a roommate. I can't make ends meet on that pittance of a salary Dr. Mathis gives me." He paused. "Maybe I could kick him out and you move in."

Heather was calming down, but still glaring. "We're not at that level in our relationship, and you know it."

Dex used the opportunity to push his research methods. "You know I can help you with that anger. Just go to sleep a few times listening to the recording I give you or maybe watch a video I've made. Anger management is just one of many benefits of my sleep and memory research."

"Let's don't go there . . . especially not now. I've got to go. We can talk about it later."

Dex walked Heather to her car and planted a kiss on her cheek. "Call me tonight."

She muttered something, cranked the car, and shot out of the parking lot.

That hadn't gone well.

After seeing Heather off, Dex went back inside, pulled a beer out of the fridge, and sprawled out on the couch, mindlessly flipping through TV channels.

Vince Bonamo emerged from the back bedroom. He was a medium-sized, muscular man in his late twenties with beady eyes and hair growing low on his forehead. Dex had often thought Bonamo had the smallest forehead of anyone he'd ever known.

"What's Heather's problem?" Bonamo asked, taking a seat on the couch. He leaned over and grabbed the television remote from Dex's hand. "I could hear her hollering from the back room."

Dex shifted uncomfortably. "Uh, to be honest, it's you she's fussing about."

"Aw, she's hated my guts from the day we met." He clicked the channel to ESPN. "I wouldn't worry about it too much if I were you. She'll get over it."

Dex shot Bonamo a hard look. "She *is* my girlfriend, you know. I can't just ignore her."

"You know as well as I do that she's not *really* your girlfriend. . . ."

Dex shrugged. He didn't know how to respond to that. His relationship with Heather was indeed not much more than a good friendship. "You're no better at love and relationships than I am. Otherwise, you wouldn't be stuck here with me."

Bonamo didn't flinch. "I know what it's like to be in love." He looked away. "No matter. I'm only here with you until I decide what to do with my life."

"You need to decide something, all right." Dex's frustration with Heather spilled out. "Louisiana boy moving to Ole Miss to be a glorified campus gardener isn't much to write home about."

"Why I moved up here is none of your damn business!" Bonamo threw the T.V. remote across the room and exploded with such a loud voice that it shook the walls. His eyes were bulging and filled with rage.

Dex was terrified at the Jekyll-Hyde transformation and feared a physical attack. He couldn't decide whether to run to another room or try to calm Bonamo down. "Sorry. I didn't mean to offend you."

Bonamo inhaled deeply as if trying to collect himself. Dex wondered what was coming next.

He suddenly jumped up, pointing to Dex's beer. "I'm gonna get me one of those."

When he returned, he had both a beer and a notepad in his hands. Gone was the anger. His eyes suddenly glowed with excitement and there was an unusual niceness about him. "Dex, tell me more about your memory research. I'm fascinated by it. And also that colleague of yours, Dr. Mathis, who I think is totally hot."

"Could I ask why you need a notepad if you're asking me about Seetha Mathis?"

"Oh, just to keep it straight in my own mind. The memory research, that is. Me thinking Dr. Mathis is hot is just a little side road." He paused. "Is she married?"

Dex wasn't about to go that way with Bonamo. Seetha Mathis' love life was not any business of his.

The notepad thing really made him nervous. Sure, he loved the fact that someone was interested in his research — that someone appreciated his genius — but to write down specifics of his research was another matter altogether. He made a mental note not to reveal too many details. Unfortunately, that was something he had failed to do three months ago when Bonamo had first shown interest in his memory research.

"I'm not sure about her marital status. I just don't know."

Bonamo drilled him with his eyes, but apparently let it go. "Let's see," he said after a long pause, "tell me again how the hippocampus in the brain regulates memory."

Dex lit up. This was his thing. His baby. "Well, this is how it works. There are particular neuron firing patterns in a small part of a person's brain — the hippocampus — which are specifically linked to recalling past experiences. Researchers, I mean, I have recorded several snippets of these neuron firing patterns with specialized electronic equipment."

"Is it possible for you to know what the person is remembering?"

"No." Dex shook his head. "Not unless they tell us that sort of thing and we label the recording with that information."

Bonamo scribbled notes. "And tell me more about how you get people to *act out* certain memories."

Dex blushed. Bonamo was smart. Maybe too smart. *I've got to be careful what I reveal here.* "Well, that's a whole different thing from the hippocampal firing patterns. All I can say about that is what I've told you before. Certain brief visual or auditory snippets of an activity, appropriately translated into a pattern of lights and colors, when played to a person can sometimes — and I repeat, sometimes — cause that person to have mild-to-moderate urges to repeat those activities."

"Like playing them quick, instant, almost imperceptible colors, frames, or flashes in a video something like that?"

"Well, yes, I suppose . . ." Dex's palms became sweaty.

"Would the person receiving the treatment, the one who acts out the memory, recall doing so afterwards?"

Dex was becoming alarmed at the direction of the conversation. "Well, no, I don't think so."

"Then why doesn't a researcher like yourself seek ways to get government approval to conduct experiments and see if that indeed is what happens?"

Dex stood up. "Oh, I haven't ever done anything like that . . . uh, it would be unethical to conduct such experiments."

Bonamo smiled impishly. "I didn't ask if you had *done* it."

Later that night, Dex's mind whirred like an electric motor. All sorts of things were bothering him. One, his pressing financial needs. The payments on his student loans resulting from the ten-year trek to getting his Ph.D. were more than a home mortgage, and he owed over $23,000 on credit cards. He was barely able to pay rent and a car payment, much less ever move out on his own. Two, his rocky "relationship" with Heather, and three, his research. As his roommate, Bonamo, had correctly perceived earlier, Dex was indeed close to being able to induce certain behaviors in people by way of his memory devices using translated brain firing patterns. As best he could tell from his animal experiments, a person with these induced behaviors wouldn't know they had done them. It would seem like a dream.

Dex stuffed a pillow behind his neck. Bonamo was a loose cannon. He knew too much and Dex hated himself for being too open with the guy. Oh well, he would just have to deal with him later. But first, could it be possible to use the memory research to get money? Maybe, but only if he could patent the technology. That might take years. He needed money in the short-term. Like now. Lately, he hadn't even been able to pay the interest on his credit cards.

Then he recalled the gas station pay booth with the AC duct opening at the top and all the coke machines stacked around it.

"A really small person could climb through that opening when the attendant checked the pumps before closing at night," he muttered. "It wouldn't take but a minute. They lock the door, but probably not the cash register."

He sat straight up in bed as if some one had shocked him with a cattle prod. "Such a person would need to be both tiny *and* agile. Like a gymnast."

# *Chapter Seven*

*D*etective Fox studied the records of the murder case of Hope William's most recent boyfriend, Frankie Peterson, before talking with her again. She was in the waiting room out front. By now, Fox's assistant had generated a small mountain of paperwork on many of the ex-boyfriends, the current victim, his family and background, and his relationship with Miss Williams, the college coed. Nothing about this recent victim stood out as strange or unusual. He had been a fairly clean-cut, average American kid.

Fox rubbed his face in frustration. The only risk factor for crime this kid seemed to have was being a boyfriend of Hope Williams. He punched the intercom button on his desk.

"Amber, bring her on back."

When Amber escorted Hope into the room, Fox noticed how pale and scared she looked. One thing was sure, there was an innocence or naiveté about this girl. She was no black widow.

"Hello, Miss Williams, please have a seat." He pointed at a chair as he sat behind his desk.

"I appreciate you coming back for another interview." Fox smiled at her. "First, let me say that you're not under arrest or anything like that. We're just trying to gather as much information as we can about your ex-boyfriend." He paused. "Is there any thing I can get you? Coffee or a soft drink?"

Hope seemed to relax a bit. "No, thanks."

Fox began the interview by asking once again to define her

relationship with Bonamo.

"He and I dated for a year or so when I was living in Baton Rouge, but we broke up, and then I never heard from him again until I was up here at Ole Miss. He said he was living in town and wanted to get together sometime. "

"So, he's up here?"

"Yes, sir."

"When did you know he followed you up here?"

She bristled. "I don't know that he *followed* me. He told me he got a good job here."

"Okay, we can check that out." He paused, looking over his notes. "How many boyfriends have you had, let's say, since your junior year in high school?"

Hope huffed as if her reputation was now in question. She named off five names, touching her fingers with her thumb upon calling each one.

"And how many of those have died tragically or unexpectedly?"

Now she looked offended.

Fox saw it and knew he needed to reassure her. "Hope . . . may I call you Hope?"

"Yes." She avoided eye contact.

"I realize these may seem like harsh questions. I just don't want you to be the next victim. We've got to get to the bottom of this, so there's lots of questions that must be answered. You may have a hard time believing it, but I'm here for you. I want to help you any way I can, so I need to know what happened in the past."

"I understand." Eye contact again. "Okay, what do you need to know?"

He began again, this time trying to be more reassuring in his tone. "How many of your boyfriends have died unexpectedly?"

She methodically named three of the boys who had died.

"Bonamo is number two of five?"

"Yes, but one of the ones that died was my first one, so it couldn't be Vincent harming them."

"But, don't you see, he died *after* you had dated Bonamo."

"Well, yes."

"What if he killed forward *and* backward, so to speak?"

Hope shrugged. "I wouldn't know about that. I guess it's possible."

Fox walked over to a bookcase, picked up a decorative antique clock and wound the key on the backside. "Hasn't it occurred to you, Hope, that it's strange that so many of your boyfriends have died mysteriously, and the last one, Frankie Peterson, was killed right here in Oxford, the same town your ex-boyfriend number two has followed you to?"

"Of course, it's unusual." She was getting agitated again. "It's downright scary, but I don't know who did it, or even if it was on purpose."

Fox sat down on the edge of the desk, facing her. "During the time you were dating Mr. Bonamo, did you at any time see any behaviors you thought were illegal, immoral, or suspicious?"

"No, I can't think of any. He was always a perfect gentleman."

"You sure?"

Hope backtracked. "Yes, well, other than having a bad temper. But he always apologized later."

Fox let that sink in. "You know anything about his family? Did he ever talk about them?"

"Not much, other than they live in New Orleans."

"You ever meet any of them?"

"No, seems like he always went out of his way to keep me from meeting them." Her head went down. "Maybe he was ashamed of me . . ."

"Could there be other reasons why he wouldn't want you to meet his folks?"

"I don't know, unless maybe they're in the Mafia or something," she said in a sarcastic tone.

Fox reassured Hope he was going to solve the case and handed her some forms to fill out detailing the last times and places she had seen each of the former boyfriends. Then he let her leave.

Fox re-read the files his assistant had compiled on the case.

He punched the intercom button. "Amber, get in here." He drummed his fingers on the desk until she appeared.

"Yes, sir?" the perky twenty-five-year-old asked.

"Anything new on the ex-boyfriends?"

"Only one thing so far." She checked a small notepad in her hand. "Apparently, the one named Vincent Bonamo is now living here. His folks are from New Orleans."

Fox knew that already from talking to Hope. "What's he doing here?"

"Works at the university — landscaper or something like that."

"How much do they still talk?"

"I don't know, sir."

"I must speak with him. Find out where he lives or the building on campus where he works."

"Yes, sir." She scribbled notes. "There's more."

"What?"

"N.O.P.D. says he's trouble."

"What do they mean?"

"Some kind of connection to organized crime."

Fox looked out the window. He wasn't scared. If the guy had anything to do with the murder, then he would arrest him, simple as that. Mafia or no mafia.

"Oh, changing the subject, did you ever find out anything about Rodney Mathis, the guy in the federal pen? Has he been released?"

"Yes, sir. Just got an e-mail about him not ten minutes ago. I forwarded it to you. Apparently, he was released three weeks ago. And nobody seems to know where he went."

"Not even a parole officer?"

"Never reported to one. And you know how overwhelmed parole officers are these days. They probably won't make much of an effort to find him . . . since he was only in for money laundering. "

"I figured as much. That certainly complicates things. Get me the phone number for Seetha Mathis over on campus. I need to tell her the bad news." He paused. "No, wait, just get me her work number; I think it's the biology department. Maybe this kind of news needs to be given in person. I'll call tomorrow and see if I can stop by and see her."

"Yes, sir."

"Oh, and get me that Bonamo information ASAP. We've got to talk to him right away."

\*\*\*\*\*

The morning of March twenty-third broke cold and raw, with a north wind swaying the newly-budding trees around the Ole Miss campus and rattling loose-fitting windows in the forty-year-old biology department.

Seetha and Dex saw patients in the sleep lab that morning. The elderly patient, A.D. Smith, came back, but this time escorting her grandson to the clinic. Seetha heard her talking loudly out at Tonya's receptionist desk.

"Oh, hi, Dr. Mathis," A.D. smiled when she saw Seetha coming. "I brought you another patient." She stepped aside to introduce her grandson, Stephen, who was tall and lanky and appeared to be about fifteen years old.

"It's very nice to meet you, Stephen." Seetha tried hard to make direct eye contact with him. "You're a nice looking young man. What can I do for you?"

"I have bad dreams." He looked down.

Seetha glanced at him, then A.D. "Are your dreams bad enough to interfere with your daily life at school?"

He nodded shyly.

"Okay, let's get some forms filled out, then we can talk about that. All sorts of things can lead to nightmares." She waved toward one of the treatment rooms. "Let's go in there. Tonya, bring us those forms we need."

Inside the treatment room, Seetha found out that A.D.'s grandson was suffering from recurring nightmares. He reported often waking at night, with profuse sweating and his heart racing.

"This could be something simple like caffeine," she said. "Do you drink coffee or sodas at night?"

"No."

"How about chocolate?"

He shook his head.

"Hmm." She bit her lip, thinking.

"How about those energy drink things?"

Stephen's eyebrows shot up. "Yeah, I do drink those little four-ounce power drinks, but I don't think they have caffeine."

Seetha knew she might be on to something. "Stephen, I know some of those products claim to have no caffeine, but believe me, they're high powered stimulants, equivalent to several cups of strong coffee. No matter what name the company gives them — all natural or whatever — they're just like drinking a bunch of coffee."

"You sure that's all there is to it?" A.D. said. "He says he has the same dream each time."

Seetha paused. That could indeed indicate something deeper, but she knew she should try the obvious first. "Interesting, but let's first try restricting your energy drinks to morning only. Then, if things don't get better, we'll revisit the issue."

A.D. didn't seem convinced. "Do you think Dr. Poindexter would agree with this assessment?"

Seetha's face reddened. Why had she said that? The woman barely knew Dex. Why would she bring him into the conversation? "I don't think we need to consult Dr. Poindexter in this matter. It seems fairly straightforward to me."

Later that afternoon, Seetha and Dex made their way to the main building to attend Duke Livermore's "philosophy club." Classes had just let out so the hall was crowded with students, many headed home for the day. A dark-headed student suddenly ploughed into Seetha, pressing her against the wall. It was Robbie Obergon, the geeky student with the crush on her.

"Excuse me; I'm so sorry . . . oh, hi, Dr. Mathis," he gushed. "I didn't know it was you. I mean, even if I did know it was you, I wouldn't have crashed into you. I'm sorry — it was an accident. I wasn't paying attention where I was going and tripped." He reached and touched her arm. "Hope I didn't hurt you." His cheeks turned pink. "Oh, please forgive me, Dr. Mathis. I'm such a dufus."

Seetha jerked back when he touched her, but then tried to ease his embarrassment. "It's okay, Robbie. Things like this could happen to anybody. Don't worry about it."

"But I feel awful. You're my favorite person." He nervously swiped the hair on his forehead to one side. "I mean, you're my favorite teacher."

"We've got to be going." Seetha stiffened her back and ignored his remark.

"Okay then, I guess I'll see you in class tomorrow."

She nodded.

Shawanda, the departmental secretary waved her down in the hall. "Dr. Mathis, a detective from the police department called for you a few minutes ago. I rang your office, but you weren't in."

Seetha felt embarrassed, and even more so because Dex was with her. Police detectives calling her at work? That couldn't be helpful for promotion and tenure. "Yes, I know him. It's a personal matter, not some big crime or anything like that."

Shawanda eyed her carefully. "Okay, well, he asked if you were going to be around the next hour or so. Said he was going to stop by."

*Stop by. That's bad.* "I'm scheduled to speak at Duke Livermore's philosophy club in the next few minutes." She pointed toward the small auditorium. "If he shows up, and I'm not finished, he can come in. I think it's open to the public." She paused. "Better yet, maybe you should just come get me."

A few doors down, Seetha and Dex found Duke setting up a LCD projector and computer to enable a PowerPoint presentation. A young Chinese-American girl and a red-headed guy in his late twenties were assisting him while other students made coffee and arranged snacks on a table in the back of the room.

"Oh, hi, Seetha!" Duke said, smiling widely and shaking her hand. "And you too, Dex. Come on in, buddy. I'm glad you're both here."

He turned toward the people helping him. "This is Meha Wu, one of our biology Ph.D. students, and Dr. Jeremy Allen from the Math Department. They're the foundational pillars of the group. The philosophy club was actually Jeremy's idea. He's sharp . . . you wouldn't want to get into a deep philosophical discussion with him. Sometimes I call him 'Little Einstein.' "

Jeremy's face flushed, matching his untamed red hair. "I don't know about all that."

Seetha extended a hand. "So nice to meet you both. I hope we won't be involved in any deep, soul-searching discussions. I'm no good at that."

Instead of shaking hands, Dex just nodded at them.

"Did you bring your talk on a flash drive?" Duke asked.

Seetha looked at her hardbound notebook, then at Dex. "I really didn't prepare a formal talk. Just made a few notes. I thought we might make it interactive."

"I prepared a PowerPoint presentation on memory and learning, if that's all right," Dex said, shooting a condescending look toward Seetha.

"Of course." Duke slapped his shoulder, obviously not catching the tension between them. "We'll take 'em both. We're not picky."

Seetha excused herself to go to the restroom while Duke helped Dex load the computer program. She felt inadequate and hoped Dex wouldn't try to embarrass her. He often seemed competitive and self-promoting. Sometimes she wished she hadn't hired him, though he *was* brilliant and often had cutting-edge ideas for memory research. Seetha had known from the start that Dex condescended toward the sleep disorder work and really wanted to just do pure memory and learning research — nothing practical or applied.

She was washing her hands when a memory hit her like a dart deep in her psyche. "You're fat and lazy and will never amount to anything!" The thought was so strong it sounded like a real voice there in the restroom. She could even vividly remember her father's bulging eyes and red face as he screamed at her. It began to play in a loop, making her want to run and escape.

"You're fat and lazy. You're fat and lazy. You're fat and lazy."

*Jerome & Rosella Goddard*

Seetha reeled from the onslaught. *I've got to regain control.* She shook her head as if flinging the old memories aside, checked her face in the mirror, and forced herself to walk out the door.

She hoped others wouldn't see the sweat on her forehead or terror in her eyes.

When she returned, the room was dotted with professors and both undergraduate and graduate students. Duke made a few introductory remarks and then turned the meeting over to Jeremy.

"Thanks folks, for coming," he began. "There's one little item of unfinished business we've got to deal with, then we'll get to our guest speakers for today."

He flipped through a loose-leaf notebook. Apparently the philosophy club discussions were recorded by someone. "Oh, yeah, Kaitlyn was discussing ancient beliefs and how people used to think everything was caused by demons or evil spirits, especially mental illnesses like what we now recognize as schizophrenia." He read on. "Then, she said scientists now know that these things have organic or biological mechanisms and there are no such things as evil spirits. Let's see." He turned a page. "William said he had heard of childhood mental disorders in which little three or four-year-olds compulsively holler out really gross, vulgar, and sexual talk. Stuff they've never heard or learned. He offered that as proof that maybe there really are demons. Then he quoted the psychiatrist, M. Prescott, who wrote a book about this sort of thing, saying that Dr. Prescott investigated this subject and became convinced that there really was such a thing as demon possession."

He rose up. "And that's where we ended. I don't think we came to any sort of closure on the subject. Anyone want to comment?"

Duke rubbed his chin and leaned forward. "It's my understanding that the word 'demon' actually has a number of meanings, all of which are related to the idea of a spirit that inhabited a place, or that accompanied a person. Whether a demon was benevolent or malevolent, the Greek word meant something different from the later medieval notions of 'demon,' and I think scholars have debated the time that its original Greek sense became transformed to the later medieval sense. Many Christians believe that demons are dis-embodied spirits, though I should mention that some Christian denominations include fallen angels as de facto demons."

"But do you think they're real or not?" William prodded, apparently not wanting to hear a definition.

"To be honest, I don't know. I used to be totally skeptical of anything so-called 'spiritual' but not so much anymore." He paused. "I really don't know what I believe about such things."

"You *don't know* . . . or *can't decide*?" William continued.

Duke shrugged and smiled. He'd learned the precise time to shut up from many arguments with his wife, Liz.

A psychology major named Lucinda's hand went up. "I wasn't here last time, but it's my understanding that the famous psychiatrist Kurt Schneider said that schizophrenics have the distinct impression that thoughts are being inserted into their conscious minds by an external force. That's why some say it's a demon or something like that." She paused. "But it's really not. They just have the feeling that's the case. I personally think it's a chemical imbalance."

Nobody offered any analysis on that statement.

After a few minutes Jeremy spoke up. "Anybody else have a comment on this 'devilish' issue?"

Several people laughed at that comment, but none one else took the bait.

"Okay, I guess we'll leave that unresolved for now." He turned to Seetha. "We're delighted to have with us today Dr. Seetha Mathis and

Dr. Gregory Poindexter from the sleep disorders lab to speak to us on the subject of sleep and memory. Dr. Mathis, I'll turn the program over to you."

Seetha stood nervously, unsure of herself. Feeling that something was expected of her, she managed a smile. "I'd really prefer to let my post-doc go first." She nodded toward him politely. "Then I'll follow up." She wasn't about to go first and give Dex the chance to rip up her comments. She knew her stuff, but Dex was able to twist things around to make himself look good.

Dex rose, clicked the PowerPoint slide on the screen, and began his lecture about human memory and all the complexities of its operation. He started with the basics of memory function and how the hippocampus plays a key role in it, then he dove off into the mysterious world of animal research. It was obvious right away that he had much more than a cursory knowledge of lab animal research.

Seetha watched with fascination at first, then irritation, as Dex delved into his animal research projects on memory function. This guy was doing *way* more research than he was supposed to! And he hadn't told her. She tried staring hard at him, but he refused to make eye contact.

"Recently," Dex lectured on, "researchers have demonstrated that the structure of sleep in zebra finches is remarkably similar to that of mammals." He paused, waiting for that to sink in, then continued. "It is now apparent that sleep plays an important role in bird learning and memory."

Seetha's cheeks burned. That's why he had ordered those birds a few months back. Dr. Jackson was right. He had lied to her, saying he was only purchasing them for Lindsey Southward, the biology department's bird expert. All that about holding them in his research facility until Dr. Southward could get to them. Now, Seetha knew he was doing research on them . . . and without Institutional Animal Care approval. Didn't he know the University could fire him for such behavior?

Dex seemed unfazed. He had the crowd hanging on his every word. "Working with birds, I — I mean, other researchers — have found that for a bird to remember a particular song, it must sleep fairly soon after imprinting. Therefore, sleep somehow consolidates the memory. That's where we're going next with research. Trying to further investigate the link between sleep and memory."

He smiled widely, which was unusual for him. "I guess I'll stop there and turn it over to Dr. Mathis." He swaggered to the very back of the room and took a seat.

Members of the philosophy group apparently missed the significance of Dex's statement about where the research was headed next, apparently thinking he only meant researchers in general. But Seetha didn't fall for it. She was going to have to confront Dex about the secret, unsupervised research and soon. But first, she had to get through this talk.

She rose and opened her notebook, nodding courteously toward Dex, though still steaming over his speech. "Thanks, Dr. Poindexter, for that very enlightening presentation. Ladies and gentlemen, it would be hard for me to top that. I guess what I want to do for a few minutes is go over some of the basics of what we do in the sleep lab . . . a little more of the practical or applied end of the sleep research."

She shifted her weight and proceeded to tell the group about the common problem of insomnia in America. "According to the National Sleep Foundation, about seventy million Americans suffer from some form of sleep disorder. And this is big business, folks, at least twenty-three billion dollars were spent last year on sleep aids . . . all the way from high-powered prescription pills to buckwheat pillows to self-help recordings and videos. What we do in the Ole Miss sleep lab is try to help people with these disorders. But to be honest, most often, all we do is help *identify* what the problem is, not *cure* it, though we certainly give advice on treatment methods."

For the next few minutes Seetha explained about the lab and how they processed and evaluated patients. She sprinkled in a few funny stories about eccentric or crazy-acting patients she had had through the years and some of the odd gadgets and devices that supposedly helped with sleep disorders.

While she was speaking, she noticed that Dex suddenly had a strange look on his face, as if startled. Then, he began moving his hands in the air out to both sides, as if trying to hold an invisible object. Since he was in the very back of the room nobody else noticed the odd movements, but they broke Seetha's train of thought. Was he purposely trying to distract her or mock her? But why the terrified look on his face? Was that part of the prank?

Fortunately, Meha, the Asian graduate student raised her hand to ask a question. "Dr. Mathis, can I ask you a question?'"

"Sure, I'd like for this to be informal."

"My aunt in California is a terrible insomniac and she bought some kind of silly watch that measured her arm activity or something like that. She said it would wake her up at just the right time. Are you familiar with that product? How does it work? If a person has a hard time sleeping, how could waking you up be a *treatment*?"

"Great question." She looked back at Dex, who had his head down on the desk now. "That watch is called something like the Sleeptracker. It works by sensing your movements while asleep, because in theory, your arms move around more during lighter stages of sleep. The watch gives you an analysis of how well you sleep at night."

Just then, the door in the back opened and Detective Fox slipped in and took a seat. He nodded toward her and smiled.

Maybe this was going to be a cordial visit after all. The guy didn't seem harsh or intent on arresting her or anybody else.

Seetha walked around to the front of the desk and sat on it. "Ah yeah, as for the watch that treats insomnia, the thing also supposedly wakes you up during one of the light stages of sleep, making you feel better because you awakened during an almost-awake moment."

Meha popped her hand half way up, "But is it worth several hundred dollars?"

"I guess that's up to the patient. If it helps them—"

Just then, Shawanda eased the door open, pointing and gesturing toward Seetha.

"Me?" Seetha responded. Why all of a sudden was everyone wanting to talk to her?

"Yes, sorry to interrupt, but your daughter is on the phone. She says it's urgent."

The blood drained from her face as Seetha ran toward the door. She could have kicked herself for turning off her phone during the philosophy club meeting, especially in light of the stalking incident the other day. She turned back toward Duke Livermore. "Sorry, but I've got to take this."

At the departmental office, Seetha snatched the phone from across the desk. "Sam, is everything all right?"

"Yes, I mean, I'm okay, but it's you somebody ought to be worried about."

"What makes you say that?"

"I checked the mail when I got home from school and there was a weird letter in there."

"What do you mean, 'weird'? And why did you open my mail?"

"Mom, I opened it because it was in a pink envelope and had little red hearts glued all over the outside. No normal person would send you something like that. I knew it had to be a prank or something."

Seetha's pulse quickened. She remembered Detective Fox saying he was going to find out if Rodney was now out of prison. Maybe that was why he was here to see her. "What did it say? Who was it from?"

"It was anonymous, Mom . . . but creepy. And I mean *really* creepy. All kind of rambling about how much he loves you and a bunch of sex stuff in there, too. About touching you. He says he's gonna get you."

Seetha wilted to the edge of the desk. This had to be Rodney tormenting her again; she would need to show the letter to Detective Fox as soon as possible. She tried to regain composure. Remembering that Fox was already just down the hall to see her, she paused. "Sam, I've got a couple of things I've got to do, then I'm coming home as soon as I can. Don't go anywhere . . . and especially don't let anybody in the house."

"Okay."

"And, dear, please call me instantly if you get scared, or if anything else happens, or if you need me."

"Mom, it's just a letter that came in the mail. I'm fine."

When Seetha got back inside the auditorium, Duke Livermore was apparently wrapping up the philosophy club because he was commenting on when they would meet again and who they might get as a guest speaker. Oddly, Dex was standing next to Duke.

Seetha stood at the side of the room with her back to the wall. Why was Dex up there again? Had he been lecturing about his illegal research? If so, that could be bad. She feared the worst.

People stood to leave and soon there was a mix of chatting students and faculty. Part of her wanted to confront Dex and ask him what he had been saying while she was out of the room, but another part of her wanted to see why Detective Fox had come to see her.

The Fox option won out because he was already making his way through the crowd toward her.

"Hello, Dr. Mathis." He extended his hand. "I hope it's okay for me to drop in like this. I tried to call first. . . ."

"Sure, it's a public meeting." Seetha swiped her hair back from her face. "Is anything wrong? What have you found out about Rodney?"

He looked around. "Is there a more private place we can talk?"

Hearing that made the back of her neck prickly. "Yes, over in my lab, but oh, let me tell you what just happened. My daughter called saying that a love letter or something like that just came in the mail with all kinds of weird stuff in it."

"From Rodney?"

"I don't know."

"Is she all right?"

"Yes. I mean, I guess. It was just a letter in the mail."

"Tell you what," he placed his hand on her shoulder, guiding her toward the door, "we're going to your place to check on your daughter and look at that letter, then we're going to have a long talk."

# Chapter Eight

$\mathcal{D}$etective Fox followed Seetha to her apartment late that afternoon so she could show him the obsessive letter and get updated about her now missing ex-husband. She looked at Fox in her rearview mirror as they made their way into the apartment complex parking lot. This was going to be interesting, if not downright scary. The man obviously had news about Rodney that he wanted to give in person. Oddly, part of her wanted to know Rodney's status, but another part wanted to remain in blissful ignorance. She would be terrified to know for sure that he's around again.

But first things first. She needed to introduce Fox to Samantha without alarming her.

Sam met them at the door. "Hi, Mom," she said, then shrunk back when she saw the large man standing behind her mom.

Seetha knew that would be the case. Of course, the girl would be suspicious of men after what she had been through. Seetha had struggled with the same thing.

"Samantha, this is Detective Fox from the police department. He's here to look at the letter that came in the mail today."

"Oh, hi," she said without making eye contact.

"Nice to meet you, young lady." He smiled.

Sam whirled and headed toward the kitchen. "It's in here on the table."

Seetha followed, got the letter, then paused. "Sam, dear, could you let the Detective and me discuss this in private?"

There was blank look, then a flash of anger. "Am I not a part of this family? What is it you can discuss with him that you can't discuss with me?"

Seetha placed her hands on Sam's shoulders. "You *are* family, dear. We just need to discuss some things. Adult things."

"Like what?"

Seetha paused. "Like your father."

That did the trick, because Sam suddenly seemed to have no interest in the matter. She grabbed her books off the table and headed toward the stairs. "I'll be upstairs."

Seetha turned toward Fox. The mystery letter could wait a minute. "There must be a reason you came to see me in person today. You could have just called." She paused. "It's about Rodney, isn't it?"

"Well, yes, actually." Fox shifted his weight. "He was released from prison about three weeks ago, and nobody's heard from him since."

Seetha's heart sank and she turned pale. There really wasn't anything she could do. Rodney would have been released sooner or later anyway. "But doesn't he have to report to somebody? You can't just get out of prison and not have to report in occasionally, right?"

"In theory, that's how it should work, but the correctional system is so overwhelmed. . . ."

Seetha fought the urge to pace the floor. "Oh my God, this is bad." She looked toward the upstairs where her daughter was. "If he comes back around here, I don't know how she'll handle it. It might push her over the edge."

"Try not to worry. I'm here to protect you, and I can ask the Chief to assign an officer to help watch over you and Samantha."

There was a long silence as Seetha tried to process the news. This would change everything about the way she and Sam lived.

"Can I see that letter? If we can prove it's from him, we can have him arrested on a stalking charge whenever he does surface."

She handed him the letter and the envelope it came in.

Fox turned the letter and envelope over and over in his hand, examining them closely. "This looks like typical stationery sold in places like Wal-Mart all over the country, except for the little hearts they cut out and glued to the outside. Anybody could have stationery like this lying around the house."

He held the letter up to the light. "Come here and look closer."

Seetha eased so close to him that she could smell his cologne and their shoulders touched. She had a hard time concentrating.

He pointed at the letter, still holding it up. "Looks like it's been run through a printer, so there's no way to trace it or analyze handwriting."

"But I've heard of the FBI connecting a typed letter to a particular typewriter. Can't you do that?"

He looked at her over his half-moon reading glasses. "Nobody uses typewriters anymore, Dr. Mathis. Of course, there could be slight variations and stray marks from various computer printers and we *might* could identify the exact printer." He paused. "That is, if we had any idea who might have sent this and where they lived so we could issue a search warrant."

"You think it's from Rodney?"

Fox bit his lip. "That would be my best guess, unless you've got other disgruntled boyfriends."

Seetha blushed. "No chance of that."

Fox removed the reading glasses and looked at her.

"I don't know about that—"

Suddenly she felt very unsure of herself. "Uh, is there anything else I need to do? I've got to go upstairs and check on my daughter. I don't want her to feel excluded or unsafe"

"No, that's about it." He walked toward the door and stopped, his left hand on the knob. "I really want to help. Please don't hesitate to call me if you get any other unwelcome cards, letters, or phone calls."

He turned to shake her hand, and oddly, she didn't want to let go. "I mean it," Fox said, "call me if you need anything."

*****

As soon as the philosophy club meeting had ended, Dex made his way swiftly toward his car. He needed to clear his head. The boating accident memory that had re-surfaced during the club meeting was strong and intrusive. He scratched his neck. *Maybe it's only because I just recently viewed that video with the memory*, he tried to reassure himself.

He gripped the car steering wheel tightly. Sweat glistened on his forehead even though it was cold outside. He had to get home to his electronic recording equipment as soon as possible. Today was going to be a new beginning, the threshold of an era. He had never used the research in this way before . . . well, not *exactly* in this way before. As far as human experimentation, he had recorded some of Seetha Mathis's fear memories and even relived them himself, which was an invasion of her privacy, but he had never implanted thoughts, memories, or urges in another person. This was entirely new territory. Sure, he had developed the technology a while back using lab animals, but had never attempted to employ it, at least not like this. He might get caught and go to jail.

Few things scared him anymore, but that possibility did.

He giggled, remembering his religious and old-fashioned mother. She would probably have grounded him for months due to the "sinfulness" of these actions. He was glad he had outgrown all that.

Dex made sure Bonamo wasn't home before entering the makeshift lab he had created in his bedroom. He didn't want the guy around, not tonight anyway. Bonamo had often questioned Dex about the equipment, displaying an uncanny understanding of it, but Dex had tried to hide its real purpose.

He went over every detail in his mind of how he was going to proceed as he made a quick sandwich in the kitchen. Hippocampal or frontal lobe firing patterns translated into short bursts of ultraviolet or infrared lights, undetectable to the viewer, along with carefully constructed dream, memory, and activity promoters placed in a video. But he needed a substrate. What could he use?

He remembered Heather's hot temper. A thought popped in his head and he darted over to the computer on the bar in the kitchen, quickly Googling anger management techniques. Soon he had located several short videos and self-help demonstrations of how to analyze and work on one's anger.

He saved them to his computer for manipulation on the video he would give Heather. When the light on the hard drive ceased flickering, he snapped his finger at the machine. This was going to be perfect and he couldn't wait for the weekend to develop his secret product.

*****

The weekend finally came and Dex was ready to devise the memory impulse video to give Heather. All the way home on Friday afternoon, he went over and over in his mind how he was going to construct the so-called anger management video, secretly implanted with brain neuronal firing patterns mimicking a dream or memory and with urges to act it out. Sweat popped out on his brow. *Would this really work?*

Dex rushed into the apartment headed toward his makeshift lab in the bedroom. He crossed paths with Bonamo in the hall.

"Where's the fire?" Bonamo said dryly.

"Oh, nothing, just in a hurry. I've got a big project due."

"Uh huh, I'm sure you do."

The next afternoon, Bonamo knocked on the bedroom door. "Hey man, you alive in there? Aren't you ever going to come out? Your part of the kitchen isn't going to clean itself up, you know." After a long pause, he continued. "What's going on? I hear a lot of commotion in there."

Dex went to the door, opening it just enough to see his face. The last thing he needed was Bonamo snooping around. "Been busy, Vince. Lots of work these days." He looked at his watch. "I'll get to the kitchen soon, I promise."

Bonamo was holding a hand towel. He eyed Dex suspiciously. "Aren't you going to see Heather this weekend?"

"Sure, yeah, but it'll probably be Sunday. I'm just so busy."

Bonamo wiped his hands on the towel and turned to go. "So you say."

Monday morning at daylight, long before Bonamo was up and around, Dex tiptoed out the front door of his apartment to check the mailbox, hoping that no one would see him checking his mail before the postman made his rounds. He trembled with fear and excitement and pulled his jacket tight against his chest to break the cool north wind. What was he doing? Was he crazy enough to believe it would really work?

He initially cracked open the mailbox, then threw it open. He gasped. It was packed completely full of cash — mostly all fives, tens, and twenties, but still cash nonetheless. He nervously looked both ways before stuffing hand loads of it into his coat pocket.

"Unbelievable," he muttered. He hoped it would be enough to get him caught up on his bills. Just this one time, he told himself; he wouldn't do it again.

Dex was at work by seven a.m. trying to act as if it was just an average day, although he was now over seven thousand dollars richer and much happier than most days. He plotted in his mind which bills to pay the money to first. Maybe it would be enough to make the bill collectors stop calling him.

He sat at his desk, thrumming his fingers on it. He couldn't believe it. Getting that money had been so easy. Apparently there was nothing linking him to the crime. Did he dare try it again sometime?

Dex got up to check his research animals in the lab, made a few notes in his secret logbook about several ongoing experiments, and checked the day's list of sleep disorder patients. He figured most of the patients would say the same old boring, run-of-the-mill, "I can't sleep at night" junk. That changed when he saw A.D. Smith's name on the list. She was one patient he was keenly interested in because she had traumatic memories resulting from a tornado the year prior.

He bit his lip, thinking, *I've got to keep my interactions with this patient off the books and hidden from Seetha.*

At eight o'clock Heather called. She was frantic. "Dex, something's wrong with me."

His stomach clenched. "It's all right. Just try to calm down. What's going on?"

"I think I walked in my sleep last night. I had this dream, I mean, it was so real. I dreamed that I crawled through the roof of a gas station, stole some money, and put it in a mailbox somewhere. Then, when I woke up this morning, I had some scratches on my arms, my shoes were in a different place, and they had oil all over them. It's so creepy. I don't know what to do."

"Calm down. I'm sure it was just a bad dream. Believe me, you didn't do anything."

"But what about my shoes and the scratches?"

"Uh, I don't know. Maybe you got something oily on them yesterday and you just didn't know it. And scratches might come from anything."

"It felt like much more than a dream, Dex. Maybe I should call and make an appointment with Dr. Mathis there at the sleep clinic. She could evaluate me. This has really gotten me all shook up."

"No, no. You needn't do that. It was probably just a one-time thing, whatever it was. Just give it some time."

"But the feelings . . . I mean, they were so real. And the scratches . . . well, scratches aren't something you can make up."

"I don't know," Dex lied. "People with certain anger and anxiety disorders may scratch themselves. It's called neurotic excoriation or something like that. You may have done it during the night. That's why I gave you the video—to help you with that. You did watch it, didn't you?"

Heather seemed to calm down a little. "Well, I took your advice and watched the thing late last night figuring it couldn't hurt to try. I hope it helps me, especially if what you're saying is true. I sorta would like to watch it again today."

Dex went cold. He'd never thought of that. It might make her do it again. "No. Absolutely not. Don't watch it again. And delete it from your computer."

"What? Why?" she asked. "You said it had 'anger management substrates' or something like that that would cure me. Wouldn't it *help* me?"

"Uh, no. In light of your nightmare, I don't think you should watch the video again. Let me carefully review the master copy here to see if there's anything in it that's in any way unsettling or frightening. You should make sure that copy I gave you gets deleted. Do you need me to come help you do that?"

She paused a long time. "How could a video on anger management make a person have a nightmare?" Another pause. "But okay, I guess I can delete it if that's what you think is best."

"There's no *guessing* about it, Heather. You *will* delete it," he ordered.

*****

Seetha had a difficult time concentrating on work that morning. The meeting with Detective Fox last evening had unsettled her. The mystery letter was either Rodney tormenting her again, or it was someone else. A sicko or pervert. Both options were awful.

Dex walked in the office, even more disheveled than usual. He didn't seem himself, and that was a shame. She desperately wanted, no, she *needed*, to clear the air with him. The rivalry developing between them was becoming ridiculous, as evidenced by Dex's behavior at the philosophy club meeting. The rivalry wasn't on her part; at least she didn't think so. That's why she wanted to talk to him about it.

A midmorning break provided the opportunity. Seetha followed Dex into the animal research room. He walked straight for a cage containing white rats with electrical wires surgically implanted into their heads. Dex checked a device, then a computer screen, which was connected by the wires from the lab animals.

"What's this experiment about? Tell me again," Seetha asked as non-threateningly as possible. She knew if she didn't handle Dex just right, he would clam up.

"It's about traumatic memory recall and various interventions to mitigate that." He never made eye contact with her, pushing a computer key to get a printout of the patterns displayed on the screen. "I've been working on ways to block expression of fear memories using replication-defective herpes virus vectors." He looked toward the door of the animal room. "You know, I've actually come to think that the human brain has some sort of 'immune' system that prevents, blocks, or heals traumatic memories."

Seetha had recently heard of a possible brain memory immune system from a scientific paper she had been reading, and knew by his comments on defective herpes viruses that he was injecting the animals with disabled viruses to "kill" certain subsets of neurons involved in traumatic memories. Even though she had included provisions for preliminary work in lab animals in her protocols, she knew he was taking it too far.

"Dex, can we talk?"

He kept working. "Sure, what about?"

"Well, it just seems like something isn't right between us lately. You seem so—"

"So *what*, Dr. Mathis?" He made direct eye contact this time.

"Defensive maybe, or secretive."

"Dr. Mathis, you are my boss, and I respect you in that capacity. If there are *specific* things you want me to do work-wise, just tell me. Otherwise I'd really appreciate being left alone. I can run my own life, secretive or not."

Seetha noticed his plastic smile. He wasn't about to reveal how he really felt. She guessed he would probably continue his pattern of passive-aggressive behavior. Her cheeks flushed. Such a shame, because he was a talented researcher with great potential.

"Dex, your personal life is your personal life. But when it comes to research in this lab, I'm responsible to the department chairman and the university dean of research. Please understand that I *want* you to do your memory and sleep research. It's something you're really good at. But I get the distinct impression from your comments at the philosophy club that you're conducting experiments which haven't been appropriately cleared by the animal use committee and institutional review board, and I won't allow that."

"Which ones?" He waved his arm widely. "Which experiments are not approved?" He glared again. "You know full well that we included this virus vector experiment in the protocol."

He was right about that, but the approval had only been for an initial pilot study with just a few lab mice. He was obviously performing the experiment with rats and who-knows-what else.

"What about the zebra finches? I never wrote a protocol for research on birds."

He crossed his arms. "I told you I ordered those for Lindsey Southward."

"She told Dr. Jackson that she never wanted them. How do you explain that?"

His gaze fixed steady. "Maybe she forgot our arrangement. I have an e-mail from her requesting me to purchase and hold the finches."

"I don't know about that—"

"You calling me a liar?"

Seetha knew e-mails could be cut/pasted and otherwise faked and that Dex was smart enough to hide the complicated and illegal aspects of his research. This certainly wasn't the time or place to get into an argument with him. She had at least accomplished one objective for now — to let him know she was on to him and would not tolerate unethical research in her lab.

Francis broke the tension by sticking her head in the animal room. "Doc Mathis, you got a call. It's a teacher from Samantha's school."

"Oh, I hope nothing's wrong . . ." she said, pushing past Frances toward the reception area.

Frances turned to follow, arms upraised. "Who said something's wrong? They only asked to speak to you. I'm sure everything's okay."

Seetha reached for the phone, expecting the worst. Had Rodney kidnapped her? Or worse?

"Hello, this is Seetha Mathis. . . ."

"Dr. Mathis, this is Donna Jones, principal at Samantha's school—"

"Is everything all right?" Seetha interrupted. "Is Sam okay?"

"Actually, no, Dr. Mathis, that's why I called. . . ."

The room swirled.

"I thought you should know," she continued. "Another student saw her in a bathroom stall a few minutes ago, cutting herself on the arm with a knife from the cafeteria. The girl ran and told a teacher on duty in the lunchroom who confronted your daughter about it. It was only a minor wound, but she was bleeding, so I instructed her to be taken to the school nurse. I'd like for you to come get her and take her to a doctor. And, more especially, I'd like for you to get her some help. She obviously needs counseling in light of this and other behaviors."

Seetha sunk to the top of the receptionist desk. Tears welled up in her eyes. "Are you absolutely sure? And what other behaviors are you talking about?"

"I'll answer the latter question first. Lately, our teachers have noticed that Samantha seems to have spells of forgetfulness and 'zoning out.' It could be a medical issue." She paused a second. "As for this most recent incident, yes, I consider the report truthful. Your daughter *was* found with a knife, and her arm *was* bleeding. Also, the student who reported the incident is fairly quiet and shy. There's no reason for her to make up a story like this."

The scientist in Seetha temporarily over-rode her parental concern. She could deal with spells of forgetfulness later. "But if the other girl was not in the stall, how do you know that's what happened? Maybe there's another explanation. Maybe someone else cut her. She told me she's been having to put up with a lot of crap at school lately."

The principal's tone turned stern. "The girl said she was using the bathroom, heard someone crying in the stall next to her, and was horrified to see spots of blood on the floor — as far as she could see under there — in the stall where Samantha was."

"But how do you know she cut herself?"

A long silence ensued. "Look, Dr. Mathis, this is not the time to argue. I would appreciate you coming on down her as soon as possible."

Ms. Jones' authoritative tone knocked Seetha back to mother mode. Her voice quavered, "I'll be right there."

# Chapter Nine

*D*ex worried himself sick over the next twelve hours, thinking the cops might show up any minute and arrest him for committing a crime through behavioral manipulation of Heather. At home that night, he carefully examined all of his electronic equipment and recordings he had made over the last few months, deleting anything that might seem suspicious. "Surely the police would understand that a university memory researcher does work at home from time to time," he muttered. "Nothing strange or unusual about that." He broke a blue-ray recording of one of the traumatic memories into several pieces and carefully placed it in a small sack containing other items he planned to toss in a garbage dumpster far away from his apartment. He sat back in his computer chair and blew out a long breath. Sweat popped out on his forehead. *What if there were security cameras at the gas station?* Dex shook his head. "No way. There's no way a little dump like DeeVo's would have cameras."

He jumped up, remembering a stack of notes he had made on transferring traumatic memories from one animal to another. Even they were written in coded wording that only he could understand, he still needed to add those notes to his trash bag.

The doorbell rang and Dex almost peed in his pants. He darted to the bedroom window, trying to see who might be parked in the parking lot. Even though it was dark, a streetlight illuminated a white police cruiser in front of his building!

"What am I gonna do now?" Dex's head whipped around, quickly glancing in several directions. Had he destroyed all the evidence?

Then he remembered the sack of trash he was still holding. With a little de-coding, it contained enough information to send him to jail . . . or, at the very least, to get him fired on the spot from the university.

The doorbell rang again, followed by loud rapping on the front door. That wasn't the Avon lady.

Dex started to stuff the trash sack under the pillow on his un-made bed, then changed his mind. He couldn't take a chance on someone else like Bonamo finding it. He would just have to hold on to it until he made sure it was properly disposed of. At least it was in his hands and under his control.

He hurried to the door, paused momentarily to gulp air and steady his nerves, then opened it, all the while holding the little sack low and to his side.

"Yes?"

A big guy with salt-and-pepper hair loomed in the doorway. He was obviously some sort of plain-clothes cop.

"Hello, I'm Detective Jonathon Fox from the Oxford Police Department. Are you Mr. Bonamo?"

Dex was taken aback. Bonamo? Why would the cops be looking for Bonamo? Had Vince ratted on him?

"Uh, no. He's not here right now. Is something wrong?"

"Who are you?" Fox sidestepped the question.

"I'm Gregory Poindexter." He managed to move the sack to the other hand in order to shake the policeman's hand. I'm a, uh, well, I work out at the university. Vincent and I are roommates."

Fox seemed to notice the sack, then scanned Dex for every bit of non-verbal information he could get.

"What department at the university?"

"Biology. I work in the sleep disorders unit."

"Hmm." So this guy worked with Seetha Mathis. "How well do you know Mr. Bonamo?"

"Not well; we're just roommates. We're not *together* if you know what I mean."

"How long have you two lived together?"

"Almost a year, I guess."

"Then how did you meet?" Fox asked mechanically.

Dex paused. Why the interrogation? "Have I done anything wrong, detective? I told you he's not here. You could probably come back in about an hour and he'll be home."

"How do you know that?"

"Because he's one of the Ole Miss indoor landscape technicians. They water and maintain the indoor plants all over campus and that often requires late evening work."

Just then, Dex spotted Bonamo's car zip into the parking lot. "In fact, there he is right now." Dex pointed with relief. "You can ask him anything you like."

Fox turned and headed toward Bonamo, who was now beginning to come up the walkway.

"Are you Vincent Bonamo?"

Bonamo glared at Dex, but was cool and smooth toward the cop. "Yes, can I help you, sir?"

Fox introduced himself as an OPD detective and asked if they could talk for a few minutes.

"Sure, come on inside, sir." Bonamo smiled and waved his arm. "I'll be glad to answer any questions you have."

Fox followed Bonamo and Dex inside the apartment where they took seats in the living room. Dex sat beside Vince on the couch, still clinging to the bag of evidence he needed to destroy. He eagerly awaited a chance to excuse himself. He didn't know why the cops were interested in Vince, but it was rapidly becoming apparent that it had nothing to do with him. At least not yet.

"Mr. Bonamo, I'd like to ask you a few questions about your relationship with a college student here at Ole Miss named Hope Williams, and also where you were on the night of March tenth."

This was his chance. Dex interrupted. "Sir, if this interview has nothing to do with me, may I be excused? I've got some pressing research that I need to get done at the university. Animal research."

Fox glanced at his watch. "At eight-forty-five?"

"Yes, I've got experiments underway with some lab animals and need to check on them at nine-o'clock."

Fox nodded toward the bag in Dex's left hand. "That's not an animal in there, is it?"

"No, no." He looked at the sack, hoping Fox didn't see his hands shaking. "No animals in here. Just some old papers I need to take up to the lab."

Long pause. "Okay, but I may have questions for you later."

Bonamo leaned into Dex and whispered coldly, "Don't think I don't know what you did."

Dex tried to ignore the comment and shot off the couch, bag in hand, but then checked himself. He shouldn't be too eager to leave. Soon as he got out of sight, he almost ran out the front door of the apartment.

Whatever Bonamo was in trouble for, or what he meant by his threatening comment, didn't really matter to Dex at the time. Just as long as it wasn't him the cops were after.

*****

The next day, Seetha sat in a small waiting room across from Dr.

Rajnese Sinkot, the psychiatrist assigned to Samantha's case at the Behavioral Unit of the Northwest Mississippi Hospital. He was quite blunt in his assessment.

"At a minimum, Dr. Mathis, your daughter needs a four-week inpatient-care program. My initial interview with her suggests deep-seated mental and emotional issues, leading to an eating disorder and self-mutilation. I'm afraid that if we don't do a significant intervention at this time, she might have a psychotic break."

"What kind of deep-seated emotional issues are you talking about?"

He paused for a long time. "My assessment is preliminary at this time, but—"

"But what?" Seetha had a difficult time speaking the words. She could barely breathe.

"Surely you've noticed her blunted facial affect and clearly asocial behavior? In the couple of interviews I've had with her, I can see that her thinking is disorganized. It's like her dreams and memories are all mixed together with reality and she's having a hard time telling them apart."

"What does that mean?"

"I'm going to be honest, Dr. Mathis," he said with devastating candor, "it could be the beginnings of a serious mental illness." He raised his right hand as if to stop her before she commented on that. "But we don't know for sure, and if we treat early, the condition may never fully manifest."

"Oh God, are you sure can you help her?" Tears welled up in Seetha's eyes.

Dr. Sinkot smiled. "I think so. At least, that's been my experience with patients like this. Going in big, not holding anything back, can stop, even turn around, the mental deterioration. We have some fairly good medications nowadays."

"Mental deterioration?" Seetha shuddered, repeating the words.

The doctor leaned forward, placing his elbows on his knees and his hands steeple-like in front of his face. "Maybe that wasn't the best choice of words, Dr. Mathis. More like, 'path of intellectual-slash-emotional decline.' "

Seetha nodded, still reeling from the doctor's assessment. "Whatever you need to do, I'll agree to it."

Dr. Sinkot rose from his chair. "Okay then, I'll ask my assistant to generate the necessary paperwork to get the ball rolling."

With that, he turned and walked away. Seetha threw her hands on her face, fresh tears gushing from her eyes. She hadn't known Sam was that bad off. A million regrets shot through her mind. Maybe she should have divorced Rodney earlier in the marriage. Sam obviously was suffering terrible memories and damage from her past. Then Seetha remembered the sleep-memory-therapy Dex had devised for her which had obviously helped. Perhaps that technology could help Samantha.

No. She stood up as if to shake off the thoughts. That wouldn't be ethical. That would be human experimentation without appropriate oversight.

*Chapter Ten*

Two days later, late in the evening, Dex made his way from his apartment to the lab to work on his memory experiments. Driving on the Ole Miss campus was like entering a beautiful state park. Perfectly placed lights around the campus accentuated its beauty. The grass and landscaping were expertly trimmed and lush, adorned in early spring green, and huge oak trees, way bigger than a person could reach around, dotted the campus, giving the place an ambiance like the grounds of an antebellum home on a plantation.

Once on campus, Dex had to drive by the guard gate preventing cars from entering the "loop," an older road that encircled the center of campus and main administration building. Cars were now prohibited from the heart of campus. Seeing the guard shack worried Dex. At first, he didn't know why, then it hit him. The shack was similar in size and shape to the pay booth at DeeVo's gas station. Lots of glass and just enough room for one person. What if Heather felt an urge to climb that structure?

*Uh oh. That's something I never thought about,* he thought, rubbernecking the thing and hoping the scenario in his mind would never come to pass. He had failed to insert in her video some sort of shut-off code or "ending" to her compulsion.

Walking into the sleep disorder lab, Dex quickly reviewed his situation. Seetha's problems with Sam lately had worked out well for him. She had been so preoccupied the last couple of days getting Sam admitted to the behavioral unit that she barely paid any attention

*Jerome & Rosella Goddard*

to her own work, much less Dex's research. That was good, since he desperately needed to perfect some of his techniques. He had found that animal research was long and tedious, often needing to be repeated over and over to verify results.

Dex thumbed through his secret logbook. He had several different projects going on at the same time; one was trying to figure out ways to heal or erase traumatic memories. That project was the only one officially sanctioned by the university, with appropriate methods and plans all approved by the various safety committees. Of course, he was taking the research further than the approvals allowed. They just didn't know it. The second major project he was doing was trying to figure out ways to make people "act out" memories, and the third one was trying to figure out how to transfer memories from one person to another. He was at various stages of progress in each area. For example, he was already fairly sure how to make people act out memories or dreams as evidenced by Heather stealing money for him from DeeVo's gas station. But the other projects were in the infancy stage. One thing complicating his research on erasing traumatic memories was the fact that the erasure process sometime overwrote areas of normal brain and memory function. He had theorized that the human brain, at least in some people, could naturally protect itself against fear memories by isolating them, but experimental erasure was inexact and sloppy.

He drummed his fingers on the lab counter-top. That thought made him re-evaluate the brain memory immune system hypothesis again. Perhaps the human brain indeed had an immune system that could sequester unbearable thoughts and memories and only let them surface when the patient was able to face and deal with them. Therefore, numbing and amnesia resulting from traumatic experiences was somehow a good thing, preventing unresolved and un-integrated thoughts from causing untold destruction within a patient until they were better able to handle them. If true, then strengthening that immunity would be a way to treat traumatic memories. But, conversely, if that immune system was damaged in a person, then the memories might multiply and run rampant, totally out of control.

He turned to go to the animal cages. If so, what would that look like? What kind of person would that be, one with rampant memories out of control?

*Perhaps a mentally ill patient.*

Dex walked to one of the cages containing a white rat with three wires coming out of its brain that were attached to a computer. He had surgically implanted the wires into the naive rat just two days prior.

"Good," he mumbled. "This one's never been traumatized — a blank slate."

He turned on the electronic equipment, slipped on a pair of latex gloves, and then retrieved a foot-long piece of rubber tubing out of the cabinet. He opened the top of the cage. A frown turned down the corners of his mouth. To him, making a fear memory was a necessary evil. Dex whacked the rat with the rubber tubing as hard as he could.

The rat tried to dive out of the way. Sawdust and wood shavings lining the bottom of the cage flew in all directions. The rat made a high-pitched squeak. Dex attacked again, this time non-stop, beating the rat until it was lying on its side quivering.

The computer monitors lit up like NORAD tracking a Russian attack. Lines and squiggles danced on the screen as the machines recorded the brain firing pattern of the rat's trauma.

Dex walked to the sink and washed hair and blood off of his rubber tubing. He slowly caressed the wet tubing. There must be no sign of the torture, anywhere in the lab. That had been the reason for using rubber instruments in the first place.

He went back to the rat cage and carefully stroked the rat's disheveled fur back into place. The few places where he had broken the skin were now appropriately hidden. Then he got a broom and dustpan to sweep up around the cage.

After cleaning up and making notes in the logbook, Dex trembled with excitement. The thrill of scientific research was settling in — finding out things that had never before been known by any human anywhere. He got on the computer and used an editing program to cut snippets of the neuron firing patterns from the rat's hippocampus and recorded them to the computer's hard drive. Next, he used a computer software program he had devised to encode those patterns into a series of light and color flashes. Then he got a new naive rat and attached a mask which contained a tiny video screen to its head. He then proceeded to hook the mask to the computer system with a cable so the rat would be forced to view the neuron firing pattern as a series of carefully orchestrated light flashes.

Dex began to talk to himself, his common practice. "This specimen's brain is pristine. Clean as the fresh, wind-driven snow."

The white rat was younger than the first one, being smaller, with neatly aligned fur. It had been grooming itself frequently, which was a sign of good health. Dex had learned a long time ago that when animals lost their "conditioning," they were ill.

As soon as the cable was connected and in place, Dex held his breath and pushed the play button on his makeshift computer program designed to replay the brain firing patterns.

Almost instantly the rat emitted a squeak, more like a whimper, ducked its mask-covered head, and darted to the side of the cage. It kicked wildly and kept lowering its head repeatedly as if a mighty invisible hand were pressing it down. Soon the rat urinated, defecated, and flopped on its side, breathing rapidly.

Dex tried to rationalize the otherwise normal rat being tortured by the fear memory of another rat: *It's for the good of humanity.* After all, if traumatic memories can be transferred, they can be moved. And if they can be moved, they can be *removed.* This was the stuff Nobel Prizes were made of. Money, fame, and fortune would surely follow, not to mention the respect he deserved.

By nine-thirty p.m. Dex had completed the animal traumatic memory experiments and recorded the data in a secret logbook he kept stashed in his backpack. He rubbed his temples. *So much to do.* His efforts to block expression of fear memories using replication-defective herpes virus vectors were producing good results, but other areas of memory seemed to be affected as well. Dex knew that might or might not be a serious problem, depending on what was overwritten. For example, if one's ability to tie a knot in a string was affected, no big deal, but if the ability to walk was affected by the memory treatment, well, that would be disastrous.

He would have to deal with that later. Like everything else.

Dex sneaked to the front door of the sleep disorder unit and looked outside. He had to be extra sure nobody was around for the next experiment. He darted back inside the lab, dug out a memory device containing human hippocampal and frontal lobe recordings from a hidden stash, and popped it into the computer. He scrolled through the various clips, each containing a brief "leader" labeling the date, source/ person, and duration of the traumatic memory recording. He smiled when he saw one labeled, "28 Mar 2009, A.D.S. grandson, 5 minutes." That had been the newest addition to his collection. He would need to analyze that one soon. He continued searching the recordings looking for the particular one he had in mind to use.

"Aha! There it is," he said, smiling again. It was labeled *20 Feb 2009, S.M., 7 minutes.*

Dex quickly used the "copy" function to move that specific neuron firing sequence, which had already been translated into a complex pattern of lights and colors, and pasted it to the desktop. He then took a few minutes tinkering with various ways to arrange and present the neuronal firing sequence data in different light wavelengths, something he had done before on Heather's video. He did it in ultraviolet light and then infrared, and then using all kinds of different colors, figuring that if ultraviolet light worked, he could secretly transfer the recording to unsuspecting persons. The main point, however, was the *pattern* of neuron firing. That was the message he had to somehow convey to the brain. Then he used a computer program to insert ten copies in a row of each of the sequence variations to a video.

"I hope this works," he mumbled as he removed the flash drive from the computer and walked to one of the sleep evaluation rooms. He already knew how to use the memory/dream firing patterns embedded in a video to cause someone to "act out" a dream or impulse. What he didn't know for sure was how to transfer specific traumatic memories from one human to another. He had tried it a few times using Seetha's memories with mixed results, but had never perfected it. Dex lay down in one of the recliners used for sleep research, placed the portable memory stick in another computer, and began watching the neuronal firing patterns presented as flashes of lights and color. Of course, the images on the screen meant absolutely nothing to his conscious mind, but he hoped his brain understood what the patterns displayed on the screen meant.

A dark shadow passed over Dex. The darkness was like an opaque wall that shut off most of the light in the room. His chest suddenly pulled hard for air, and he felt like he was wrapped tightly in a blanket.

Startled, he jumped up and ran toward the main room, crashing into the wall two times before making it through the door. He fumbled until he found his desk and sat down. The room swirled. He felt sick.

Light returned, but his vision was blurred. Gray iridescence like shiny fog circulated in his peripheral vision.

He was in the boat again, in the Tennessee River, with a terrible storm approaching. Panic seized him when the wind began to howl out of the northwest which was, unfortunately, perfectly in line with the direction of the river. Wind barreled down the natural corridor, whipping the river into an angry frenzy. Waves slammed the boat from the side. Dex knew what was coming next — he would be thrown headfirst into the icy river.

Dex suddenly grabbed his head, trying to ease the intensity of the memory. He grabbed at the air as if holding on to the sides of the boat, then fell into the floor, flailing wildly, unable to stop the sensation of sinking in the water. He kicked his feet and waved his arms, desperately trying to swim upward.

Dex grabbed his head, fighting to control the panic and regain control of his emotions. Maybe he could ride it out and the world would right itself soon. Surely this traumatic memory intrusion was only temporary, sparked by viewing the neuron firing patterns.

He climbed back into the desk chair. Then there was motion. Something in his right periphery was moving. Maybe this was real this time. His heart began to race and a sense of impending doom swept over him. He suddenly felt terror. Not just terror — *intense terror.* Like a real person was in the room.

The movement in his peripheral vision came closer — a dark form was coming from the right. It *was* a person! Dex whipped his head in that direction and struggled to see who it was, though his vision was still blurred. All he could tell was that it was a man. Had someone entered the lab? He hadn't heard the door open.

"Hey! Who are you?"

The man slapped him squarely across the face with such force that

*Jerome & Rosella Goddard*

Dex fell from the chair to his hands and knees. He waved his hands wildly to the right trying to deflect further hits. His face burned with intense pain. "You fat slob," the man shouted. "You disgust me!"

Again, Dex felt a wave of intense fear and terror, unlike anything he had ever experienced before. He rubbed his eyes, trying desperately to look up and see his attacker. The man kicked him in the stomach, bowling him over. He could barely breathe.

"If you *ever* pull a stunt like that again, I'll kill you. Understand? Some things are better left alone." The attacker placed an exclamation point at the end of that statement with another swift kick to the gut.

Dex collapsed flat on the floor again, not able to breathe or think, his mind seized with raw fear.

It was four o'clock in the morning before Dex awakened in the floor of the sleep disorders clinic. He felt like he'd been run over by a truck. Pulling himself up into a chair and rubbing his temples, Dex tried to make sense of what had happened. Then he stood up to clean up the place and retrieve the memory stick from the computer before anyone came to work later that morning.

His knees wobbled. He felt of his ribs. Had he *really* been attacked, or was it the traumatic memory from the experimental transfer? He knew the storm experience was only Seetha's traumatic memory resurfacing, but the second experience — of the man entering the room— well, he wasn't so sure. It had certainly seemed real. The man had clearly said something about "pulling a stunt" and "leaving things alone."

# Chapter Eleven

**S**eetha could hardly bear the separation from Sam. The hospital's behavioral modification program prohibited Sam from contacting anyone on the outside for the entire first week, even close family members. The only communication Seetha had with Sam was indirectly through her doctor who called daily with a sterile, clinical statement.

After a quick dinner of tuna salad, crackers, and bottled water, she paced the floor in her apartment, worrying herself sick. She knew better; this was plain-as-day obsessing that didn't help the situation whatsoever. No matter. It was *her* daughter who was ill.

A brief moment of sanity peeked through the dark clouds of her mind. What if someone saw her through the window pacing the floor and chewing her fingernails like a caged animal at the zoo? Although the sun had set an hour earlier, it was not yet totally dark outside. She walked to the living room window to close the curtains.

A dark form darted from a tree in the open yard into the hedges not fifty feet away. She shook her head. It was too big to be a dog.

She jerked the curtains tightly shut. *Maybe it was only a deer*, she tried to convince herself into believing, knowing full well that the form had seemed more human than animal. But deer have been found in towns more and more lately, she thought.

On the other hand, what if it was a person out there? Rodney maybe?

Seetha took a seat in the recliner, but dared not turn on the TV or any music. She needed to listen. Too bad the neighbors in the apartment next to her were out of town. If not, she could go visit with them for a few minutes to calm her nerves.

After fifteen minutes of quiet solitude, examining every sound inside and outside the apartment, Seetha loosened up. Maybe she was just too jumpy lately, especially with Rodney on the loose. She tried to think rationally. Surely he wasn't stupid enough to come around harassing her. That would be a one-way ticket back to the slammer. Part of Rodney's prison sentence had been to stay away from her and Sam — forever.

Seetha considered calling Detective Fox. After all, he had seemed really nice and helpful the other times she had interacted with him. And hadn't he given her his number and instructed her to call anytime if she felt threatened? She reached for the phone on the end table by her chair, but changed her mind.

Her thoughts wandered to how he made her feel when she was around him. Safe. Secure. The scientist part of her wondered if that was only because he was a cop. No, that wasn't it, another part of her protested, it was because he seemed so real and genuine. She wondered if he was married. He wore no wedding ring. No. She stood to break that chain of thought. If she called, Fox would think she was over-reacting or plain crazy. Besides, he was probably with his girlfriend, or significant other, or whatever. Heck, for all she knew, he was living with some woman and had five kids. Happy as a lark.

He certainly wouldn't want an overweight woman of Indian descent with a messed up kid. Besides, she wasn't even sure she *could* be with a man again.

Just then, something tapped the window. Or at least, it sounded that way. Was this a traumatic memory attacking her again?

The tapping occurred again. That was no fear memory.

Seetha grabbed her chest to keep from screaming. Her legs turned to jelly and her mind raced with fear. What was that noise?

She stood like a statute, listening. Nothing. Then she slowly eased toward the phone on the kitchen bar. If someone tried to break in, she wanted to be near the phone.

Then shadows began dancing on the window and she heard a faint rumble in the distance. Thunder.

"It's about to rain." Relief spread through her entire being. Maybe that's all it was. The wind blowing debris against the window.

When another rumble of thunder rattled the apartment, closer this time, Seetha had the nerve to walk back to the window, push aside the curtains, and peek out. Trees and shrubs swayed in the onslaught of the approaching thunderstorm. For an instant, brilliant lightning illuminated the entire yard, allowing her to see that no one was lurking outside.

Her tension eased. I've got to lighten up, she thought. I've been way too jumpy lately.

Seetha went back to the recliner and sifted through some magazines in a rack by the chair. Heavy rain pelted the roof and windows. Lightning flashed. Thunder boomed. In some ways, the storm comforted her. She smiled. There was one good thing about stormy weather — it was too bad, even for the boogers. Even criminals stayed inside in bad weather.

Just then the doorbell rang.

Seetha jumped out of the chair as if it were suddenly electrified. Her heart jumped into her throat. Who was that?

She tiptoed to the door and stood there listening. For what, she didn't know. The storm was in full fury. She couldn't have heard a bomb go off out there.

"Who is it?" she hollered above the storm.

Silence. Or at least, just the storm.

She ran back to the window, looking outside again, trying

desperately to see the parking lot, but it was not in the line of sight. Lightning again illuminated the yard. Nobody there.

The doorbell rang again.

*There's no way I'm opening that door.*

She ran to the phone and punched in Detective Fox's number.

"Fox," the man answered with a deep voice.

Seetha wilted. What had she done? "Uh, Detective Fox, this is Seetha Mathis, I hope you remember me . . ."

The voice on the other end was suddenly mellow and protective. "Of course, Dr. Mathis, is everything all right? There's a terrible storm out."

"Yes, well, that's why I called. Earlier I thought I might have seen someone in the yard, and now — in the midst of this terrible storm — the doorbell has rung twice. I didn't know—"

"Don't open it. I'm on my way. Give me that address again."

Relieved, she gave him the address.

"Keep the phone in your hand and call 9-1-1 if anything happens. Don't open the door till you know for sure it's me. Understand?"

"Yes."

Seetha hung up. Now all she had to do was wait.

Minutes seemed like hours. Something tapped the window again, but maybe it was just shrubs hitting the glass as a result of the wind. Each crash of thunder caused her to jump and look around, thinking someone was kicking in a door or breaking out a window.

Eventually, there was a knock at the door accompanied by a deep male voice. "Dr. Mathis, it's me, John Fox."

Never had she so wanted to fling open a door and dive into a man's arms. As much as she had issues with romantic relationships, she knew this was different. Then, another part of her argued that Fox was only her security at this moment in time. That was it. Or so that's what she told herself.

Seetha ran to the door and opened it. Fox stood there in the doorway, but he wasn't looking at her. He was shining a flashlight to the base of the door frame where a single red rose and a greeting card were propped. The card was pink, with the name "Seetha Mathis" hand-printed in ink on the outside. Even though there was a porch and a section of roof over her front entrance, the card was partially wet.

Fox looked up. "Are you all right? Has anything else happened?"

She crossed her arms tight across her chest. "I'm fine, I guess." Her eyes went toward the card and rose. Terror, like a wave, washed over her again. "What's that?"

"Don't touch it. I'll get some gloves and evidence bags out of the car. Then, we'll open it."

By now, the thunderstorm was retreating to wherever storms go, leaving only a steady rain. Fox darted out to his car and returned with two gallon-sized resealable plastic bags and a pair of blue latex gloves.

He carefully opened the card at Seetha's kitchen table. It was a standard greeting card about romance, which could have come from any discount store in America. Printed in ink at the bottom were the words, "I love you, Seetha. Can't wait until we're together. Looking forward to touching you." The letters were large and oddly shaped, as if someone were trying hard to make them look weird. For example, the tail of the "y" curled down and to the left like a snake.

"Does your ex-husband print like this?"

Seetha leaned forward, pushing a clump of hair away from her eye. "No, he wrote in longhand, but I guess he could be doing it that way on purpose."

Detective Fox carefully placed the card and rose into the bags and sealed them. "I'll get it checked for prints tomorrow." He looked toward the door. "And don't touch the doorbell or outer door knob till

I can get them dusted for prints first thing in the morning."

He stood up. Seetha's fears flooded back in. *What will I do when he leaves?* Nobody had ever made her feel so safe to be around, especially no man. She didn't want that feeling to leave.

He grabbed his flashlight. "I need to check around outside for footprints."

"But what about the rain?" She reached her hand toward him, then pulled it back. "Wouldn't it wash them away?"

Fox reached the door and turned back. "Yes, most likely, but there could be a place under a tree or bush where they're still intact. I'll be right back. I'll knock and let you open the door from the inside so I won't have to touch the knob."

Seetha followed him to the door. She wrestled with an urge to go with him outside; she didn't want to be alone.

After twelve long minutes Fox knocked on the door and she let him back inside. He peeled off his obviously worn-out raincoat, wet almost head to toe. His hair stood out like he'd just gotten out of bed. "I'm afraid there's no sign of anyone out there. No prints or anything. We have the storm to thank for that."

Seetha watched Fox as he walked into her living room, scanning the place. She knew he was analyzing everything. That's what detectives did. He took out a small pad and a pen. "Dr. Mathis, could you list for me every possible person who might write a card like that and leave it on your doorstep?"

"Please call me Seetha."

"Okay, Seetha." He smiled. "You can call me Fox if you like. Everybody else does."

"Why not 'John'?"

"That'll work too." He nodded. "Anything but Jonathon or Theodore."

She fought the urge to giggle, even at such a serious moment. The names parents give their children . . .

"Who would do this?" Fox reverted to cop mode.

She blushed. She had no boyfriends. "Uh, well, maybe Rodney, my ex, just to torment me."

"Anybody else?"

"There's only one other possibility . . . I have a student worker who seems to have a crush on me, but I'm sure it's nothing."

"Oh? What's his name? We can't overlook anyone."

"Robbie Obergon."

"How do you know he has a crush on you?"

She blushed. "A few times he's made inappropriate comments to me."

"Sexual?"

"I think so. Depends on how you interpret them."

"Threatening?"

"Well, no."

Fox rubbed his chin.

"Are you going to talk to him?"

Fox shook his head. "No. No crime has been committed here. But I do want to check him out. You're his supervisor and have his social security number. Tomorrow I want you to call me with the number so I can run him through the computer. Also, do you have papers with his writing? We can get that analyzed by a handwriting expert."

She nodded. "I'll call you tomorrow with the number and look for a writing sample. I'm sure I've got something in his student worker file that's not typed."

Fox paused a long time, looking at Seetha, as if wanting to say more but couldn't find the right words. His gaze was different this time. She thought she caught a glimpse of something in his eyes that she hadn't seen in years. A certain look. The look — *that* look. Like he was interested in her.

No, she tried to convince herself. It couldn't be. *Not me.* She needed to guard her heart from this kind of thing. Rodney had seemed nice too, and look how that had turned out. Just then, the traumatic memory erupted again. "You're fat and lazy and will never amount to anything."

Seetha stood quietly before Fox, hoping to appear normal. She desperately hoped he wouldn't see World War Three raging inside her.

"Would you like for me to stay awhile and make sure he doesn't come back?" His brown eyes held hers and he smiled almost imperceptibly.

She tried to avoid eye contact. "No, I'll be fine."

*I don't want you to go.*

"Well, please don't hesitate to call me if you have any more problems. I mean it." He caught her eye again. "Anytime."

Seetha followed him to the door, fighting urges to let him stay. She had stopped shivering; now she started again.

He would think I'm totally unstable, she thought.

# *Chapter Twelve*

*T*he sight of Bonamo in the living room of their apartment made Dex uneasy. They needed to talk, but Dex was apprehensive. No, that was understating it; he was plain scared of the guy. Bonamo had an uncontrolled temper and seemed jealous of everything. They had spoken only briefly since the evening the cop came, and each time, Bonamo showed little or no interest in anything other than surface talk. And in one instance, he had clearly scowled at Dex in a threatening manner.

Now, Bonamo was in the living room watching TV and Dex was forced to walk past him. So he mustered all the nerve he could and took a seat directly across from him. "How's it going, Vince?"

Bonamo barely looked away from the TV. "Fine. And you?"

"Okay, I guess. Busy up at work. I've got several experiments running right now."

"Uh huh." He never looked at Dex. "I'm sure that's so."

Dex's irritation temporarily overrode his fear. "Look, Vince. We need to talk. Please believe me when I tell you that I had nothing to do with the police coming over here."

Bonamo clicked off the TV and turned to face Dex, his face showing absolutely no emotion. "Doesn't matter now. What goes around comes around, if you know what I mean."

Dex wasn't sure how that applied to him. Did that mean the guy was going to get his mafia family to beat the mess out of him?

"Why was that cop here anyway? I mean, what's going on?"

Bonamo's nostrils flared, showing his anger, then he softened. Dex could tell that he was trying desperately to control his emotions. "Just a misunderstanding, that's all. Apparently, a boyfriend of my ex-girlfriend got whacked."

"You never told me you had a girlfriend here."

"I don't have a girlfriend. That's the misunderstanding. I've had nothing to do with her or her several boyfriends since we broke up."

Dex shifted uncomfortably. If Bonamo had nothing to do with the girl, how did he know she had "several" boyfriends since they broke up?

"What's the girl's name?"

Bonamo paused a long time. Dex could have sworn the guy's hands were trembling. "Hope Renae Williams."

He pronounced her name slowly, emphasizing each word.

"Is she a student here?"

Bonamo stood to his feet. "I've got some things I need to do. Talk to you later."

*****

A few days afterward, Seetha was finally allowed to visit Sam in the behavioral unit. Gaining entrance to the place was like entering FBI headquarters or the Pentagon. At first, her purse was searched, then she was patted down by a security guard, then she was "counseled" by a nurse practitioner about what she could and could not say to her daughter. Lastly, she had to sign a form stating that she clearly understood the medical center's visitation policy. But just before being escorted to visit Sam, Dr. Sinkot, Sam's physician, poked his head at the door and motioned for her to come with him. Seetha had learned to study the faces of physicians she had worked with during her career as a researcher. She knew they might say one thing, while conveying something entirely different with their facial expression. Today she could have sworn Dr. Sinkot was nervous, even afraid of seeing her.

How could that be? The man was a psychiatrist.

"Dr, Mathis, may I speak with you a minute before you go see Sam?"

She nodded.

"Let's step into my office."

Seetha smiled, hoping he was about to give her a report of the progress Sam was making during treatment. After all, the daily clinical updates had been generally positive.

Once inside the office, Dr. Sinkot pointed for her to take a seat and then his face turned solemn, like a Centers for Disease Control official reporting an outbreak of bird flu on the nightly news. "I'm sorry, Dr. Mathis, but the news is not good, and you need to know that before visiting Sam."

"What do you mean, 'the news is not good'?" Seetha crumbled. "She's under professional care. She *has* to be getting better."

"No she doesn't *have to get better*," Sinkot popped off nervously, then seemed to feel guilty for saying it. He ran a hand through his hair. "What I mean is, not all patients in our unit progress at the same rate. It takes longer for people with deep-seated issues which are compounded —"

Seetha's voice became shrill. She was losing it. "What do you mean, 'compounded'?"

Sinkot looked down momentarily. "I'm sure you recall that we spoke about this upon her admission. I think Sam has several mental and emotional deficits, but as to the most pressing issue, she appears to have a self-loathing resulting from her verbally abusive father which prompts her toward self-destructive and anti-social behaviors."

Seetha nodded. She had seen that first-hand.

Then his tone turned even more serious. "And just recently I've noted a predilection toward multiple personality disorder, and perhaps something even more serious."

"What?" She stood up. "How could that be? That's nonsense."

"We think she's been sexually abused," he said flatly.

Seetha wilted back into the chair and all the blood drained out of her face. "Oh, my God." The words seemed to scrape in her throat. "I had no idea. Rodney?"

"We're not sure yet. We haven't gotten that far because she's so withdrawn."

"Withdrawn?"

"I just want you to be aware of Sam's fragile condition and not upset her in any way when you go in to see her. And *please* don't question her or press her in any way. Just let her know how much you love her — unconditionally. If she happens to say anything weird or strange, don't call attention to it. Just ignore it. Understand?"

Seetha nodded, numb from the shocking news.

Sinkot stood. "Any questions?"

"Can you explain to me more about her condition . . . or *conditions*?"

"Not now. Trust me, there'll be several patient/parent conferences later. Our policy is to limit our discussions until the patient can be part of the conversation."

He stood up. "Now, let me take you to her."

Seetha was devastated when they entered the room and saw her daughter. What had once been a beautiful, vivacious teenager was now a sulking, whimpering mental patient. Sam was lying in bed in a fetal position, pillow clutched tightly against her chest, and with eyes dark and hollow. Fear — no, more like terror — was clearly displayed on her face. Back in her college days, Seetha might have easily studied Sam clinically as a case of early teen psychotic break, but this was different. This was *her* daughter!

Seetha reeled, her knees weak. The utter wretchedness of it all threatened to swallow her.

"Samantha," Dr. Sinkot said calmly, patting Sam's shoulder. "I brought someone to see you. Someone who loves you very much . . ."

Seetha eased nearer and stroked her daughter's cheek, trying to display her bravest face. "Hello, Sam. I've been so excited about coming to see you. I miss you, dear. Dr. Sinkot tells me that you've been having it pretty rough lately. But he also tells me that you're going to get better." She glanced at Dr. Sinkot. "Please hang on, sweetheart. Things will get better, I promise."

Sam recoiled and jerked the pillow over her face. "Don't touch me."

Tears poured down Seetha's face, but she tried to remain calm and upbeat. "I can't wait until you get better. There're so many things we can do this summer, just you and me. We'll have so much fun."

Dr. Sinkot raised his palm toward Seetha with his five fingers outstretched. She knew that meant "five minutes."

Seetha scooted her rear end onto the bed beside Sam, edging the frail girl over enough for her to sit down. "Sam, I love you very, very much." She stroked her hair. "We're going to face this together, I promise. There's nothing so big or so serious that we can't face it together. Trust me."

Silence.

"Sam, can't you talk to me? Isn't there anything you want to say to me?"

Sinkot shot her a stern look.

After another couple of minutes of silence, Seetha leaned over, hugged Sam, and told her goodbye. Then she and Dr. Sinkot left the room.

On the way out to the car, Seetha felt like the weight of the entire world crashing down on her. She felt a powerful urge to do the same thing Sam was doing — crawl into bed, lie in a fetal position, and withdraw from the world.

# Chapter Thirteen

Thursday night at one o'clock, Heather McHann robotically drove her Nissan Altima to Oxford Middle School. If anyone had been there to see her, they would instantly notice the faraway look in her eyes and zombie-like facial expression. She was dead asleep.

She parked in an empty lot across the street, grabbed a plastic bag out of the back seat, and took off toward the tiny guardhouse located at the entrance of the school grounds. What she didn't know was that the school guard was only on duty during regular school hours.

Once beside the guardhouse, Heather struggled with a compulsion to make sure the guard was out checking the gasoline pumps before closing for the night. The feelings were so real. So strong. She looked around for the gas pumps. There were none, nor was there a gasoline attendant.

She thought it strange, but the always-awake portion of her brain reminded her that dreams are often illogical.

Heather then clawed and scratched her way like a spider monkey up the side of the brick building and up onto the roof. She looked a lot like Cat Woman in a *Batman* movie except she was dressed in a white T-shirt and blue shorts. She squatted and looked around, again confronted with a dilemma. The dream she was having and the world she was currently in stood in stark contrast to each other. There was no hole in the roof, no air conditioning duct entrance. No cash register. No gasoline pumps.

She sank to the roof, sitting Indian-style, plastic bag in hand.

Frustrated. Asleep.

Soon she was jolted into reality by a spotlight trained on her from a police cruiser in the road. "Hey," a deep voice commanded. "What are you doing up there?"

Heather shielded her eyes from the bright light. Normal-ness crept back into her mind, like the way it does when someone comes out from under anesthesia.

She was sitting on the roof of a tiny guard shack in the middle of the night!

*I must be absolutely crazy!*

*****

Detective Fox worked the graveyard shift on that Thursday night. He was bewildered when Patrolman Ogilvie brought Heather McHann to the station about two o'clock, describing where she had been found and relaying to him her explanation. Something about having a recurring dream of sneaking in a gas station pay booth from the roof and stealing the money from the register. She had reported being asleep and possibly acting out the dream.

Fox ordered her held in the conference room temporarily. Heather seemed harmless enough and perhaps the event tonight at the school was genuinely just a case of sleepwalking. He had heard of such things, especially in people taking certain prescription sleeping pills. He would definitely need to ask her about that.

Fox rubbed his chin, then punched the intercom. "Monique, would you please come in here." Monique was the nighttime clerk.

Presently she appeared in the doorway. "Yes sir."

"Pull me the report on the robbery at DeeVo's gas station."

She whirled and disappeared. Fox sat down. He distinctly remembered the DeeVo theft a couple of weeks back. One explanation at the time had been that someone might have crawled into the pay booth from the roof.

Monique returned with the file and Fox studied it carefully for a few minutes. The similarities between the DeeVo theft and Heather McHann's sleep walking urges were striking. Small, pay-both type building. A compulsion to climb to the top of it to find a way in.

It was now time to talk to the young lady.

In the conference room, Fox found her to be cooperative and genuine, yet fearful. Probably not fearful of her potential legal troubles, but instead, fearful that she was going crazy. Mascara was streaked under her red and puffy eyes. She obviously had been crying.

"Should I call my parents? Am I being charged with a crime?"

Fox took a seat across from her. "No, not yet. Let me be clear. You're free to call your folks anytime. But at this point, you're not under arrest, so let's just talk for a few minutes. How's that?"

Heather swiped hair away from her teary eyes. "Okay, I guess."

Fox scanned the police officer's report in his hand. "According to this report, you were a student here at Ole Miss until last year when you graduated."

She nodded.

"What have you been doing since you graduated?"

"I teach gymnastics at a local fitness club. Mostly little girls."

"I see you live in an apartment on Gandy Street. Still there?"

"Yes."

"Married?"

"No."

"Boyfriend?"

"Yes, but we don't live together. I live alone."

"What's his name?" Fox scribbled notes.

"Gregory Poindexter."

Fox rubbed his face. Wasn't this the same guy he met when interviewing Vince Bonamo? And the same one who spoke at the philosophy club. "What does he do?"

"He's a researcher at the university."

"What department?"

"It's a sleep disorders clinic or something like that."

Two thoughts immediately popped into his mind. One, this was the place where Seetha worked, and two, this was definitely Dex, Vincent Bonamo's roommate. *How weird that all these people are connected.*

"Have you ever met your boyfriend's roommate, Vince Bonamo?"

Heather sat up, apparently shocked that Fox knew about her boyfriend's roommate. "Why, yes. Why do you ask?"

"You know anything about him?"

"Not much, other than he's a creep."

"What makes you say that?"

She tossed her hair. "Oh, I don't know, nothing particular. He just gives me the heebie-jeebies."

"You ever heard of a guy named Frankie Peterson?"

"No . . . well, should I?"

"Just asking."

Heather nonchalantly crossed her legs.

Fox figured she knew nothing of the Peterson boy murder. "Miss McHann, isn't it odd that your boyfriend, Gregory Poindexter, works at a *sleep disorders* clinic, and now someone, that being you, is sleepwalking and possibly robbing stores. Seems like a strange coincidence. "

"I never robbed a store," she protested. "I only had a dream that I did. I made that clear to the officer who brought me in."

Fox re-read the report. "It says here that you had an 'uncanny feeling' that you really had broken into a gas station."

"Yeah, but it was only a dream."

"Have you ever heard of DeeVo's gas station?"

"No. I mean, maybe." She fidgeted. "Why?"

"It was broken into less than two weeks ago and we think that whoever did it climbed up on the roof and came down through an air conditioning duct."

Heather turned white as a sheet. "I didn't do it! I promise."

"Maybe you did."

Heather sunk her face into her hands, crying. "I didn't do it. Or, if I did, I must have been asleep. Oh my God, I must be losing my mind."

Fox paused a long time. "Tell you what I'm going to do, young lady. The incident tonight at the school seems to be a legitimate case of sleepwalking. I'm not going to pursue that. But, we're gonna have to look into that DeeVo's gas station thing. This is what I want to do: I want to talk to you and your boyfriend both at the same time about it."

He let that sink in, then continued. "Like I said, it sure seems odd that your boyfriend is a *sleep* researcher and he can't even cure his own girlfriend, who is a sleepwalker."

"He's never tried to cure me of sleepwalking," she popped off.

"Then what *has* he tried to cure you of?"

She paused and Fox made a note of that. "Anger. He's tried to help me with my anger issues."

"How?"

"By watching a video of anger management techniques."

"And that's all? No hypnotism or any other hocus-pocus stuff?"

"Nope. Just a video."

"Okay." Fox stood up. "We'll re-visit the DeeVo's thing in a day or two. You're free to go for now."

After she left the room, Fox fell back in his chair thinking. What a strange set of events, all associated with the university sleep clinic. He worried that perhaps Seetha was somehow mixed up in this. No, she couldn't be. She'd apparently had a difficult life. Besides, what could possibly be her motives?

Fox got up to re-wind the clock on his bookshelf even though it didn't need it. He refused to allow himself to think Seetha could be involved in these crimes. With the problems her daughter had been having . . . no, Seetha had to be innocent. He rubbed his chin.

Maybe there was a lot more going on with Dex than Seetha knew about.

*****

Dex was terrified when Heather called at daylight with news of her encounter with the police and subsequent questioning by Fox. He immediately asked her to meet him at Little Pete's for breakfast. Little Pete's was a local mom-and-pop, Waffle House-like place where breakfast was served twenty-four hours a day. Besides, the restaurant was big and spacious with lots of room for private conversations.

At the restaurant door Dex greeted Heather with a stiff hug and quickly ushered her to a small table in one of the side rooms. They needed to talk and *now*.

Dex ordered coffee and a sweet roll for them, mainly just to justify using the restaurant for a meeting place.

"What happened?" he snapped as soon as the waitress left. "And what's all this about the police questioning you about DeeVo's gas station?"

"I had a bad dream . . . I guess I was sleepwalking . . . and they said I might have had something to do with a recent robbery at DeeVo's. Can you believe that?"

Dex raised his palms. "No, no. You're getting ahead of yourself. Start at the beginning and tell me everything that happened."

Heather looked out the plate-glass window and took a deep breath. "First of all, let me emphasize that some of what I'm going to tell you is what the police *said I did*, and not necessarily what I remember doing."

She then recounted the entire night, beginning with going to bed around ten-thirty and later ending up on top of a guardhouse at the Oxford Middle School. "They said I was holding a plastic bag and examining the guard house roof for an opening. How crazy is that? Why would I be up there in the first place? And why try to get inside the thing? There's nothing inside it."

Dex suddenly had to work hard to keep his hands from trembling. He knew *exactly* why she had done the deed. She was merely following urges planted in her brain by his "anger management" video. Preventing re-occurrences of the urges was something he would have to work on in future experiments. He would have to get to that later.

"How did the DeeVo's issue come up?"

"They said there had been a robbery at DeeVo's recently and that whoever did it went down through a hole in the roof." She paused, white-faced. "I think they suspect me."

"Of course not. I can verify that you and I were together that night," Dex deftly suggested that he might provide an alibis for her.

"But you and I don't sleep together." She looked at him strangely. "And you don't even know what night the robbery occurred."

"Yeah, but maybe I could cover for you, if you know what I mean. It's important for me to support you in this time of need. This sleep walking problem of yours could get you into all kinds of trouble."

Tears rolled down Heather's cheeks. She was visibly shaking. "But I've never been a sleep walker. I didn't even know I had a sleepwalking problem. Why would it start all of a sudden?"

Dex shrugged. "Maybe you're just having too much stress right now. I think I can help you through this."

"Like with another video?"

That statement deflated Dex's self-confidence and jolted him back to reality. "Did you tell them about that?"

"Yes, as a matter of fact, I did."

"Did you delete the thing from your computer like I asked you to?"

"No. In fact, I've watched it again two times."

"Why would you do a crazy thing like that?"

"I don't know. I guess it's like a compulsion. You know how OCD I am. But hey, it's actually helped with my temper."

"Oh no." Blood drained from his face.

Heather studied him closely when he said that, then smiled. "Oh, the detective said he wanted to meet with us *both* in a day or two to answer some questions."

"Good grief . . ."

# *Chapter Fourteen*

*A*t work on Friday morning, Seetha sat at her desk, thoughts and emotions swirling inside her like bees around a hive. She was deeply concerned about Sam, and now, the stalker. If Rodney was indeed back, why all this secret admirer stuff? She placed a patient record in her desk drawer and slammed it shut.

"That's not Rodney's style," she muttered. He was an in-your-face kind of guy. She mused a minute.

Unless he had changed.

She knew she needed to talk to someone about these things. Her gut feeling was to ask Dex to treat Sam's traumatic memories. Although he was difficult to get along with, Dex was an excellent researcher who seemed to be making great strides in memory treatment. On the other hand, she knew it might not be wise or ethical. Maybe she could ask Duke Livermore for an opinion in the matter. He seemed like a nice guy who wouldn't judge her.

By ten-thirty that morning, she could no longer fight the urge to speak to Dex about Sam's traumatic memories. Surely it couldn't be wrong to just ask his *opinion* about potential treatments.

Dex was in his office studying graphs containing brain scan-type lines.

"Hi, Dex, can we talk?"

He never looked up from studying the graphs. "Okay."

Seetha pulled up a chair, sat down, and leaned toward the man. She resisted the idea to fall on her knees before him. After all, this was the man who might could save her little girl.

"Dex, I know you know that Sam's in the behavioral unit at the hospital. Well, it's worse now." Her voice cracked and she had to pause to regain composure. "She's a mess. Dr. Sinkot says her memories and her perception of reality are all jumbled together. He thinks she's been severely abused."

Dex looked at her and smiled. "As if the memories are multiplying and running wild inside her head, taking over?"

Seetha was stunned and angered. Why had he smiled and asked that question? Did he somehow understand all the inner working of fear memories and mental illness?

"What makes you say a thing like that?" She drilled him.

"Oh, just speculating. It's perfectly natural for the human mind to attempt to 'wall-off' intense trauma, but sometimes, I think, the memories break out and multiply unchecked—" He stopped mid-sentence, apparently not wanting to talk about it any further. "Do they think it was Rodney?"

"Yes," she answered, but made a mental note to ask him later to explain his comments.

He put the graphs down and looked at her. "How does that pertain to me?"

"I guess I was hoping you could help her cope with these traumatic memories, or maybe come up with a treatment to remove them." She paused, reality setting in. "Or, at a minimum, help *me* know how to help her."

Dex looked back at the brain scans. "I don't think I can help. I'm just a post-doc at a sleep disorders clinic."

Seetha's cheeks reddened. "Oh cut the crap, Dex. You and I both know that you've been secretly conducting animal research on fear memories and, I'm convinced, you're further along in this area than anyone else in the world. Besides, you helped me with mine—"

"We shouldn't have done that," he interrupted. "You yourself said that." He placed the graph in a folder. "I might be out of the memory treatment business."

Desperation swept over Seetha. "I'll let you continue your unorthodox research here, anything, just please help me. I won't tell anybody."

Dex again made direct eye contact with her, an action rare for him. "Are you absolutely sure? Do you realize what you're asking me to do?"

She didn't answer. Just a pleading look.

His eyes rolled and he looked away. "I don't know. I'm so busy right now with the research."

She reached for his hand. "I think your work is really important." Long pause. "Please, I'll beg if I have to."

The corners of his mouth turned upwards in a tiny smile. "Yes, I do think my research has far-reaching implications, but I'm not convinced we should do this work on a child. Not yet, anyway."

She leaned back in the chair. Dex was right. What was she thinking? She couldn't experiment on Samantha, no matter the potential benefits.

Unless things got worse. Much worse.


Seetha spotted Duke Livermore in the faculty lounge when she turned in her monthly activity report to the departmental office. The biology department's faculty lounge was across the hall and only two doors down from Duke's office. She had once heard him say that he liked the location because he could slip over and get coffee without a major disruption. Plus, he could smell fresh coffee as soon as it was made and could grab a cup before the others even knew it was done.

Duke was leaning against the counter top in the lounge. "Hey, girl.

What's going on?"

She leaned against the doorway. "Not much. Just turning in my monthly report. How are you?"

"Fine. Taking a break from the snakes and lizards. Coffee's almost done, want some?"

"No thanks." She looked down. "I've been wired enough lately without adding any caffeine. My daughter Sam is in the hospital."

"I'm sorry to hear that." His face was kind. "Anything Liz and I can do to help?"

"No, but thanks for asking." She turned to go, then checked herself. Maybe she could ask him about Dex and his unapproved memory treatments.

"On second thought, could I ask your opinion about something?"

"Sure, shoot."

She looked around. "Not here. It's a private matter."

Duke poured a cup of the freshly brewed coffee and waved his arm. "Let's step into my office."

Seetha took a seat in Duke's spacious office/lab combination. He closed the door behind them and plopped down in his leather desk chair.

She was impressed with the pictures and awards on his wall, especially a plaque that read, "Best Academic Instructor."

"What's going on?" he asked.

Seetha's emotions were on the verge of breaking loose like waters behind a crumbling dam. She wondered how much to reveal to Duke and whether or not she could do it without totally breaking down. If too much, Duke might become concerned and report Dex's animal research to the department head and the animal use committee, eventually implicating her. At a minimum, she was guilty for allowing her post-doc to perform un-sanctioned work in her lab.

"As you know, my daughter is in the hospital, but the truth is, she's in the behavioral unit."

"I'm sorry to hear that."

"Thanks. Problem is, she's suffered mental and emotional abuse from her father and suffers from traumatic memories."

"Aren't you divorced?"

"Yes, but she's suffering from abuse that happened years ago. It's just now coming to the surface."

"Isn't that good? I mean, that it's coming out? Maybe now she can get the help she needs."

Seetha shook her head and her eyes misted over. "Duke, it's much worse than you can imagine. She's in a fetal position—a whimpering mess." She buried her face in her hands momentarily. "Sometimes, I swear, I just want to run and hide from it all. I don't think I can take it anymore."

She was openly crying by now.

"Before we go any further, let me just say, hang in there. Life is extremely difficult sometimes and we have to just hang on until it passes. Believe me, eventually things will get better."

She shook her head. "I don't know. Everything inside me is urging me to run, to hide, to withdraw."

Duke bit his lip as if choosing the precise words. "You've heard me talk about my wife, Liz, haven't you?"

Seetha nodded. She'd heard of his saintly wife who had a master's degree in philosophy and religion. Everybody around the biology department had.

"Well, she would probably tell you right now to use your *willpower* and not give in to your emotions." He paused. "It's an important concept, you know. The human will is stronger than emotion and acts like the rudder of a huge ship, guiding it along, whereas emotions can toss the ship around like giant waves."

She thought that sounded corny. "That might be helpful to me, Duke, but what about my daughter?"

"Aren't the psychiatrists helping her?"

"Maybe." She rubbed her face, trying desperately to recover from her temporary breakdown and stuff emotions back inside the dam. "Anyway, that's not the point. I wanted to ask your opinion about something else. Something peripherally related."

Duke leaned forward, elbows on the desk. "Okay, I'm listening."

Seetha wiped her eyes again. Enough blubbering. She first offered background information about Dex, his insights about traumatic memories, his official research, and all that. Duke seemed confused about how that related to Samantha, but listened attentively.

"But lately," she continued, "he's been developing techniques to mitigate and even possibly remove traumatic or fear memories."

"What kind of techniques? How do you do that kind of thing?"

She carefully chose her words. "Uh, things like listening to recordings and other 'sleep-learning' kind of things. Nothing invasive. I think he's just trying to soothe or overwrite the fear memories."

Duke rubbed his chin. "That doesn't sound so bad, but I had no idea he was pursuing this kind of research. Why hasn't he presented some of his findings at our departmental seminars?"

Her cheeks felt warm and she knew he could see it. "Uh, I think it's just in the formative stages. He's pretty private."

"If you don't mind me being blunt, Seetha, something's not right here. I can see you're uncomfortable defending Dex and his work. Is his research unethical or illegal? Believe me, I know something about that."

The emotional dam was about to break again. "How?"

"A while back, there was a guy here in this department who was conducting illegal research on animals trying to develop a way to alter the perception of time. It ended badly." He shook his head. "Very badly."

Seetha's pulse quickened and her palms became sweaty. "How so?"

"He and one of his graduate students were killed in a terrible car crash while fleeing the authorities."

"Wow," she said flatly. "Sorry to hear that. To be honest, I think some of Dex's work is off the books and not approved by the research committee, but it holds great promise to help people with traumatic memories." She raked a hand through her dark hair. "And I wanted to ask you about a specific aspect of that."

"Okay, I'll hear you out, but I don't want to leave unresolved this matter of Dex's research which you say is off the books. Unapproved research, no matter how potentially wonderful, can be dangerous. Believe me."

"We can talk about that later, I promise. But here's my question for now. If Dex has developed a technique that can help erase traumatic memories, why shouldn't we use it on Sam?"

"I don't know." Duke shook his head. "Sounds dangerous. Have there been any controlled studies? What are the potential side effects?"

Seetha couldn't let herself think along those lines. "How could there be side effects? It's only sleep-learning kind of stuff. Listening to soothing recordings and the like."

"Is that all there is to it?" Duke cocked an eyebrow. "Nothing invasive? No chemical agents or drugs given?"

Drugs or chemical use was something Seetha didn't know for sure. She did know about the virus vector injections, but that wasn't a drug *per se*. Besides, she didn't want to leave that door open for further inquiry.

*Jerome & Rosella Goddard*

"No, that's about it. Harmless efforts to re-write or cover up the bad memories."

Duke leaned way back in his chair. "This is out of my league. I'm only a snake man, but personally, I wouldn't do anything without the approval of Sam's doctors. Why don't you sit down with them and discuss this new technology. See what they think."

Seetha struggled for an answer to that. "I don't think Dex would go for that. He's so protective of his research ideas that he wouldn't allow me to tell them to anyone."

Duke stood up. "I've heard that before. Kirk Swartz used to say things like that."

"Who's Kirk Swartz?"

"The professor here in our department who did the illegal research and got himself killed."

# *Chapter Fifteen*

*D*uring a quick lunch consisting of a chicken salad sandwich and diet Coke, Seetha thought about her conversation with Duke. His comments hadn't helped much. While she certainly understood Duke's concern, waiting for controlled studies of Dex's new treatments could take years. That would be way too distant in the future to do Sam any good.

She glanced at her watch. Thirty minutes left on her lunch break and five and a half hours before her next visit with Sam at the hospital. Her stomach clenched. What would she do this evening if Sam was still a total basket case? Or even worse?

Seetha looked out the window. A walk in the April sunshine might help clear her mind.

She made her way down the hall and outside toward the Grove, a park-like area in the middle of the Ole Miss campus carpeted with lush green grass and dotted with lots of huge two hundred year-old oak trees. She took a seat on a bench hoping Nature's beauty would soothe her troubled soul.

The air was deliciously cool. A few students meandered along, mostly in pairs, snuggling and cooing, uncomfortably reminding her of her single status. For some reason however, it did make her recall John Fox, wet from head to toe after searching for her mystery stalker in the rain. He had been so sweet to come help her during the storm. He seemed so different from other men in her life, making her feel safe and affirmed.

*Jerome & Rosella Goddard*

That's it, she thought. *Affirmed.* Fox made her feel affirmed. No one had ever seemed to acknowledge her strengths and contributions. Not even her own father or mother. Father because he was just plain mean, and Mother because she was afraid to stand up to Father.

The more she sat there thinking about John Fox, the more something seemed to be pulling her toward him.

Seetha turned and stretched her left arm along the top of the bench. She sighed. What was she doing? She didn't want to get back into a relationship again. She forced herself to look around the Grove to break that chain of thought. The weather was wonderful. Why couldn't her life be like that? The sky was robin-egg blue, with only a few wispy clouds drifting along high above. The crisp, cool breeze tickled her face. The Grove looked like a serene pastoral scene right out of a jigsaw puzzle; however, the peaceful scenery outside stood in stark opposition to her inner being, where the major storm was.

"Why hello, Dr. Mathis," a male voice spoke from behind. "What a delight!"

Seetha whirled to see Robbie Obergon coming around the bench. He took a seat on the bench beside her, getting a little too close for comfort, and smiling widely like somebody who had just won the lottery.

"Hi, Robbie," she replied flatly. Maybe if she didn't encourage him, he wouldn't stay but a minute; otherwise she would have to go back inside to get away from him. "What're you doing out here?"

"Just watching over you—" He seemed to catch himself mid-sentence. "I mean, just watching over this beautiful Grove. It's such an ecological treasure, don't you think?"

Seetha steamed. He was obviously obsessed with her. She now regretted hiring him as a student worker.

"Wonderful day out here, huh?" he waved toward the sky.

"Yes, very."

"There's so much beauty in the world." Then he looked at Seetha. "All around."

Seetha knew that was aimed at her and it caused her to think. Could Robbie possibly be the one stalking her? If so, maybe she should confront him. That might shake him up enough to make him stop. She would have to wait for the right moment to do it.

"I'm sad about the semester ending soon," Robbie said.

"Is that right?"

"Yes, it'll mean the end of your class, my most favorite class and teacher ever." He shifted on the bench and turned toward her.

That was enough. "Robbie, I need to be brutally honest with you about something."

"Yes? What?"

"You say entirely inappropriate things that make me uncomfortable."

Something appeared in his eyes—either coldness, disappointment, or fear. "I'm sorry. Like what? Give me one example."

He had her. None of his comments today could be considered offensive. They were vague and at most, mildly flirtatious. She would have to resort to previous encounters with him for an example. "Well, that time recently when you called me 'sweetheart.' "

"I never said that," he said, seeming indignant. "I only said, 'let me help you with that chart.' "

"Let's not play games, Robbie. You know as well as I do what I'm talking about."

A blank look of innocence appeared on his face. "I'm sorry you feel that way, Dr. Mathis, but I haven't once been inappropriate with you, either in class or at work."

"Were you outside my house a few nights ago?"

He blushed. "Absolutely not."

Pause. "What night?"

She stood to leave. If Robbie wasn't hanging out in her yard, why did he have to ask what night? Did that mean he *had* been out there on *some* nights?

Anger swelled within her. "I'm not kidding, Robbie, if you don't get over this silly adolescent crush-kind-of-thing and leave me alone, we're gonna have to move you to another department for your work study." Her lips formed a tight thin line. "I want you to stay away from me. Do you understand?"

"But I work for you part-time."

"You know what I mean. *Personally.* Stay away from me personally."

A red-faced Robbie looked down. Seetha couldn't tell if he was furious or about to cry. "Yes ma'am. I didn't mean any harm."

She jumped on that. "So you *have* been stalking me and sending those notes."

He stared blankly back at her. "Well, no, I haven't done all that. What are you talking about?"

Seetha drilled him with her eyes. "This had better stop, young man, and I mean *now.*"

On her way back inside the biology department, she considered what had just transpired. Even though he had mostly denied it, Robbie was obviously the one stalking her and sending strange notes. She had noticed him blushing during his denial; the boy wasn't a good liar. And although it was creepy, she actually felt relieved. It made perfect sense. Robbie was "in love" with her or something like that, and that infatuation was causing him to act out. This was just a silly crush on a teacher, she reminded herself. Plus, if it had been her ex-husband Rodney, he wouldn't have been so passive. He would have been at her door, screaming at her, face red as a beet, veins bulging out of his neck everywhere. Maybe even with a knife or gun in his hand.

She made a mental note to call Detective Fox about this new development as soon as possible. Oddly, something inside her was tingling with excitement to do just that.

*****

Dex was back in the sleep lab, lines, flashes, and colors on the electronic display screen wriggling like honeybees doing their primeval dances. Just like all the times before, Dex slipped into a dream-like state and was enveloped in a thousand sensations; he was re-living a memory. One of Seetha's fear memories he had recorded. Yellow iridescent light swirled in his periphery, but the center of his field of view remained clear.

Memories again began to play out before him. The office had been stuffy. Sweat popped out on her forehead, but not from the heat. She worked through the stack of patient files as quickly as possible because she simply *had* to get home before Rodney did. She dared not allow him to be there alone with Samantha. Not since *that* time. The time she came home and found him pressing her against the wall, screaming obscenities into her face. Telling her how overweight and ugly she was. All the poor little thing could do was try to pinch him. Seetha couldn't allow that to happen again.

A flash of light shot across Dex's view, interrupting the scene. He tried desperately to see what it was, but the memory trance was so strong, so dominant, that nothing could break its spell. It seemed as if a personality or spiritual being were living inside his head, forcing him to re-live events whether he wanted to or not.

The memory switched to a different one.

She was in a car. The radio was playing. All of a sudden a dog ran out into the road in front of her. The woman screamed and swerved hard to the right. Everything went black.

More flashes of light. Dex's face tingled. From what, he didn't know.

She was at a residence now, looking outside the window. Maybe it was her home. It was nighttime. A storm was coming. Someone — or something — darted out from behind the bushes. Her heart raced. Someone had been watching her!

Two hours later Dex woke up, his head resting on the lab table. He ached all over and his eyes felt strained. What had just happened? The memories had been jumbled this time.

He scrambled for the lab notebook lying open nearby. He needed to make notes and observations while they were fresh on his mind.

"Let's see," he said, picking up an ink pen at the lab counter top. "First of all, moving memories from one host to another isn't very precise," he wrote. "Memory transfer may be sloppy, with no clear-cut beginnings and endings. Apparently, memories can be jumbled or mixed with other ones. Work on this later."

"Secondly," he wrote, "traumatic memories can be life-like, even personality-like. Do a literature search on that later as well."

He paused a minute trying to put into words what he had experienced. This was otherworldly.

# *Chapter Sixteen*

*O*n April 22, Dex and Heather met with Fox in his office at the police station. Since the guardhouse incident had occurred almost a week earlier, Dex had begun to think nothing would ever come of Fox's investigation. No such luck. The detective had called yesterday, asking for a joint interview with him and Heather.

"As both of you know," Fox began after a brief introduction, "Heather was found on top of the guard house at the Oxford Middle School, apparently attempting to break in through the roof."

"You have no evidence that she was trying to break in," Dex interrupted. "She told me that she was sleepwalking and just ended up there. Sleepwalking can do things like that to people, you know."

Fox seemed irritated. "Not correct, young man. She told our officer that she had been dreaming about climbing down through the roof of a gas station and that's what she was trying to do at the guardhouse. She was acting out her dream." Fox rose and placed his hands flat on the desk. "Please let me finish before saying anything else."

He walked around the desk. "I've heard of people acting out their dreams, but that's not what bothers me about this case." He gave Dex a stern look that pierced his soul. "What bothers me is that you are a sleep researcher and, oddly, your girlfriend here suddenly begins acting out her dreams."

"You have no evidence of that." He shifted his weight uncomfortably. "You can't put that on me. That's just coincidence. She could've just seen a movie or something about climbing on buildings."

"Coincidence? I assure you, this is more than coincidence."

Dex fell silent. What else did Fox know?

"And, compounding the situation," Fox continued, "someone broke into DeeVo's gas station in a similar manner a few weeks back. According to our police report, Ms. McHann, you denied having had anything to do with that break-in, but during the Oxford Middle School incident, you said you kept having a compulsion to look for a hole in the roof and to check for a gasoline attendant. Why would you be looking for a gasoline attendant at a school?"

"See, that's all it was." Dex waved his arms. "She had just seen a movie or something about buildings and roofs, and gasoline stations. She was obviously sleepwalking."

Fox reddened. "Do *not* interrupt me again."

He turned to Heather. "Do you have an explanation for these compulsions of yours?"

"No, sir." She shook her head. "I can't explain it."

Fox leaned against the front of the desk, watching them both. "Doesn't it seem odd to you that all these things are related?" He focused on Dex. "The one common thread in all this is *you* and your sleep research."

Heather looked over at Dex, seemingly confused. Dex rubbed his hands on his thighs, hoping their relationship ran deep enough to withstand this scrutiny. He reached for her hand. "Perhaps she read about the robbery at DeeVo's in the newspaper or heard about it on the news, and then dreamed about it. Things like that have been reported in the scientific literature. I've seen them."

"So you say." Fox smiled. "Tell you what, bring me copies of such science papers that report these things and I'll be satisfied."

"Uh, well, I'll have to look them up."

"You do that." He walked to the door and opened it for them. "I've got time. I can wait a week or so for you to find and copy the papers."

Dex turned several shades of red.

\*\*\*\*\*

That evening at home Seetha desperately tried to relax, but it wasn't possible. Not until Sam was home from treatment and everything was back to normal. At least, as "normal" as could be expected for a single mom raising a young teen. She sat in a recliner, thumbing through magazines and science journals, though she couldn't concentrate. She looked toward the window, recalling the night of the storm and the mysterious love letter at her doorstep.

Chills crept along her spine. *What if he's out there again?*

She pitched the science journal aside and tiptoed to the window for a peek outside. Night was falling, casting shadows along the ground and yard outside. The hair on the back of her neck stood up.

No one in sight. Or was there? Dark shadows hung around the trunk of every tree. He could be out there watching her.

The phone rang. Seetha jumped as if she'd seen a snake.

She ran to pick it up, but hesitated. Was this him?

"Hello?"

"Seetha—"

John Fox! Relief instantly spread through her.

"Oh, hello, Detective Fox." She tried to conceal the shakiness in her voice. "I'm *so* glad you called."

"I was just calling to check on you. Are you okay?"

"I think so, maybe." She ran a hand through her hair.

Fox paused. "You sure?"

"Yes, absolutely." She tried to infuse confidence into her voice.

"How about Sam?"

"Maybe a little better today. I talked to Dr. Sinkot earlier and he

*Jerome & Rosella Goddard*

gave a fairly good report. He's hoping she can come home in a couple of weeks."

"Good news. That's very good news."

Long pause.

"How about you?" she asked. "Anything happening in the investigation? Any word on the whereabouts of my ex?"

"Some progress." Pause. "Uh, but mostly not in regard to your situation. No sign of Rodney."

Seetha shuddered. "I hope to God he stays away from me and Sam."

"You still think it's him?"

"Maybe." Chills again. "He hates me, John. I tell you, the guy hates my guts."

"That may be true, but it doesn't mean it's him stalking you. Could be that Obergon kid."

Seetha sat down. "I guess you could be right. Speaking of him, I confronted him a few days ago about being obsessed with me and he sort of admitted it. When I asked about being outside my house on the night of the storm, he didn't act surprised. It made me think he's watched me from the yard on more than one occasion."

"Good. Keep being firm with him and he'll get the message. I'm planning on talking to him myself soon. I don't want anyone bothering you."

Awkward silence.

"Thanks, I appreciate that. But, he's my student worker. I'd rather you not be too hard on him."

"Don't worry. I won't."

Pause again.

"Well, I guess I'd better go," Fox said. "Like I said, I was just checking on you. Hey, maybe we could meet sometime for a cup of coffee."

She smiled and leaned back in the recliner. "I'd like that very much."

"Okay, I'll look at my calendar tomorrow and call you to set something up. Deal?"

"Deal."

With that, Fox hung up, leaving Seetha to bask in thoughts of dating and romance. Something she hadn't done in a long time.

# Chapter Seventeen

*T*wo and a half weeks later Seetha made her way across town to the behavioral unit at the hospital. She was anxious. This was Sam's release date, at least release into outpatient care where she could stay at home. Even though Sam had clearly made progress during treatment, she had a long way to go. She could now talk and had returned to some semblance of normalcy. Dr. Sinkot said she should come in for counseling five days a week for the first two weeks after release, then three times a week for another month. Fortunately, school was almost out and Sam would be available for these treatments; Seetha just needed to make arrangements with the school principal.

At the hospital, Seetha met Sam in Dr. Sinkot's office. She found her dressed in jeans and a pullover, not unlike any other youth her age, and had her hair neatly brushed. However, she was standing by a chair, arms to her side, with an emotionless look on her face, like someone numb to the pleasures or pains of life. Seetha grabbed her and hugged her tightly. "You look so good, sweetheart. This is your big day. You've made great progress and I'm very proud of you."

"Okay, Mom. I feel fine, and fine is a grade used by coin collectors."

Seetha looked her in the eye. *What kind of strange answer was that?*

Dr. Sinkot intervened. "Let's sit down for a minute. I need to give you some 'out-processing' advice and instructions."

Seetha took a seat, but Sam remained standing. Seetha motioned downward with her arm. "Have a seat, dear. It's okay. I'm sure this won't take long and then we can go. I'm excited about us going home together."

No comment, just a blank stare. Sam looked straight ahead at Dr. Sinkot. Oddly, he didn't force her to sit down, but instead, acted as if this defiance was normal.

"Dr. Mathis," he began, "Samantha has had a difficult time here in the program, especially the first week, but she's made a lot of progress. You should be aware that she's in a *process* of healing and restoration that may take some time. Her thinking and speech may at times seem unorganized, but neither one of you should be alarmed or worried." He paused. "She's going to be just fine."

As was the case the first time she had met with Sinkot, Seetha again noticed that his face and eyes didn't match his words. He probably had no idea if she was going to be 'just fine' or not. He was just saying a bunch of doctor talk and she knew it.

"It's very important for you to continue with the treatments and the medications." He looked at Seetha. "Please don't let her miss a session or even be late. This is crucial for Sam's recovery. Understand?"

"Of course."

He handed Sam a hardbound notebook similar to the logbooks Seetha was accustomed to using in the lab. "Now Samantha, each day, I need you to write in this journal your deepest thoughts and feelings. Try your best to describe exactly how you feel so we can talk about it when you come in for your appointments. You think you can do this for me?"

She nodded, but her eyes conveyed a fearful or pleading look.

"Perfect. I'm confident you'll do this for me." He reached for a large stack of paperwork bound with a large black binder clip. "One

*Jerome & Rosella Goddard*

more thing, Dr. Mathis, here's a prescription for her meds, and uh, I need you to sign these release forms. It's a routine matter, I assure you. They're just saying that you're pleased with the way we handled things while Samantha was here."

Sam walked to the door and stood there waiting, while Seetha grabbed the written prescriptions and stack of forms which had a legal form letter on top containing several signature blocks. She thumbed through the stack which appeared to be daily observation records and treatment notes. Nothing seemed unusual until she read the legal disclaimer on the top page, which read:

*I understand that during treatment of my daughter, various events, traumas, and experiences may have occurred which were beyond the control of the hospital or its staff and management. Therefore, I agree to hold harmless and not pursue legal action against the hospital, its physicians, staff, owners, and operators for any such occurrences that may have happened during her treatment. I understand that her best interest was always the utmost concern and that, ultimately, my daughter was not harmed during her treatment in any way, emotionally, physically, or otherwise.*

Red flags went up everywhere in Seetha's mind. "I think I need time to read this before I sign anything. Can't I do it later?"

Sinkot blushed. "I'd rather you not. Our regulations require that these be signed and filed before anyone is released."

Seetha vacillated. Maybe it wasn't a big deal. "Let me ask you a question, Dr. Sinkot, and I want an honest-to-God answer."

He shuffled his feet. "Okay, sure."

"Is there anything in these patient records that *you think* I would be displeased with?"

Long silence. She now knew something had happened and they were trying to cover it up.

"Only one thing, actually," he said. "But Sam's safety was never in question that we know of."

"That you know of . . ." Seetha's voice became loud. "What happened?"

"Mom, can we just go?" Sam interrupted. "It was nothing, really."

Seetha whirled to face her daughter. "What happened? Did these people hurt you in any way?"

"No, Mom, nothing happened. Could we just go?"

"Just wait, Darling, we'll go in a minute." She turned back to Dr. Sinkot. "Tell me right now, or I'm calling an attorney."

Dr. Sinkot seemed embarrassed. "As I said, Dr. Mathis, Sam had a very difficult time the first week. We had a hard time, shall we say, 'stabilizing her.' Well, during that time, she escaped for a few hours."

Seetha blew up. Her faced burned and she blinked back angry and humiliated tears. "You mean my daughter, a patient in your care, got away? For how long?"

"Only a few hours. But she came back. Maybe she just needed some time to think."

Seetha looked at Sam. "Is this true? Where did you go?"

"Oh, Mom, it was nothing. Give it a rest. Like Dr. Sinkot said, I just needed to clear my mind for awhile."

"But you could've been hurt or injured."

"But I wasn't."

"Where were you?"

"I just went for a walk around town, that's all. I came back . . . and back is good. Like I said, no big deal." She waved her arm toward the door. "Now can we please go?"

"But how did you get past the hospital security? Seetha shot a glare over at Dr. Sinkot.

Sam shrugged.

"I'm not signing this until I know more," Seetha pitched the stack of papers back on Sinkot's desk.

"Well then, I guess Sam can't be released today." He crossed his arms across his chest.

Seetha paused for a long time, looking from Sam and then back to Dr. Sinkot. "Okay, I'll compromise. I'll promise to be open-minded and not be so quick to sue you for this obvious breach of patient safety and security, if you'll agree to let me take my daughter home right now. I want to talk to her in private about what happened during her stay here. If, and only if, she convinces me that her safety and welfare were never endangered, I'll drop the matter. Deal?"

Dr. Sinkot seemed relieved. "Okay, but I can assure you, there was no breach of patient care or safety. Let me reiterate that it's not unusual for a patient to have a difficult time here the first couple of weeks. When someone *is determined* to sneak out, there's not much we can do."

Seetha wasn't so sure, but at the moment it didn't matter. She could re-visit the matter with Sinkot when Sam wasn't around.

Within fifteen minutes she and Sam were on their way home.

*****

Two days later, Fox called Seetha asking her to meet him for coffee and dessert at Newt's located just off the square in Oxford. The invitation caught her off-guard. She had been so pre-occupied with the situation with Sam that she had forgotten his promise three weeks ago to get together.

Seetha hung up the phone. The guy obviously didn't get in a hurry. But that was okay. At least they were finally going to meet for a social outing. The thought of a "date" made her at once both excited and scared. She wasn't sure if she was ready for the dating scene.

Maybe . . . because Fox seemed different from other men she had been around.

Seetha juggled her patient schedule around the next day so she could meet Fox for coffee after lunch. Sam was at school until three-thirty so Seetha had an hour or so free.

Walking through the streets of the small town, Seetha checked her appearance reflecting back at her from the storefront windows. Seriously, why would Fox want to have coffee with her? She wasn't much to look at, and emotionally she was about as stable as a leaf lying on the ground on a windy November day. Surely he could see that. He was a detective.

The restaurant was a local coffee shop with charming wood tables scattered among islands of potted plants and small indoor trees. Fox rose from one of the tables to meet her, smiling and extending a hand.

Seetha immediately noticed a difference in his demeanor and guessed this was the "off duty" John Fox. There was definitely more kindness in his face than she had ever seen before.

"Have a seat." He waved an arm. "Thanks so much for coming. I hope it wasn't too much trouble."

"No trouble."

"How's Sam?"

Seetha smiled. "Home now. So far, so good." She dared not tell him about Sam's escape from the behavioral unit. She needed more time to process all that. At least she had Sam home again.

"Great news. I hope she continues to improve." Fox looked at his watch. "How long do we have?"

Seetha moved the napkin holder aside when the waitress came with a list of specialty coffees and teas. "Until Sam gets out of school. I don't have to go back to work right away. There's considerable leeway in scheduling our research projects and sleep disorder patients. Besides, I have a nurse who works for me who does much of the clinical testing for our patients, then either Dex or I review the test results and schedule a consultation with the patient.

"Do you like working there?"

She twiddled with her hair over her shoulder. "Yeah, it's a satisfying job . . . most of the time."

Fox suddenly seemed to be studying her face for clues.

"Oh, it's not what you may think. I really do like helping people with sleep disorders, and the research is intellectually stimulating. It's just—" Seetha stopped short.

"Just what?"

She didn't want to talk shop, so she tried to sum it up quickly. "Personnel issues."

"Like that guy, Dex, your loose cannon?"

She nodded.

"I see."

What else could the detective see? That made her nervous. The traumatic memory reared its ugly head again, as if someone were shouting in her ear, "You're fat and lazy and will never amount to anything."

Seetha sat quietly before Fox, probably looking like an idiot.

He seemed to sense her inner struggle. "Seetha, I really appreciate you meeting me like this." The kindness of his face soothed her. "It means a lot to me. I'd really like to get to know you more."

She blushed and mumbled who-knows-what in response. Probably incoherent babble.

That didn't deter the guy. Fox continued gently asking questions and making conversation until she finally was able to relax and enjoy being with him. Soon she found herself wishing this could last forever.

"Tell me something about yourself," he continued, then placed his elbow down on the table, resting his cheek in his hand, as if eagerly awaiting an answer.

Seetha wandered about conversationally, telling him bits and pieces about her Indian-borne, physics-professor, father and her upbringing in the college environment at the University of North Alabama. She left out most of the negative aspects, though she figured Fox was good enough to read between the lines.

After an hour and a half, Seetha realized she needed to go, but she certainly didn't want to leave. Fox seemed to genuinely care for her and made her feel safe. "Well, I guess I need to get home to check on Sam," she said reluctantly. She finished off her coffee and wiped her mouth with a napkin. "Ever since she got out of the hospital, I've been trying to run home every day after school to check on her for a few minutes."

"I completely understand."

He escorted her outside to the street. Seetha turned toward him. She didn't want to break the romantic ambiance, but desperately needed to know if anything new had been found out about her ex-husband. "Have you found out anything more about Rodney?"

He paused. "You're convinced it's him coming back to stalk you? You know it could be the Obergon kid. Rodney's gotta know coming back here to harass you is a one-way ticket back to jail."

She shuddered. "It's Rodney. He hates me, and I'm afraid he wants me and Sam dead."

He stepped up to her, put his arm around her, and pulled her close. A wave of peace washed over her.

"Don't worry. I'm not going to let anything happen to you or Sam."

*****

By nine-thirty the next morning, Seetha was busy at work when Tonya tapped on her door. "Dr. Mathis, there's a walk-in out here who says she needs to talk to you. Apparently, she knows you."

"Who is it?"

*Jerome & Rosella Goddard*

"Heather McHann."

"Oh, of course I know her, that's Dex's girlfriend." She stood to go out front. "But he's not in this morning. Wonder what she wants?"

Seetha found Heather standing at the receptionist desk and immediately noticed the dark circles under her eyes. She appeared emotionless, if not downright depressed.

"Dr. Mathis, I'm so glad you're here." The darkness on her face temporarily brightened.

Seetha shook her hand. "It's nice to see you, Heather. What brings you in? Dex is out this morning."

Heather glanced toward the door. "It's actually you I wanted to talk to . . . but I don't have an appointment."

Seetha leaned over Tonya's desk to see the appointment calendar. Their nine-thirty appointment was already checked in. Seetha pointed at the name. "Where's this patient?" she asked Tonya.

"In with Frances for the preliminary work-up."

Seetha turned back to Heather. "Okay, I might can squeeze in a few minutes." She pointed toward a door. "Let's go into one of the patient rooms."

Inside the room, Heather unloaded. "Dr. Mathis, I'm sorry to bother you like this, but I need help. Two times over the last few weeks I've apparently sleepwalked."

"Sleepwalking is a fairly common condition—"

"Oh, it's more than simple sleepwalking," she interrupted, locking eyes with Seetha in a pleading look. "I actually go places and climb up on things."

"How do you know that? Maybe you just have the impression that you do."

She shook her head. "No, in the latest incident, I was arrested for being on top of the guard shack at the Oxford Middle School in the middle of the night. I *really* was there. I *really* was arrested. That was no impression."

That got Seetha's attention. "What about the first time?"

"Well, that's one I'm not for sure about. I just woke up with a strong feeling that I had climbed into a pay booth at a gas station. And there was grass in my bed the next morning."

"But you don't know for sure that you did it?"

Heather inhaled deeply. "Well no, but the police detective seems to think I did."

"Would that be Detective Fox?"

"Yes, do you know him?"

"Uh huh."

"The cops said someone stole money from DeeVo's gas station the same night that I had the intense dream or feelings or whatever you call them."

Seetha made a mental note to speak to Fox about the incident, then had second thoughts because of patient confidentiality rules. Then a thought hit her. How much did Dex know about this? Worse yet, did he have anything to do with it?

"Heather, have you spoken with Dex about this?"

There was a long pause. "Yes, he and I were both interviewed by the detective about the DeeVo's incident."

"I see. But have you asked Dex about these urges that occur during your sleep?"

Another pause. "To be honest, I'm beginning to not trust him like I used to, and I don't know what to believe or not to believe anymore about sleep and memory."

Seetha looked at her watch. Heather had dodged that question. "Okay, maybe we can re-visit that later. Tell me more about this sleepwalking and your urges to climb up on things."

"I know it sounds weird, but the best way I can describe it is like there's a renegade thing running around inside my subconscious. It pops up every now and then, even when I'm awake sometimes, urging me to climb up on top of small tower-like structures—" She stopped short. "And there's more, but I'd rather not tell you that right now."

"Does this urge prevent you from sleeping?"

"Not really. It's *me* not letting myself sleep, afraid of what may happen if I do go to sleep."

"Hmm. This 'thing' you call it, running around inside your head, tell me more about it." Seetha picked up her notepad and a file folder. She would need to start a file on Heather.

"I'm sorry, but that's the only way I can explain it. It's as if my mind contains the urge temporarily, then it breaks out and moves to another location." Heather's hollow eyes suddenly looked sadder. "It's very scary. Is my brain out of control? Can you help me?"

Seetha drew in a breath. "It's not your *brain* out of control, Heather, but possibly the thoughts within it, or at least your *impression* of those thoughts. I might could help you with the non-clinical aspects of insomnia, but this might require a medical consult." She reached for Heather's arm. "It could be something relatively simple like a chemical imbalance or dietary deficiency. Please try not to be afraid."

Heather grabbed Seetha's hand. "How can I *not* be scared. It's like I'm possessed by these thoughts."

Seetha stood, signaling that she needed to get to her next appointment. Heather stood up as well, but seemed reluctant to leave. "What should I do?"

Seetha hugged her. "First, we're going to schedule you for an appointment where we can do a more thorough work-up." "We'll get Tonya to set that up." Then she reached for a note pad. "Here, let's exchange phone numbers. Please call me anytime if you need to talk."

She placed her hands on Heather's shoulders. "I mean it—anytime."

# *Chapter Eighteen*

*L*ife continued to stabilize the next week, or so it seemed. Seetha enjoyed having Sam back at home and tried desperately not to upset her or confront her about anything. For the most part, Sam seemed lucid and stable, although emotionless about half the time. There was still a considerable intangible "distance" between her and Seetha, but Seetha hoped that distance would fade with continued outpatient care.

Personally, things were better for Seetha. Her interactions with John Fox by phone and in person continued. She often reflected back upon her date with Fox at the coffee house and his strong arms around her before their departure. Was she falling for him? Everything about being with him seemed so natural. She found herself thinking of him often and anticipating their next encounter. This man was definitely nothing like her father or Rodney. Maybe he was different enough that even Sam could trust him. Thoughts of the three of them together excited her like nothing had in years.

\*\*\*\*\*

"You sure you're okay leaving Sam a couple of hours?" Fox asked when he picked up Seetha at seven o'clock to go to a movie. He didn't want to go too fast in their relationship, especially with her having a sick child.

"It'll be okay." She buckled her seat belt in Fox's shiny black Murano. "She seems to be doing pretty good so far. I was glad I could get Ms. O'Brien to watch her tonight."

"Who's that?"

"Her friend Molly's mom." She smiled. "There are only a few people in town I'm comfortable letting Sam stay with. The O'Brien family is one of them. Stable home, good, honest church-going folks."

"Actually, that's becoming a minority these days."

"What do you mean?"

"The traditional nuclear family with a mom and dad and children." Fox paused, thinking it odd that he would say that. Did that mean he longed for that kind of family himself?

When he turned out on Highway 7, Fox reached over and took her hand. "I want you to know how much I've enjoyed the times we've been together recently."

"Me too." She squeezed his hand.

The newly constructed Royal Cinema 10 Theater was just outside town, located near the Kroger store where the stalker had first been seen. Seetha must have noticed it because she immediately brought the matter up, reminding Fox about her confrontation with Robbie Obergon.

"Like I told you before, that day out in the Grove when I pressed Robbie about stalking me, he all but admitted it, even writing the love letters."

"What do you mean, 'all but admitted'?"

She paused, apparently caught off-guard by his cross-examination. "Well, he didn't deny it." She rubbed her palms on her thighs. "And he blushed, looking guilty."

"Looking guilty or not can fool you sometimes, I've learned that the hard way. But you needn't worry about him. I'm gonna have a talk with the boy soon and put the fear of God in him."

"Like I said before, please don't be too hard on him."

"Oh, I probably won't slap him around or anything like that." Fox laughed. "But, if he doesn't cease and desist this stalking, I've got ways to help him come around to my way of thinking."

"I feel relieved that at least I now know where all this stuff has been coming from. The worst part is not knowing . . ."

The movie was a combination sci-fi techno thriller about a guy who had been implanted with a computer chip to make him recall training and experiences he had never had. Apparently, the CIA did it to the poor guy to prompt him to do things they wanted.

Fox shook his head when the movie was almost over. What was the world coming to? Implanted memories and urges. Before long, how would anybody know what was reality and what wasn't?

Just then, the phone in his pocket vibrated. He stretched out his legs to retrieve it.

The screen showed that it was Monique, the night clerk at the station.

"Sorry, I need to take this," he whispered, standing to leave.

"Is everything all right?"

"Probably. I'll be right back."

In the hallway, he hit the "call" button to re-dial the station.

"John, I'm sorry to bother you, but I thought you might want to know that the university police are chasing a guy who apparently had been snooping around inside the sleep disorder unit. It's all over the radio. I think they want to talk to Dr. Mathis to see if anything's missing." She paused. "I figured she might be with you."

"Have they caught him?"

"I don't think so."

"Tell Chief Chapman at UPD we're on our way."

Fox went back inside, got Seetha, and headed toward campus. He whipped the car into a no-parking zone behind the biology building and noted a white University Police Department van parked beside of the structure. Two campus policemen stood just outside the double doors. One was a tall, older gentleman, and the other, a thirty-something African American female. The older guy was Chief Dean Chapman; the woman was Officer Tonisha Travis.

"Good to see you again, Dean," Fox said, shaking his hand. "Been a long time."

"Yeah, great to see you too." Chief Chapman replied. He looked like a statesman instead of a hardened policeman. "You didn't have to come. We don't even know that a crime has been committed."

Fox stepped back to introduce Seetha. "This is Dr. Seetha Mathis, director of the sleep unit."

Chief Chapman nodded. "Great. I'm glad you're here. We tried to call you."

She grabbed at her purse. "Maybe I had my phone on silent in my purse." She looked past the policemen toward the building. "What happened?"

"Apparently, one of the cleaning crew noticed a light on in your lab after she had previously cleaned the place and cut it off. She knew that no cars were in the parking lot, so she peeked in to see who it was."

"Who was it?"

"Don't know. Said it was a male figure sitting at one of the lab benches with some of the electronic equipment turned on. She called security, but the guy took off before they arrived. Supposedly, they chased him momentarily out in the Grove."

"Any signs of forced entry?" Fox asked.

"No,"

Seetha brushed past the officer. "Let's see what he was looking at."

Nothing seemed amiss inside Seetha's lab. In fact, everything was in perfect order. Too much so. The electronic brain-scan equipment was turned on, with the Blue Ray/CD drive still open.

"Whoever was in here grabbed the disc and ran." Seetha closed the drive door. "Wonder what he was looking at?" She ran a hand through her hair. She hoped it wasn't one of the fear memory discs she had allowed Dex to make. One of *her* memories. That would be embarrassing.

Seetha turned and walked to her desk to see if anything was missing there. Oddly, all the papers and file folders on her desk were neatly stacked and perfectly aligned with the folder tabs exactly lined up.

"Hmm." She thumbed through them.

"Hmm what?" Fox asked.

"See how neat all this is?" She pointed. "Anybody that knows me, knows I'm not that neat." She looked around the office. "Somebody's been here all right, going through all this stuff on my desk."

"Could it be Dex?"

"Dex certainly works up here occasionally at night, but he would have no reason to run away."

Who else would have access to the lab?" Chief Chapman asked.

"Nobody else but the medical director, who is *never* here, my nurse, Frances Flowers, and my student worker, Robbie Obergon."

Fox reddened. "That boy better not be behind this."

*****

Even though school was almost out for the summer, Seetha knew Sam would still be required to attend the remaining few weeks. The first few days back at school had gone well. Seetha had spoken with Sam's teachers and the school nurse, giving them a heads-up about her condition, along with instructions from Dr. Sinkot, and apparently, no catastrophes had occurred upon her return. Or, at least, no one reported any.

That all changed on Tuesday of the next week. The Principal called, reporting that Sam had been found displaying inappropriate behavior with a male student in a storage room during lunch. Seetha knew she must confront Sam about it as soon as she got home from school. Acting out sexually was fairly common for persons who had been sexually abused.

Maybe that wasn't what had happened. She hoped to God not.

Seetha left work early that day to be there when Sam got home. The school bus usually dropped her off about three-thirty. While waiting, she paced her living room floor in the habitual pattern, chewing her fingernails and trying to rehearse what she would say to Sam when she walked through the door. This had to be handled correctly or Sam might clam up, explode, regress, or worse.

Seetha heard the key in the lock and ran to open the door. Sam was wide-eyed when she saw her mother. "Mom . . . I didn't know you were here?"

"Hello, sweetheart. Come on in. You and I need to talk,"

Sam pitched her backpack on the couch, her face reddening by the second.

"Have a seat, honey."

Sam sat on the very edge of the couch like a runner ready to jump at the sound of the starter's pistol. "So, what's this all about? Am I in trouble?"

"Should you be?"

"I don't know what you mean."

"I mean, is there something you want to tell me? Like, how things may have gone at school today."

"No, everything's fine." Sam looked straight ahead like a zombie. "I had a great day at school."

"Sam, the Principal called. I know about you and the Thompson boy."

"We weren't doing anything. We were just playing around. It's all a misunderstanding."

"That's not what the Principal said."

Silence and an even redder face.

"Look, I'm concerned that some of your . . . shall we say . . . damage from childhood is causing you to act out in this way."

Sam pounced. "I have no idea what you mean by that. Are you now my psychiatrist too?"

Seetha leaned forward. "I just want what's best for you, honey. And becoming sexually active is *not* what's best for you at this time in your life."

Sam jumped up, headed for the stairs. "Gross, Mom. I don't want to be talking to you about sex."

"We're not done yet."

"Oh yes we are." She ran upstairs.

Seetha sunk her face in her hands. What was she going to do?

*****

"I know you have some kind of fixation on Dr. Mathis out at the university." Fox was grilling Robbie Obergon in his office. The college student squirmed in his chair like a kid caught telling lies. "And I want to know every time you have made contact with Dr. Mathis over the last three months. Even times when she *didn't know* you were there."

"But I work for her. I see her almost every day."

"You know what I mean," Fox growled. "*Other than* school or work-related activities."

"Uh, I've already apologized to her. I never meant any harm."

Fox knew that was a confession of sorts, but only a partial truth. The guy hadn't actually apologized, but had told Seetha he meant no harm when she confronted him on the issue. "You're not answering the question. Tell me about your contacts with Dr. Mathis."

"Like I said, I see her three times a week in class, then at work." He smiled pleasantly as if remembering.

Fox's temper flared. "Not that," he hollered. "I want details of all the other ways and times you've seen her."

He looked startled, then hung his head. "I've bumped into her a few times in the hallway."

"Did you do that on purpose?"

Silence for a long time. "Well, maybe a time or two. But it was harmless." He crossed his legs like a girl. "I just wanted to see her. To watch over her."

"What do you mean by that?"

Robbie shifted his weight in the chair. "Nothing weird or perverted. I just care for her and wouldn't want anything to happen to her. After all, her husband's gone and she needs protection."

Fox walked around and took up position directly in front of Robbie. "Her personal life is none of your damn business, Robbie. You have no right to intrude. Now, I know there's more about your interactions with her than you're telling me. Believe me, young man, this'll go much easier and be over sooner if you just tell the truth."

"I am telling the truth."

"Were you in her office at the lab the other night, going through her files."

"No." Long pause. "I told you I work there, sir."

"But were you there the other night, looking through her files?"

"What night?"

"Saturday."

Robbie looked confused. "I don't think so."

"Have you ever stalked her?"

"No . . . unless you call watching from a distance 'stalking.' "

"Explain 'watching her from a distance.'"

"Oh, nothing except I've stayed late at the biology department a few times to make sure she got out to her car safely."

"Nothing more?"

"No, sir."

"So you've never followed her in a car."

He rubbed his palms on his pants. "Only once."

"Did you try to hit her car with yours?"

He seemed indignant. "I most certainly did not. I guess I just got a little carried away."

Fox knew he was getting somewhere. The boy seemed to be telling the truth now, if only partially. This was like pulling teeth. "So you did stalk Dr. Mathis from the Kroger parking lot into town?"

"Yes, but only that one time. I didn't mean to frighten her. I just wanted to watch over her. She's my favorite teacher."

"And what about the love notes, and the roses, and you hanging out in her yard on the night of the storm?"

"I have no idea what you're talking about. I did none of those things."

"Yes, you did and you know it."

"No I didn't." He shook his head vigorously, then slowed, as if questioning himself. "At least, I don't recall doing that. Unless I did it in my sleep."

Fox threw up his hands. He'd heard that excuse a lot lately.

Just then his assistant, Amber, stuck her head in the door. "Detective Fox, there's a call for you."

"Can't they leave a message and me get back to them?"

"It's Vincent Bonamo. He says it's urgent."

That got his attention. "Tell him to hold for a minute."

Fox turned back to Robbie. "Okay, young man. That's enough for now. I'll have to get with Dr. Mathis and see if she wants to press charges."

Obergon looked like he was about to cry. "Please don't. I didn't mean to do anything wrong."

"I'll tell you one thing, you'd better leave her alone." Fox eased into the student's face. This thing with Seetha was beyond his ordinary cop role. "Stay the hell away from her. No calls, no letters, no reading her files, no following her, *nothing*. Understand?"

"Yes, sir. I'll try."

"You'll do more than try, young man!"

Robbie left the office white as a sheet.

Fox snatched up the phone. "Jonathon Fox."

"Detective Fox, this is Vince Bonamo."

"Yes, Mr. Bonamo, what can I do for you?"

"Well, maybe it's just the stress of all this investigation, but I've been having problems lately."

"What kind of problems?" Fox huffed. He didn't have time for a whiner. He'd just interviewed one. "I mean, what does this have to do with the police department or our investigation of your ex-girlfriend?"

"I know this sounds crazy, but I've been plagued with nightmares recently. And I've never had bad dreams before."

"What kind of nightmares?"

"Dreams of me attacking and beating a young man." There was a pause. "So realistic. I know this sounds really bad and it scares me to death—"

"Mr. Bonamo, you need to stop right there and think about what you're saying. You've recently been questioned about the beating death of a boyfriend of your former girlfriend. And now you're telling me that you've been dreaming about beating up some guy? Why are you telling me this now?"

*Jerome & Rosella Goddard*

Then Bonamo dropped the bombshell. "Because I'm afraid I might have attacked Hope's boyfriend while asleep."

Fox was stunned. "Can you come down here and give us a formal statement?"

"Yes, sir. I'll be there in a few minutes."

Fox hung up the phone. He wanted to run to the window and scream out into the streets, *Does every crime in Oxford lately involve sleepwalking?*

# Chapter Nineteen

**M**onday morning Seetha went in to work at seven-fifteen, hoping to talk to Dex about Sam's condition before things got cranking. She found him in the animal room. The guy was a mess—hair all greasy and not combed, and clothes looking like they had been slept in for days.

"Hi, Dex. How's it going this morning?"

He recoiled at her greeting. "Okay, I guess." He shuffled papers onto a logbook lying open on the counter top. "I was just double-checking the animals."

She knew he was covering up his notes in the logbook. "Were you up here all night?"

His face hardened. "Were *you*?"

"Of course not. I just got here."

"But that's just what you *say*," Dex snapped.

Seetha decided not to pursue this line of crazy paranoid talk. Dex was obviously sicker mentally than he had been just a few months earlier. If he continued to decline, she would have to write him up or talk to the department head about it.

"Truce!" She held up her hands. "Dex, I need your help."

"Help with what?"

"You know what."

"Samantha? Surely you're not going to ask me again to treat her for traumatic memories."

Seetha gave him a pleading look. "I've thought about it all weekend

*Jerome & Rosella Goddard*

and the risks involved far outweigh any risks of not acting. Sam's on the cusp of spiraling out of control. Please help me."

Dex slammed shut the logbook and stuffed it under his arm. He fiddled with the controls on a piece of equipment.

"I'll pay you," she begged.

After a long silence, Dex looked her in the eyes. "How much?"

"Whatever you want . . . I mean, within reason."

He sat down at the lab bench and she followed, taking a chair nearby. "Okay, I'm willing to talk about it, but I'm not going to do anything that'll get me in trouble." He looked both ways. "If there's a way for me to tell you what can be done, and then *you* do the treatment, I *might* be interested. But it's gonna cost you $40,000."

Seetha swallowed hard. She had no idea where she would get that kind of cash. "I'll do it any way you want, and I promise not to implicate you if we get caught."

Dex eyed her closely. "You're something else. One minute you're all high and mighty about not doing illegal research, then the next, you're begging me to do illegal research. You can't have it both ways, you know."

He had a point. "It's only for Sam. She's my daughter and I'm convinced that you can help her."

"I might can help her, but I'm not absolutely sure."

"If we decide to go through with this, what would you do? I mean, give me a thumbnail sketch of the treatment plan."

A twinkle appeared in his eyes, like that of an artist seeing his painting displayed in public for the first time. "I think I would try two things. One, the defective herpes virus vectors to block expression of fear memories, and secondly, I'd like to try to over-express the protein $\alpha$CaMKII, at the very moment she recalls the memories. That should erase them."

Seetha was taken aback. She didn't know he had developed the technical capability to over-express that particular protein. Lately, every time she spoke to Dex about his research he had a new idea. How in the world did he have enough time to pursue these things?

"What would be involved?" she asked.

"Maybe watch a video, and during it, get her to recall her worst traumatic memory. Also, swallowing a steroid pill and receive one injection. I think I can combine all the ingredients into one shot."

"Are you sure this won't harm Sam?"

He seemed irritated. "Quit cross-examining me. You're the one asking me to do this. If you want to do it, fine. If not, fine."

"I'm sorry." She raked a hand through her hair. "I just don't want anything to happen to my daughter."

He rose and reached for the doorknob. "Let me think on it and come up with a detailed plan. Like I said, if it's *you* doing the treatment — which you stole, I mean, 'learned' from me — then maybe we can work a deal." He gave her an icy stare. "But believe me, I'm *not* taking the heat if anything goes wrong. I'll deny everything and say that you pursued the therapy on your own because of the problems with your daughter."

Seetha felt like throwing up. This was sleazy. "Don't worry."

"Like I said, let me try to come up with a way to do this."

Seetha attempted to work the rest of that morning, but her guts churned. Her scheme with Dex violated every moral and ethical standard she had been taught. On the other hand, this was *her* daughter. This was different. She didn't want Sam struggling with traumatic memories her whole life like she had. This pattern of generation-to-generation abuse had to stop. And it had to stop now.

After lunch, the phone rang. It was Donna Jones, the Principal at Sam's school.

"Dr. Mathis?"

Seetha went numb. The Principal never called unless something was wrong. "Is everything all right? How's Sam?"

"She's fine, Dr. Mathis, but I wanted to discuss a particular matter with you."

"What kind of matter?"

"Sam visited the school nurse today and asked for birth control and also for the cervical cancer vaccination. We usually never disclose the nurse-student interactions, but in light of Sam's recent medical issues and Dr. Sinkot's instructions about her return to school, I thought you should know."

"Birth control? And a vaccine to prevent cervical cancer?"

"Yes."

"Why would she need that?" Her voice was becoming shrill. "She's not sexually active."

A long pause ensued. "Are you sure about that? The evidence seems to point otherwise."

Seetha fumed. "You have no right to say things like that," she said loudly. "That's none of your business."

"Please calm down, Dr. Mathis. I understand your frustration, but it *is my business* what goes on in my school."

"Are you saying Sam has been having sex at school? The very school you are in charge of? The school in which I entrust my child's care and well-being to?"

Silence. "I just thought you should know about her visit to the school nurse today, that's all. I can see that this conversation isn't beneficial to either of us at this point, so I'm going to end it. Please call me if you have questions or want to discuss the matter further. But I would very much appreciate it if you would try to calm down before calling back. Good day."

Seetha steamed and stewed about the call from Donna Jones until three-thirty when she drove home. She needed to confront Sam again, and unfortunately, this was becoming way too routine.

She slammed her palms against the steering wheel. *Why me? Why Sam?* Her once sweet and loving child was becoming some sort of nymphomaniac, acting out her sexual abuse. The thought horrified Seetha.

On the way home, she called Dr. Sinkot from the cell phone and relayed to him the disturbing phone call from the Principal, but he didn't seem overly concerned. Apparently, this kind of thing was nothing new to him. The good doctor only said he would "visit" the matter upon their next appointment. He emphasized that unless Sam seemed to be a danger to herself or to others, immediate intervention wasn't needed.

"Immediate intervention isn't needed," she repeated after he hung up, so angry she could barely drive.

When Seetha got home, Sam was defensive as usual. When asked about the school nurse visit, she turned beet red and crossed her arms over her chest. "Mom, please . . . it's not your business what I talk to a school nurse about. That's my private life."

"Honey, you're just a child. At this point in your life, *your* business is still *my* business. We're a family, remember?"

"Okay, sure."

"You don't think we're a family?"

"Family. What's a family?" She mocked in a disturbing tone. "We haven't been a family in a long time, Mom."

That hurt.

Seetha could tell she wasn't going to willingly cooperate, so she tried a bolder approach. "Who have you been having sex with at school? Tell me now, or you're going to be grounded forever."

Silence. Just the arms across the chest.

"How long have you been sexually active, young lady?"

Silence.

Seetha tried several other lines of questioning, to no avail, then gave up.

After a few minutes she took a seat on the couch across the room from Sam, waited a long time in silence, then switched the subject altogether. "Sam, I know that you've had some terrible things happen to you in the past, and for that, I'm very sorry that I failed to protect you. But now, I might know of a way to possibly heal you of those terrible memories."

Sam softened, looking up and oddly, seemed interested this time. "Really?"

"Look, I'm working with Dex to give you a treatment to try to remove those memories. Would you agree to let us do that?"

Sam seemed skeptical, but at least she was talking again. "Would it hurt?"

"No, Dear. I think it's mainly just watching a video or listening to some audio recordings, although there may be one injection involved. I'm not sure."

"I don't know."

"Listen, it's worth a try. It couldn't hurt anything, could it? Just to see if it works."

"How do you know it works?"

"Because Dex has been conducting research on this subject for a long time. He's been doing animal studies."

"I'm no animal."

"No, but he's progressed to the point that he's ready for human trials." A lie, and she hated herself for saying it.

Sam shrugged. "I might be interested, but only after I know for sure what he's going to do to me *before* he does it."

Seetha took the opportunity to go over and hug her. "It's all right dear. Everything's going to be all right. I promise."

*****

John Fox noticed immediately that Bonamo was totally different from the first time he had interviewed him. Gone was all his confidence and smugness. Now the guy was either putting on a great con or was literally scared to death. But knowing what Amber had found out about his family in New Orleans, Fox felt Bonamo was probably faking.

"It's a dream, I tell you, and I can't get out of my mind." Bonamo was pale. "I see myself beating some poor guy senseless."

Fox opened his desk and retrieved a picture of Hope William's boyfriend who had been found murdered. He slid it across the desk to Bonamo. "Is this the guy in your dreams?"

Bonamo winced and recoiled from the photograph as if it were a rattlesnake. "My God, it's true. It's him."

"So, are you saying you *did* kill Mr. Peterson?"

"Uh, no. I'm just saying that's the guy in my nightmares . . . well, uh, I'm not sure what I'm saying."

"But in our last interview, you provided me with an alibis for the night of the murder. Are you now saying that was a lie?"

Bonamo's eyebrows shot up. "No, well no, that was the truth. I think. At the time, anyway."

"What do you mean, 'I think?'"

He shook his head. "Maybe I was asleep."

"How do you know you were asleep?" Fox huffed. "What makes you say a thing like that?"

"I know this may sound strange, but my roommate is a sleep researcher and does experiments on animals about all kinds of stuff. I think he may even be able to make them do things they don't want to do through some kind of sleep learning or something like that."

"Is that right?"

"Yeah, and anyway, I was shocked when I saw pieces of a blue ray disc in our garbage one day recently labeled, 'memory prompting experiment, intervention one.' And then, another time, I found some wires and earphones in my room." His eyes became wide. "That really scared me."

"What are you saying?"

Bonamo sat up, looking directly at Fox. "I think my roommate Dex may be secretly performing memory or sleep experiments on me."

Fox knew the idea wasn't too far-fetched in light of the Heather McHann's situation. She too had possibly been 'prompted' to do things, perhaps via a sleep or mind treatment from Dex. But he wasn't buying this story. Dex had no motive to kill Frankie Peterson.

"Then, why would Dex want to kill Mr. Peterson, who he doesn't even know?"

Bonamo shrugged. "Beats me. You never know. Maybe he does know him."

Fox turned dead serious. "You realize, Mr. Bonamo, that your statements here today may lead to you being charged with murder?"

Bonamo gasped dramatically. "I was only doing what I thought was the right thing, telling you about the dreams. I assure you, my alibi still stands. I didn't do it."

"Then why the hell are you down here telling me all this?"

"I'm not sure."

Fox put his hands on his hips. "Let me do some investigating and we'll talk again, okay? In the meantime, don't leave town without telling me. Understand?"

"Yes, sir. Whatever I need to do to cooperate fully with you and the authorities, just let me know. I'm more than willing to help any way I can."

Fox opened the door. "Okay, then follow me to the lab. We want a DNA sample before you leave."

Bonamo appeared shaken by that statement, and for once in the interview, the response seemed genuine.

# Chapter Twenty

**S**eetha worked late on Wednesday, trying to catch up on all the work she had been missing the last week or so while dealing with Sam. She had made arrangements for Sam to stay at Molly O'Brien's house again until eight p.m. Ms. O'Brien had agreed to bring her home. Seetha walked into her apartment around seven-thirty that evening and immediately knew something was amiss. A rose petal lay on the floor right inside the front door. She looked around. There was another one on the floor toward the stairway. Then another, forming a trail of petals.

She stood absolutely still for a few minutes listening and gripping her car keys tightly in her hand. She decided that at the slightest noise she would race out the front door. The only thing she could hear was her heart pounding in her temples.

Then it occurred to her that maybe Sam had placed the petals, perhaps as a "thank you" or something like that. Maybe she was misinterpreting Sam's gesture.

She mustered up the courage to ease up the stairs. More red rose petals dotted the stairs, leading upward.

Upward to what? In the past, a trail of rose petals signaled a romantic rendezvous, but tonight, Seetha had no idea what it meant. Especially in Sam's current frame of mind.

Step by step, little by little, she tiptoed up the stairs, following the rose petals toward Sam's room.

Sam's door was closed. Rose petals lay in front of it, inviting her inside.

A chilling thought crept into her mind. *If this is Rodney, I'm dead!*

She put her hand on the doorknob and placed her right ear lightly on the door, listening for any sounds inside. She ever so slightly cracked the door and paused.

Only silence.

She pushed the door farther open enough to peep inside, keys still in her hand should she need to flee. Nothing, except more petals on the floor inside pointing the way to the bathroom.

*Oh my God, the bathtub. Who or what was in the tub awaiting her?*

Seetha again stood absolutely silent for a few minutes. She could have sworn she heard breathing coming from the bathroom, although the central heating unit clicked on and drowned out the sound.

The petals led to the bathroom door, which was closed. What lay on the other side of that door?

She thought about calling John Fox. Yes, that might be the best plan of action. She could run downstairs, out into the yard, and call him on her cell phone. He would come investigate, and, more importantly, *protect* her.

Instead of running downstairs, Seetha slipped ever so slowly toward the bathroom. Why, she didn't know. Maybe part of her was just plain mad . . . mad at whoever was tormenting her like this. It had to end.

She doubled a fist. *If it's Robbie Obergon, I'm gonna make him wish he'd never known me!*

Seetha stopped about five feet from the door. This was crazy. And dangerous. She looked around in the room for a weapon. Anything to fight off an attacker. She sneaked over to Sam's closet and gingerly opened it, looking for a baseball bat or similar item. It took a few seconds for her eyes to adjust to the darkness inside the closet, but soon was able to search the place.

No bats or tennis rackets anywhere in sight.

Then she spotted a hardbound notebook, like a journal, partially exposed under a stack of board games on the shelf. The thing looked familiar, so she carefully dug it out, trying not to make any noise. It was Sam's notebook that Dr. Sinkot had given her to record her thoughts during and after treatments.

Killer or not, Robbie Obergon or not, Seetha wanted to look inside, no, she *needed* to look inside this journal. It contained the innermost feelings and attitudes of her daughter. Pangs of guilt gripped her insides for wanting to read it.

"But maybe it'll help me better understand her . . . even help her."

She listened again toward the bathroom, just to make sure no one was coming, then opened the notebook, thumbing through the pages.

What she saw inside the book overshadowed any threat from the bathroom.

Diary entries, made in several, clearly different handwriting types, filled the pages. The first one she read seemed like ramblings of a madman.

*Mother doesn't know. She will never know. My Prince made sure of that. He has spoken, shadowy, shrill, and spectacular. The voice guides. The voice comforts. The voice condemns, but only when I deserve it. It's so real, almost like it's touching my face. Caressing my horrors away. Taking me to higher realms. Realms of the dark one. The only one.*

Seetha flipped to another page. The writing was in block print letters, not Sam's normal handwriting.

*Stay calm. The terror will pass . . . or submerge again soon. Memories can be so real. They are alive, like a person. They even multiply within me, new ones erupting and moving to new places within my mind. Guiding me. Pushing me along like I'm in a rushing river.*

Just then, a horrifying thought struck Seetha, like a punch to the belly, sucking the very breath out of her. In the writing, the tail of the "y" curved down toward the left and was curled like a snake. That writing style was familiar, *very* familiar.

She had indeed seen that same block printing before. On the "love card" found outside her door on the night of the storm.

Surely it wasn't true. Surely Sam wasn't the stalker. Seetha shook her head as if flinging off cobwebs. No, Sam couldn't even drive. Then she remembered that Robbie Obergon had admitted following her in the car that night, but denied ever sending her love notes. So maybe Sam did write the letters as a result of a split personality or something like that. Besides, she *had* gone missing for a few hours during treatment at the behavioral unit, and that was about the same time as the stalker outside her house during the storm. So then, was anyone in the bathroom or not?

Seetha carefully replaced the notebook and emerged from the closet, again tip-toeing toward the bathroom. She was about to find out.

She paused at the bathroom door, listening, then slowly reached for the door knob.

"Mom!"

Seetha almost peed in her pants when she heard that and whirled to see Samantha standing behind her in the doorway. Sam's eyes were wide, her cheeks red.

"Sam, dear." She clutched her chest like someone having a heart attack. "What in the world is going on? You scared me to death. I didn't hear you come in."

"What are you doing in my room?"

"I'm following this trail of flower petals." She pointed down at them. "You know anything about them?"

Sam looked at the petals and seemed genuinely surprised. "No, I really didn't notice them. Ms. O'Brien just dropped me off and I came up here."

"Well, there's a whole line of them and they lead into here."

Seetha reached for the bathroom door. "Be ready to run for help if someone's in here. Okay?"

Sam nodded, fear etched across her face.

Seetha flung open the door. Inside, the bathroom had been made ready for a bath. The tub was full of water, probably containing bubble bath, although the bubbles had gone flat, and with a beautiful red towel set carefully placed at the edge of the tub. The flower petals made their way to the edge of the tub and at their end lay a greeting card addressed in block printed letters, "Seetha Mathis."

"My God," Sam gasped. "He's been here."

Seetha's mind swirled. She looked back and forth between the block printing on the envelope and her beautiful daughter. In light of the notebook entries Seetha had just discovered in the closet, Sam was likely the author of the card, but didn't even realize it herself. The girl's mind had obviously split into several separate entities.

"Aren't you going to open it?"

Seetha felt sick. She had no desire to read sick or perverted comments from her own daughter which represented traumatic memories resulting from her marriage to Rodney.

She grabbed Sam by the hand and led her to the bed. "Sit down, dear."

"What? Aren't you interested in who broke into the place and did this?"

"Sam, honey, you're my precious daughter and I'll love you and support you no matter what. Understand?"

"Yes," she replied flatly.

"Well, I think we both know who wrote the card, don't we?"

A blank look. "No, I don't follow you, Mom."

"I think you — or some part of you — wrote it. Maybe there's 'another Sam' in you that protects you from the painful memories."

Sam's face twisted in anger. "Mom! What are you accusing me of?"

"I'm just saying—"

"Are you saying I'm crazy?"

"No. You know I would never say that, or even think it."

Sam's voice suddenly changed to a deeper, more mature voice. She jumped up and paced the floor like an animal. "I told her to do it," the voice said. "She's mine. My little cuddly one."

Then Sam's normal voice returned. "You didn't make me do it. I didn't do anything. Go back down where you came from." She whimpered.

Seetha's heart raced. Her daughter seemed to be dissolving into more than one personality right before her very eyes. She ran and grabbed her, giving her shoulders a swift shake. "It's okay, Sam. I understand. Don't be frightened. We can work through this together."

Sam darted toward the bed and dove into it, curling into a fetal position. Deep sobs erupted.

Seetha took up position next to her and stroked her hair. "It's all right. Everything's gonna be all right."

Nothing was said for the next five minutes. Seetha continued stroking her daughter's hair and face, trying to think of something to say. Sam's sobs finally subsided.

She sat up. A totally different look appeared on her face. It was the old Sam.

"Mom, I promise, if there *is* another Sam inside me, it's not the real me." She shook her head. "I'm going crazy. I know I am."

"No you're not . . ."

She raised a hand. "No, listen. I really do think I'm going crazy." She wiped her eyes. "For real. I hear voices, and sometimes I get the distinct feeling that I've been places and done things that I don't know are real or not. Some of my thoughts, I mean my memories, well, I can't tell if they really happened or not."

"Shh, shh." Seetha tried to comfort her. "It's all right."

"No, it's not all right. I'm scared and I need somebody to help me with these things. You said recently that Dex might could help me. Maybe do some kind of treatment. Is that true?"

"Yes, dear. He might help, but I don't want to mislead you. It may or may not do much good. I *think* it'll work, and that's why I suggested the treatment, but we just aren't one hundred percent sure. Maybe we should go see Dr. Sinkot first thing tomorrow."

"No. I gave him a chance and it didn't help. I don't care if you aren't sure it'll work," Sam's eyes filled with hope. "Dex's treatment is worth a try. I've got to get better before I go totally bonkers."

# Chapter Twenty-one

**S**eetha and Sam met with Dex at the lab late the next evening. After a few uncomfortable introductory remarks, he led them into a back room where he had a sheet of paper laid out on the lab table, along with a small stainless steel tray containing an alcohol pad, a small pill, and a syringe. Over to the side was a blue ray disc in a plastic case. Seetha could see that the paper contained a bulleted list of things to do.

Dex went back and double-checked the door. When he returned, his face was tight and the muscles in his jaw were twitching. "Are you absolutely sure you want to do this?" He looked at them one at a time.

"Yes," they both said almost simultaneously.

Dex focused on Sam. "And you, especially."

"I want it." Her eyes filled with tears. "I've been living with this crap for years and I want it gone. I want to start over."

He looked at Seetha. "What about the other matter?"

She pulled out an envelope and handed it to him. She felt like a common criminal. "Tomorrow I'll make sure you get the rest."

"Why isn't it all in here?" He glared.

"Because you haven't done the work yet."

He huffed. "All right, this is how we're going to do this. I've written out a protocol for theoretical traumatic memory treatment. You, Dr. Mathis, are going to read it, without my permission, if you know what I mean, and then do whatever you decide to do. I'm only up here tending to the animals and preparing for more experiments. I'm not responsible for what you do."

"Why is it called *theoretical*?" Sam asked. "Even I know what *theoretical* means."

"It only means I'm currently just *thinking* about how to do this research, if you get my drift. I haven't actually done any of this."

Seetha intervened. "He's just covering himself, dear. He knows exactly what he's doing."

"What's going to happen?" Sam asked. "I only agreed to this as long as I would be told exactly what would happen."

"A little steroid pill, then one shot, my dear. One tiny little injection, then I want you to watch a video before you go to bed tonight. Oh, and immediately after the injection, you must try to recall your absolute worst experience."

Sam suddenly looked pale. "The worst?"

Seetha hugged her, "Yes, but it's part of the healing, dear." She then turned toward Dex. "How'd you know about the steroids?"

"From you." Dex smiled. "Remember? You told me one time that my treatments worked better when you took a prednisone pill along with them. Well, I pursued the idea in animals and found that it indeed enhances the memory treatments." He shook his head. "Not sure how yet, but it does. That's something I've got to work on later."

"What's on the disc?" Sam asked.

"Nothing you will recognize. It's recordings of neuron firing patterns translated into lights and colors. They'll help re-write the areas of your brain where the injection has removed traumatic memories."

"But *what* cleans out my bad memories?"

"The shot contains replication defective herpes virus vectors which will block expression of your fear memories." He glanced at the tray on the lab table. "And also a chemical that will force the over-expression of a particular protein critical to brain cell communication."

Sam shook her head. "That makes no sense."

Seetha hugged her again. "I think it'll be fine, dear. There's been a good bit of scientific research on these virus vectors. They're disabled so they can't reproduce. It's a one-time effect. And the other thing is just a protein."

Sam looked at her mom pleadingly. "Are you sure?"

Seetha's insides churned again. What was she doing?

"No, dear, we're not *sure*, but I think it's best that we try the treatment."

After a long pause, Sam agreed.

"Okay," Dex rubbed his hands together, "I'll be in the next room. Dr. Mathis, the protocol is right there." He pointed at the paper.

As soon as he left, Seetha gave Sam the steroid pill to swallow and then carefully read the rationale and instructions for traumatic memory removal. She lifted the syringe out of its tray. It was loaded with one cc of the altered virus designed to find and block such memories and the chemical targeted toward protein over-expression. She looked at the thing for a long time, then turned to Sam.

"Okay, sweetheart, this won't take long, then we'll get the blue ray disc and head back home. Please sit down here at this desk. Everything'll be all right. You'll see."

Seetha wiped Sam's upper arm with an alcohol pad and then injected her with the medicine. She winced, but took the injection bravely.

Nothing happened.

"Now according to the instructions, you have to think about your worst memories for the next fifteen minutes. You must *recall* them in order for the drugs to find them in your brain and erase them, dear."

For the next ten minutes Sam put her head down on the desk thinking about the horrors of her past while Seetha stood nearby, adrenaline coursing through her veins. This was it! They were finally conducting the treatment. Hopefully it would be successful.

Suddenly Sam moaned and shook, as if being tortured. Goosebumps popped out on Seetha's arms. She leaned over and hugged her daughter. When she bent near Sam, Seetha's head tingled like being under a huge electromagnet. The room suddenly seemed to have a "presence" in it. She looked around the lab making sure no one had come in.

Seetha remained close to Sam, stroking her face and speaking comforting words. Sam quieted back down, but thoughts of Rodney then entered Seetha's mind. Intrusive thoughts. She could see a scene, like something out of a photo album, except vivid, sharp, and *real*. A dark outline of a man sitting in a chair in an office. A home office. His arms were folded across his chest like judge, jury, and executioner. Was this Sam's memory? The dark form seemed stern and demanding. Words popped into Seetha's head. It was Rodney's voice, plain as day. She would have sworn she could smell him now.

*I can't let you tell them, the man said. I won't let you tell them.*

What did that mean? Was that something Rodney had told Sam years ago?

Seetha raised up, shaking her head as if to throw off the memory attack. Was this some sort of "thought transfer"? *This is crazy. The memories are in Sam; not me.*

Fear gripped her and she fought an urge to grab Sam and go home. Maybe Dex had been right about memories traveling through a person's brain waves. This traumatic memory stuff was nothing to mess around with.

"Okay," Seetha said as bravely as she could when the time was up. She hoped Sam wouldn't sense the fear in her voice. "See, that wasn't so bad."

Sam rubbed her arm at the injection site. "Mom, he was here. It was *so* real."

"No, dear." She put on her bravest face. "It just seemed that way. They're just memories, that's all."

Sam turned toward her mom. "Well, if that's a *memory*, it's so real I'd call it *alive*."

"Don't be silly." Seetha grabbed the blue ray disc, her insides quivering. "Come on, sweetheart, let's go home."

When they arrived home, Seetha and Sam sat on Sam's bed talking a few minutes, then Seetha turned on the TV and blue ray player so that Sam could watch Dex's video before going to sleep.

She kissed her daughter and handed her the TV remote. "Now, dear, it's important that you watch the entire thing. Don't go to sleep during it. And remember, this video won't make a bit of sense to you. It's just a bunch of lights, colors, dots, and lines. But your brain will know what it means." She held up both hands with crossed fingers. "Cross your fingers that it works."

Sam's eyes were suddenly innocent and child-like, and with a new sense of warmth. She reached up with both arms, both surprising and shocking Seetha. It had been a couple of years since she had shown affection like that. "Mom, I love you."

Seetha could barely contain her emotions. "I love you too, honey. Hope you have a good night." She stroked Sam's hair. "Let the healing begin."

But in her heart, Seetha knew it had already begun.

Sam interrupted her euphoria. "Mom, I'm scared."

"Of what?"

"Not so much of the treatment, but that it won't work."

"How so?"

A pleading look erupted on her face. "You don't know how much I want to *forget* things. I want to forget every single thing that was done to me by people who were supposed to love me."

That broke Seetha's heart.

Then fear crossed Sam's face. "I can't live like this anymore, Mom," she sputtered. "The memories. The voices. The urges."

Seetha cringed when she said that. Hearing voices was serious business. She would have to leave that to Dr. Sinkot to deal with.

Unless Dex's treatment worked its magic.

## Chapter Twenty-two

*T*he next morning broke windy and wet, typical for late April in Mississippi, and Seetha was up early, trying to get breakfast and Sam's clothes ready for the day. She wanted everything to be perfect for Sam on this first day post-treatment.

She made toast and set out the cereal and milk. The events of last night still troubled her. Something very strange, almost evil, had occurred in the lab while Sam re-lived her tormented memories. They had indeed seemed so real as to be considered alive. Seetha retrieved orange juice from the fridge. "How did the memory jump from Sam's brain into mine?" she said. "I was several feet away."

She wondered if perhaps they could jump from one person to another via EEG brain waves, especially in persons standing close together. The implication of that conclusion made her want to change careers and stay the hell away from memory research forever.

She walked up the stairs and gently tried awakening Sam. Sam stirred and glared back at her. Gone were the innocence and openly loving behavior of the evening before.

"Leave me alone. I'm sleepy."

"Come on, Sweetie. You've got to get ready for school. How do you feel this morning?"

She rubbed her face. "Not too good. My head hurts and everything seems fuzzy."

"Maybe it's just a little side effect from watching those crazy light patterns on that video."

Sam threw the covers back, crawled out of bed, and started for the bathroom. Seetha noticed she wobbled as she walked.

All of a sudden her rear-end turned brown and a horrible smell filled the room. Brown liquid ran down her legs. Sam grabbed her backside with both hands and darted into the bathroom. "Mom, I can't hold it!"

Seetha was horrified to see her daughter having uncontrolled diarrhea and ran to the bathroom to help. "It's all right, dear. I'm here. Let me get you some clean clothes."

After cleaning up the mess and helping Sam get her shower, Seetha tried to get her to eat a little breakfast. "Is your stomach still queasy?"

"Yes, but I feel a little better now."

A sense of impending doom swept over Seetha, and she fought against it with all her might. "Maybe it's just a stomach virus. They're always going around, you know." She stood and walked to the window. "The weather's bad, Sam. Why don't I stay home with you today?"

"No, I want to go to school."

"Are you sure? What if you have another accident?"

Sam stood and wobbled up the stairs. "No, I need to go to school. I've *got* to go. If for no other reason than just for my own sanity."

At ten-fifteen that morning, Sam's school called Seetha at the sleep disorders unit. Seetha was paralyzed with fear when Frances handed her the phone.

"Dr. Mathis, this is Donna Jones at Samantha's school."

"What's wrong?" Her voice quavered. "I just know something terrible has happened."

Ms. Jones was somber. "I'm sorry to report that something's seriously wrong with your daughter. We can't seem to communicate with her, she can barely walk, and, well, she's been incontinent."

"What do you mean?"

"She can't seem to control her kidneys or bowels. With your permission, I'd like to call an ambulance."

"Oh my God. Is it that bad? I'll be there in ten minutes."

*****

Ever since his nerve-racking interview with Detective Fox and Heather concerning the DeeVo's break-in, Dex knew his days might be numbered at the Ole Miss Sleep and Memory Unit. With all the negative publicity, Dr. Jackson, the Department Chairman, might simply fail to renew his post-doctoral funding since it was soft money and a non-tenure track position. The situation made him determined to get as much done as quickly as possible so he could move on and continue his research at another college or university. Lately, he had become eager to explore other aspects of the memory research, especially that of acting out traumatic memories, not just implanting urges or simple impulses like he had done with Heather. For this set of experiments, he had ordered twelve young, plump guinea pigs from a laboratory supply house and inflicted upon them various types of trauma, all the way from rubbing their faces in dirt or feces, to pinching them, to beating them with a ping-pong paddle. For untreated controls, half of the guinea pigs had been left untouched.

It was now time to record the results. He grabbed a logbook and took off for the animal room so he could examine the guinea pigs and compare each animal's condition and activity with its treatment history noted in the log. Dex wanted to see if any of them were displaying the same kind of violence to others similar to what had been done to them. He watched them for a few minutes in their cages in which he had placed one "treatment" animal that had been abused and one "control" animal that had not. After fifteen minutes of watching the cages, he didn't observe any violent behaviors toward the untreated animals, but oddly, most of the treatment guinea pigs seemed unusually lethargic, as if they had simply given up on living. One-by-one, he gently lifted them from their plastic cages and slowly rotated their purring, wiggling bodies in his gloved hand. By comparing log entries with individual guinea pig numbers on their ear tags, Dex noticed that almost every one of them that had been "treatments" in experiments displayed signs of serious trauma, illness, or general disinterest in food, drink, or other activity. Some looked emaciated, some had yellow crud caked in their eyes, and some twitched uncontrollably, as if remembering their trauma or perhaps having neurological damage. Then he noticed that the last cage at the end of the shelf seemed unusually quiet. He bent over and looked at guinea pig numbers eleven and twelve. Eleven was dead, its small face giving away nothing but a cold stare framed by corncob grit. Twelve was hunkered down in the corner quivering uncontrollably. Dex flipped pages in the logbook looking for his notes on g.p. eleven. "Let's see," he muttered. "Eleven was struck five times on the dorsum with a paddle. Must've ruptured something internally." He examined guinea pig twelve again. It certainly looked and acted is if traumatized, even though no trauma had been inflicted during the experiment. Therefore, eleven must have transferred its fear memory before dying. This was the kind of result he had hoped for. Progress; real progress.

For some reason, the little white plastic cage suddenly reminded Dex of a tiny coffin. *All living things must eventually die,* he thought. Sad in a way, but really not a problem as long as it was for the good of his scientific research.

Two hours later, Dex was still in the animal room when Frances found him. She had been instructed to find him and tell him to call Seetha.

"Something's bad wrong with her daughter." Frances wore a hard look on her face like a drill sergeant. "She insists you call her right away."

A knot formed in the pit of his stomach. "Oh, hell. This is bad. Very bad."

He walked outside in order to make the call. He didn't want Frances or anybody else listening in on his call. He dialed Seetha and waited for the bad news.

When he reached her, she put him on hold while she went outside.

"Dex, what the hell have you done to my daughter!" He had to move the phone away from his ear because she was screaming. "She's regressed to a state of almost infancy."

"Calm down, Dr. Mathis. Calm down." He waved his hand downward even though no one was there to see it. "First of all, you don't know that the treatment did this to her, and secondly *you and you alone* performed the procedure. I had nothing to do with it. In fact, you stole my ideas off a sheet of paper in which I had been *theorizing* about ways to remove traumatic memories. Are we clear on that?"

"I tell you one thing, Gregory Poindexter . . . " Again Dex had to move the phone away from his ear due to her screaming and raging. All he could make out were bits and pieces about her calling the police and the FBI and all sorts of other radical actions.

Eventually she calmed enough to talk. He could tell she was crying by then. "Dr. Sinkot put her back in the behavioral unit. He says she's regressed to childhood, almost as if she'd never learned certain basic skills like walking. He's hoping it's only temporary."

She paused a long time. "Dex, I guess we can blame each other later. But tell me, from your animal research, have you ever seen anything like this before? And, if so, what was the outcome?"

He had indeed seen it before a few times—an overwriting of previously learned things in the brain. But he didn't know how much of that to reveal to Seetha. She might be crazy enough to tell the police about injecting her own daughter, get herself fired from the sleep disorders unit, and take him down with her.

"Nope, never seen any side effects at all during my research. This is all new to me. That's why I think it could just be another psychotic break like the last one she had. You know that kid's mentally unstable."

More cursing, then "click," she was gone.

# Chapter Twenty-three

*N*obody came to arrest Dex over the next forty-eight hours, so he began to ease up. The incident with Sam reinforced in him the importance of proceeding more slowly and deliberately. He had gotten ahead of himself and shouldn't have. In the future, he would need to slow down and cover his tracks better, even be more secretive than before. At any moment, Seetha could crack and spill her guts, saying all sorts of nasty accusations against him. Or Sam could too, for that matter. The kid could start rambling about her mother and him injecting her like a guinea pig to cure her past memories. Even though she was mentally unstable, that kind of accusation might get the authorities curious enough to investigate.

Sunday evening Dex worked at the lab again. Very late. He wanted to continue pursuing the "acting out" aspect of his research but had to make sure nobody was around before trying it. Results from the guinea pig experiment had suggested that traumatized animals could act out their trauma and somehow transfer those memories to others.

For this new experiment, Dex placed eight laboratory rats in a large arena about the size of a kitchen table. Each animal was marked with a small numbered ear tag in order to keep up with which one was which. The specially designed arena was equipped with cameras for twenty-four-hour observation. He then picked up one of the rats, held it up in his left hand right beside an 8x10 photograph of another laboratory rat taped to the wall. He directed the rat in his hand away from the picture, so that the rat in his hand would think the large rat in the picture was located behind him. Then he took a pair of pliers and snatched a huge chunk of skin and fur from the back of the rat's neck, simulating a bite. The rodent squealed in horror and pain. Dex then showed the rat the picture behind him one more time and returned it to the arena.

"There," he said. "The experimental rat will think the rat behind him in the picture is a real rat that bit him."

The poor rat ran to the corner licking its wounds as best it could. The "bite" on the back of its neck was obviously inaccessible, but it tried to lick there nonetheless.

Dex rubbed his hands together. He had just created a traumatic memory. Now, all he had to do was wait and see if the experimental rat "acted out" the memory, repeating the behavior by doing the same thing to others.

He switched on the cameras. Of course, they had been turned off during Dex's "treatment" of the rat. He didn't need a record of that activity which might get him in trouble. Now, the cameras were on and ready to record propagation of the traumatic memory.

He rubbed his hands together in delight. This was what science was all about.

*****

Seetha camped out in the behavioral unit waiting room for three days in a row, even though she knew she wouldn't be allowed to see Sam. She couldn't eat or sleep from worrying about what had happened and how it might turn out.

Late Sunday afternoon, Dr. Sinkot stopped by to see her after his twice daily visit with Sam. He had a look of grave concern on his face. "Dr. Mathis, you're not doing yourself or Sam any good by staying up here night and day, worrying and fretting. Please go home and get some rest."

"I can't. I feel so responsible . . ."

Sinkot eyed her curiously. "Why do you say that? This has nothing whatsoever to do with you. She was abused by *others*, not you."

Seetha swiped her greasy hair aside. If he only knew. She too had abused her daughter. Sure, it had been in a different way, and she didn't mean to, of course. Nonetheless, she had harmed her daughter.

"How is she this afternoon?" she asked.

"A little better. Brighter than she was, and even seems to be re-learning certain basic skills."

"When will she be able to go home?"

Dr. Sinkot's face turned ashen. "Oh, Dr. Mathis, I hope I didn't mislead you. Sam is *seriously* ill. She won't be going home for a very long time." He paused for an eternity as if deciding how much to reveal. "I have to be totally honest with you. Sam may have to be institutionalized indefinitely."

Seetha reeled from the sheer force of those words, rocking backward. The room swirled. She looked down at her hands and all she could see was the hypodermic needle she had used to inject Sam.

Dr. Sinkot jumped forward to support her. "Are you all right? Here, let me help you to the chair."

He stayed with her a few minutes as if to make sure she was okay, then left. Again Seetha was left alone to face demons, both her own, as well as those she had now created from half-killing her own daughter.

How could she live with herself?

*****

Dex was thrilled. Upon playing the recording of the rats' activity twenty-four hours after his inflicted trauma, he could clearly see that rat number seventeen, the traumatized one, was now going around biting other rats behind the head in a similar manner.

"Way cool," he said aloud. "It's reenacting that trauma. It has an *urge* to repeat the action, which essentially makes sure the trauma continues. The memory is repeating itself."

Dex made notes in his secret logbook, not the one that Seetha and the animal use committee folks had access to. It was the real research notebook. He smiled. The premise underlying his experiments was true. Memories can indeed sometimes act alive and spread themselves like a virus. Certain traumatic memories create an urge in people and animals to re-create the action in another person or animal, thus perpetuating the action.

"Forever, I guess," he mumbled.

He ran his hand through what little hair he had. One caveat to his euphoria was the fact that apparently in some people the brain "immune system" malfunctioned or was even non-existent, allowing traumatic memories to multiply out of control, leading to all sorts of mental illnesses. He knew that one fact alone was an earth-shattering idea totally new to science that could lead to a Nobel Prize because of the possibilities for new therapies for mental illness.

Dex huffed. He really didn't want to pursue that line of research since it revealed the dark side of traumatic memory research. Maybe he would work on that later. Much later.

Dex hid the logbook again and went over to his desk to plot out his next experiment. "I wonder if there's a way to secretly start a traumatic memory in people around here and plot its spread through the human population?"

He smiled. "Hmm, now that's an idea . . ."

\*\*\*\*\*

About lunchtime on Tuesday, Seetha was mindlessly thumbing through a *Time* magazine, when Detective Fox walked in.

"Seetha, how's Sam?"

Seetha ran and threw herself in his arms, stifling the urge to bawl like a baby. She released him and looked down, embarrassed.

Fox placed his hands on her shoulders and looked her over. "You're a mess. How long have you been here?"

"Three or four days, I guess."

"Why didn't you answer my calls?"

No answer.

He shook his head but made no further comment about that. "So how is she?"

Seetha wanted to tell him everything, to unload her burden. He seemed genuinely concerned. *But he'll think I'm a bad person, or worse, arrest me.* "She's bad off. Friday, the Principal called from school saying that Sam was having a difficult time walking, talking, and controlling her bowels. They rushed her to the hospital and Dr. Sinkot had her admitted to the behavioral unit again. He says she's regressed to a childhood state or something like that."

Her hands shook and she had an urge to wash them—to wash the image of the hypodermic needle off them. Tears streamed down her face for the umpteenth time. "I don't know what to do. I feel so bad."

Fox seemed to hesitate as if having an internal struggle, then pulled her close to his chest. "It's all right, trust me, it'll all work out."

Seetha was so torn inside that she had a hard time receiving his act of kindness. "I feel terrible."

He pulled back. Now he was in police mode again. "Why do you keep saying that? It's not your fault. I think you should be strong for Sam. Be up. Be positive."

Seetha wiped her eyes, at a loss for words.

"Come on," Fox said, "let me take you home so you can get cleaned up and get some sleep."

"I don't know. What if she needs me?"

He tugged her elbow. "Come on, I insist. You don't want me to have to arrest you, do you?"

*I deserve it.*

# Chapter Twenty-four

*O*ver the following three days, Dex worked diligently on the next phase of his experiment. He devised a plan to record the brain scan, more specifically, the neuronal firing pattern, of a human traumatic memory and then encode it into a pattern of lights and colors that could trick the brain into recording a memory. This time, though, it would be a memory he devised, so that when released, he could monitor its spread throughout the local population.

One little problem. The only human he could experiment on was himself. Seetha was pre-occupied with Sam's condition, and his girlfriend, Heather, wasn't about to cooperate anymore. So, he had to be the guinea pig this time.

Dex had developed a large clamp-like contraption on a retractable, spring-loaded device in order to jerk his hair when triggered. He needed a helper, so he would ask Nurse Frances to throw the switch and help him record the brain scan.

The indomitable nurse wasn't very amenable to the idea. "This ain't nothin' but crazy," she said when he explained the procedure to her. "And it's not a good idea. I thought this was a *sleep* laboratory. How does this contraption fit in with that purpose?" She paused. "And what about the university rules about human experiments? I didn't think we could do that sort of stuff around here."

"Trust me, Frances. I know what I'm doing." Dex tried his best to act like this was routine scientific research approved and sanctioned by all the appropriate authorities. "There's nothing wrong with experiments like this. You know that the Institutional Review Board policy on human subjects says that if you're not testing a specific hypothesis or systematically studying a problem, no human-use approval is needed. This is just a one-time observation. Besides, the department head supports my research one hundred percent, you know. And I'm doing the experiment on myself. What could that hurt?"

That was a lie. All human experiments were covered under IRB rules, even if such experiments were performed on oneself. However, Frances was a clinician, not a researcher, and he hoped she didn't know the rules on human experimentation.

"Are you absolutely sure?" Frances drilled him with her eyes.

"Yes, now let's do it before anyone comes in." He waved her into one of the side rooms. "We've got to be quick. Not everyone understands a complex protocol like this."

Once inside the research room, he adjusted the digital camcorder so that everything would be recorded for later analysis. "Now, Frances, I need you to promise you won't tell anyone about this. Understand? Like I said, most folks wouldn't understand."

She cocked her eye. "So you say . . ."

"Here," Dex said, "help me attach this clamp to the back of my head." He pointed behind his head and grabbed at his hair. "Make sure it gets a big wad of hair in it."

Frances fumbled with the thing, clamping a bunch of Dex's hair into the device close to his scalp. "Okay, that's got it."

"Now, here's what's going to happen," Dex said. "When I say 'go,' you flip that little red switch back there and the spring will jerk my hair. I'll record everything."

"What's all those wires and things attached to your head?"

"I'm doing a brain scan, uh, just to see what's going on. So I can analyze the data."

"Suit yourself, Frankenstein."

Dex finished hooking up the electrodes and got into position. He leaned his head forward, bracing for the jerking motion, then turned on the camera.

"Okay, flip the switch any time now." He squinted, knowing what was coming.

Frances threw the switch and instantly Dex screamed out in pain and horror as the mechanical clamp whipped backward, jerking a chunk of hair and scalp out of his head. He fell into a chair, writhing in pain, trying desperately to undo the wires and rub the back of his head.

"Oh my goodness," Frances cried out. "You're bleeding. Let me get you a gauze pad."

Dex held the back of his head, resisting the urge to cry and whimper like a child. "Damn, that hurt!" he yelled.

Frances returned with a handful of bandages and ointments and doctored the back of his head. She eyed him carefully. "You're one crazy guy, Mr. Dex. I've seen some silly things in my day, but this takes the cake."

His head throbbed with intense pain. "Yeah, well, just remember, don't say a word about this." He racked his aching brain for a way to keep her quiet. "I don't want any of those guys in physiology to steal my cutting-edge research. It's all about getting government grants, you know. Those guys in physiology are cut-throat, believe me."

Frances once again shook her head and turned to leave. "I've got more patients coming."

Dex unhooked the rest of the electrodes and retrieved the digital card recording from the camcorder. Even though he was still in pain, a feeling of excitement welled within him.

Now all he had to do was figure out a way to release his new traumatic memory "virus." And that would be difficult. How in the world was he going to get someone to watch the brain scan without explaining to them what it was all about?

# Chapter Twenty-five

*F*ox skipped lunch again, this time trying to plot out the various scenarios and options for the recent spate of crimes in Oxford. He used a big dry erase board on the wall to scribble on.

"Let's see." He stood back, clutching the dry erase pen in his right hand. "We have Hope William's boyfriend who was murdered. And she was Vincent Bonamo's ex-girlfriend, so Bonamo could have killed the boy out of jealousy. Bonamo's family is known to have a criminal element." He drew another circle. "And Bonamo's roommate just so happens to be Gregory Poindexter, the guy they call Dex. Bonamo claims that Dex may have been secretly conducting sleep experiments on him. He also claims he's been having dreams about murdering Hope William's boyfriend." He drew a circle at the top left. "Then there's Heather McHann, who may have robbed a gas station while sleep walking, and her boyfriend is Dex, the sleep researcher." He drew another circle low and to the side. "And someone has been stalking Seetha Mathis and sending her harassing letters and cards . . . and she works in the same lab as Dex."

He sat down and blew out a long breath. He had gone over this scenario many times, each time with the same result. There was one common thread in all these events—Gregory Poindexter. There was definitely something fishy about the guy and his so-called "sleep and memory" research.

His assistant, Amber, tapped at the door. "Detective Fox, they need you down in the lab."

He hopped up. "Okay." Maybe this was the DNA test result. He had asked the lab to run Bonamo's DNA against several samples they had taken from the Peterson boy on the day of the murder. They had gotten skin samples from under the victim's nails and on his knuckles.

Fox walked in the lab. Herb Wilkinson met him with a big smile. "We just got the DNA results back from the crime lab in Jackson. "Vince Bonamo's DNA is almost a perfect match with that we took off of Frankie Peterson, placing him at the scene of the crime when it happened. That'll completely destroy his alibis."

Fox's mind whirred like a supercomputer. He needed to be careful how he handled this new revelation. He would certainly arrest Bonamo and charge him with murder of Frankie Peterson. He just needed to figure out *when* would be the best time.

"Thanks, Herb. Great news. Don't release the info to anybody right away. I want to call Baton Rouge P.D. first. We might can tie Bonamo to one or more of the other Hope William's dead boyfriends. She's had several of them die mysteriously, you know."

Fox turned to leave. "The Baton Rouge guys will certainly want to question him, but they need the element of surprise. Right now, I don't think Bonamo knows we're on to him."

*****

That night at Dex's apartment, Bonamo was unusually nice. What had been a rude and jealous roommate for the last two months was now back, all warm and fuzzy. And Dex had no idea why.

"Hey, Dex," he said, sprawling out on the couch, "we need to hang out more often. Like we used to. Maybe watch a ballgame, huh?"

"Uh, I don't know. I've been real busy lately."

"Doing what?"

"Research. I've got several experiments going up at the lab."

"Cool. Tell me about 'em. I'm interested in that kind of thing, you know."

Dex didn't want to act *too* secretive, in case the cops ever interviewed Bonamo about his activities. He did know, however, that he wasn't going to say a word about sleepwalking, sleep treatments, "urges during sleep," or anything like that.

"Oh, mostly just traumatic memory research."

"Really. I'd love to hear about it, even help you with it sometime. I'd like to be a part of your important research."

*He might be buttering me up for something.* A light bulb went on in Dex's brain. Maybe he could let Bonamo watch the brain scan and see if the memory virus spread itself. The memory of something pulling his hair would be vague and untraceable. Bonamo wouldn't know where that memory or "urge" to pull someone's hair came from.

He scratched the side of face nervously. The idea was fraught with danger. If Bonamo experienced the traumatic memory immediately after watching the brain scan, then he would know Dex did it and beat the crap out of him. Or worse. However, if there was a delay in onset of the memory, then Bonamo would never link the two events.

This might be his one and only chance to set off the memory virus in a willing volunteer.

"Well, I could show you one thing I'm doing, if you're really interested."

Bonamo's eyes lit up. "Sure, anything."

Dex hurried to his room and retrieved his backpack containing the memory stick containing his most recent brain scan translation, the one from his traumatic hair-pulling experiment.

"Here, let's look at this video on the computer," Dex said, trying to act normal. His underarms suddenly felt moist.

"What is it?"

"It's a brain scan showing neuronal firing patterns which has been encoded into a pattern of lights and colors by a specialized computer program I wrote. This is the kind of thing I've been working on recently. I'm trying to record what a memory actually looks like, or at least, the firing pattern of brain cells during an intense memory. I mean, the pattern is only the result of the memory being put together by the Hippocampus in the brain."

Bonamo perched eagerly on the edge of the couch while Dex inserted the memory stick into the machine and turned on the computer.

"Now, it won't make much sense watching it, but I, uh, want you to see what kind of research I've been doing."

"Sure, sounds cool. Wish I could do things like this."

Presently, an irregular, dancing pattern of lights and colors appeared on the monitor screen.

"Now, be sure and watch it closely," Dex said, but himself only pretending to watch the screen. He certainly didn't want to relive that painful experience again. "You don't want to miss anything."

The neuronal firing pattern didn't last more than twenty seconds and the screen went blank. "You get that? You want me to play it again?"

Bonamo raised his eyebrows. "I guess. Is that all there is to it? I think I'm confused. What exactly is all that?"

Dex felt a little relieved. At least nothing happened immediately after watching the video. As long as some time passed between showing him the video and the urge to act it out everything would be all right. "Like I said, it's a neuronal firing pattern during a memory."

"What kind of memory?"

Dex ejected the memory device and stood up. "Uh, I don't recall. Nothing of any consequence."

"Will it make me have that specific memory?"

"Of course not." Dex's pulse quickened. Where was he going with this?

Bonamo stood up beside Dex. A shadow passed over his face. "Are you sure? How do I know you aren't giving me some kind of sleep treatment like you did last time?"

Dex suddenly felt an impending sense of doom. What had he meant by that?

"I've never given you or anybody else any sort of sleep treatment."

Bonamo smiled, retrieving a small digital recorder from his right pocket. He held it high in his hand. "I have it all right here. You *invited* me to watch your experimental research video, just like you did last time."

Dex felt faint. "Why do you keep saying, 'like I did last time'?"

Bonamo eased into Dex's face. It was like looking into the face of the devil. "Like the time you made me watch a blue ray disc implanting into my mind the idea of killing Frankie Peterson."

\*\*\*\*\*

Two days later, Vincent Bonamo was interrogated by detectives from the Baton Rouge Police Department concerning the suspicious deaths of two ex-boyfriends of Hope Williams. Both boys had been killed in car accidents involving faulty, or otherwise malfunctioning vehicle systems. Fox knew from reading the Louisiana reports that one of the cases involved brake system failure in a car traveling at a high rate of speed out on Interstate 12.

Fox sat in on the interview, but wasn't worried about the Louisiana folks getting Bonamo. He knew he had first dibs on the guy for the beating death of Frankie Peterson. Trials for manslaughter or second degree murder in Louisiana would be secondary to the capital murder charge in Oxford which was sure to be levied in a day or so.

Fox studied his own Bonamo file while the two blue suits grilled the guy. He wanted to see how Bonamo would try to wiggle out of the accusations. He knew that same kind of reasoning and "wiggling" would be used in denying the charges in Oxford.

"Yes, I worked at an oil change shop for about a year when I lived in Louisiana," Bonamo said flatly. "But I just drained the oil out of cars and changed the filters. I didn't do brake jobs. I didn't know anything about brakes." He smiled. "Still don't."

"Then how do you explain the fact that you were a mechanic of sorts during the time that Hope William's boyfriend's car had a mysterious, catastrophic, mechanical failure, leading to his death?"

"Like I said, I wasn't a mechanic then, and I'm not one now. There were other folks under the cars with me who did the mechanical stuff. Go check that out. Ask them yourself. They'll tell you I don't know anything about being a mechanic. They would have to point and tell me what to do. I didn't work there long."

The interrogation soon turned ugly. One of the blue-suited cops got in Bonamo's face. "One thing that bothers me, Mr. Bonamo, is the fact that your family is rich and powerful down in New Orleans, and yet you get a job at a two-bit oil change shop where the Braxton boy just so happened to get his car serviced regularly."

"So? My folks believe in hard work and making your own way."

"Is that so? What would you say if I tell you we've found records indicating that Ronnie Braxton's car was serviced by your shop on the day before his accident."

"I'd say I don't recall who or what person's car may have come through our shop. How would I know that? I was just a grease monkey down under the rack changing the oil and filters."

The cop shook his head. "That's too much of a coincidence, don't you think? A jury's gonna fry you."

"Nope." He remained cool. "Baton Rouge isn't all that big. There's probably not five oil change shops in the whole city. So what if the guy brought his car into ours? Besides, if, and only if, someone tinkered with the guy's car while it came through our shop, it wasn't me. Or, if it was me working on it, the shop owner must have *told* me how to do the procedure because I know nothing about cars. In that case, it was his fault that something went wrong, not mine. I'm not a mechanic. Never was. Never will be."

Fox eased out of the room and headed toward his office. He had seen enough to know the game plan. Bonamo was going to make it look like someone else did the crime, and he was plenty smart enough to cover his tracks and make it look that way. And if that didn't work, he would probably bring in the mafia to bully the judge and jury. Or worse, implement a "scorch the earth" policy wherein they kill everybody even remotely tied to the case.

He sat back in the chair and propped his feet up on the desk. That's why Bonamo was so insistent that someone had been making him sleepwalk. He's going to claim Dex did everything. It was all Dex.

Dastardly Dex.

Fox jumped up, his legs scattering papers off his desk. He looked at his watch. Five-thirty. He needed to talk to Dex as soon as possible. First thing tomorrow morning. He was the key to all this.

# Chapter Twenty-six

$\mathcal{D}$ex was in a tizzy at the lab late that night. In many ways he resembled his own lab animals in their cages, scurrying around with stuff flying in all directions. He was terrified. He must destroy all evidence of his memory research.

Bonamo had clearly trapped him.

He slammed a biohazard bag filled with blue ray discs, needles, virus vectors, and bran scan digital recordings on the lab top and began setting the dials on the autoclave machine. He knew the intense heat from autoclaving would melt the digital media. Then he could toss most of it in the dumpster although a few key items would need to be discretely thrown away, perhaps even buried in the nearby Holly Springs National Forest. Once the autoclave was turned on, he looked around nervously, then pointed at a stack of paperwork on the other counter. That had to be shredded.

Sweat popped out on his forehead. How could he have been so stupid? It was plain as day now. Bonamo was obviously the one who had killed the Peterson boy and was clever enough to use Dex's own research experience to get away with it.

He pushed the "continuous" button on the shredder and began cramming research notes into it as fast as it would accept them. He thought about Heather and the DeeVo's gas station incident.

*That's the thing that'll get me! When Fox figures out I prompted her to do that with the memory video, then Bonamo's claim that I prompted him kill someone will be fully supported.*

He retraced everything in his mind. Had he gotten the blue ray disc back from Heather, the one that he had used to transfer the video to her computer's hard drive? Had he indeed destroyed it? Was there another copy anywhere on his portable memory sticks? Had he wiped the computer hard drive?

He whipped around and faced the computer. Uh oh. The FBI had ways of examining computer hard drives, even those with all files deleted. He needed to physically remove the hard drive and maybe bury it along with the other sensitive items.

That would be his next task. But how in the world would he explain a missing hard drive?

*****

At eleven o'clock that night Fox received a phone call at home from Monique, the nighttime clerk at the police station.

"Detective Fox, sorry to bother you so late, but one of the officers suggested I call you."

"Okay. What's up?"

"They found Heather McHann on a roof again, this time at the gatehouse at Owl's Nest gated community out west of town."

"Do you have her in custody?"

"Yep, but they didn't actually arrest her. Just brought her in. She's *very* upset. Crying and wailing, saying she's mentally ill. Says she can't stop watching the video and also says she was sleep-walking and only awakened when the officers shined a light in her face."

"What kind of video? Porn or something?"

"Beats me."

Fox rubbed his chin. "Okay, Monica. This is what I want you to do. Have one of the officers take her to the hospital. I'll call ahead and speak with the doctors at the ER and see if they can get her evaluated by a psychiatrist."

"What if she doesn't cooperate? I mean, there's not really much we can charge her for other than maybe trespassing. She didn't steal anything, and the gatehouse is way out there by the highway. It's not located anywhere near the houses."

"Tell her that you're taking her to the hospital on my advice. If she balks, tell her she has two choices—either go to the hospital for evaluation or be arrested and spend the night in jail."

"Okay, boss."

Fox hung up and called the hospital ER where he explained Heather's condition to the chief admitting nurse. He suggested perhaps she be admitted into the behavioral unit for evaluation. Of course, that would be a medical decision, but he hoped they would do it. The girl was obviously having compulsions and acting out things she didn't want to do.

He hung up the phone and lay back down in the bed, thinking. Things were definitely getting weird around Oxford. Sleep and sleepwalking. Urges, compulsions, and promptings. But why? And more importantly, who?

And it just so happened that there was a sleep disorders research unit right there on campus, complete with a scientist who studied such things.

Maybe he should go ahead and arrest Dex and hold him for intense interrogation. That might crack the case wide open.

Fox instinctively knew better. The guy would lawyer up and not say a word.

Diplomacy and finesse. That's what was needed here. Maybe if he gave Dex enough rope he would hang himself.

He turned over. A plan was taking shape in his mind. He would go ahead and arrest Bonamo for the murder of Frankie Peterson and, for now anyway, keep talking to Dex without indicating that he was suspected as an accomplice in the case. Only gentle, indirect pressure would be placed on Dex for now. The boy was an egghead scientist, not a career criminal. He would surely slip-up soon and the whole thing unravel.

*****

Over the next few days, Seetha began slowly coming to terms with her situation and the ramifications of her actions. On the positive side, Sam was making slight progress, re-learning basic functions of human life like personal hygiene and walking. Lately, when visiting Sam, Seetha had found her to be able to talk, but not with the ease and clarity as before. The whole process reminded Seetha of a stroke victim's rehabilitation.

Of course, it was *possible* that Sam's mental and physical reversal was unrelated to the treatment Dex had concocted, but more than likely it was the direct cause. And Seetha wondered if she would ever be able to forgive herself for that.

She sat at her kitchen table putting together a little package of "happys" for Sam, which included her favorite candy bar, some hard candy, a decorative pen and pad of paper for her to draw or write notes with, and a few brightly-colored stickers.

Seetha ran a hand through her dark hair. "Hindsight is indeed twenty-twenty," she mumbled. As acceptance forced its way upon her, tears filled her eyes and the muscles in her face tightened. She should have never let herself become so obsessed with treating Sam that she ignored sound scientific principles and advice from trusted friends. Duke Livermore had warned her about the dangers of unregulated experimentation without proper controlled studies. But what could she do now? It was too late.

She wrapped the package in pretty red-print paper and attached a yellow bow. On a small white nametag she wrote, "To my darling Sam, the most important person in my life." She placed the package beside her purse. Duke had given wise counsel. She then recalled how he had also talked to her about using her willpower to buttress her wildly fluctuating emotions.

She made a promise to herself to try to do that more often.

*****

Dex was terrified the next morning when Detective Fox showed up at the front door of the sleep lab. He was trembling inside as he let the cop in.

"Hello, Dr. Poindexter. Nice to see you again."

"Uh, hello, detective. Is there anything I can do for you? I'm afraid Dr. Mathis isn't in yet, if you're here to see her."

"No, actually I wanted to speak to you."

"I don't understand." Dex backed up.

"I think you do." He smiled. "Is there somewhere we can speak in private?"

Dex swirled awkwardly, trying to find an empty office. He pointed. "Well, I guess we could step in there for a minute."

In the office, Fox remained standing, refusing a seat. Dex fought back the urge to break down crying. How did it ever get this bad?

Fox began slowly and deliberately. "Dex, you and I both know that you've been involved in sleep and memory research here at the university, and lately, there have been several crimes in which the suspects have claimed that they were asleep while committing them, and even feeling urges to do such things against their will."

"Yes, sir."

Fox leaned against the door frame. "I guess I was hoping you could explain these behaviors to me. Maybe even show me some of the scientific papers and articles about these things. I mean, you're the scientist. I want to understand the inner workings of the human mind and sleep and memory. And I want to know how such things could happen to apparently innocent people."

Dex was floored. Bonamo apparently hadn't yet taken the digital recording to Fox, so he wasn't going to arrest him. He said he was only asking for scientific information on sleep and memory. Dex suddenly became confused. Yellow iridescent light swirled in his periphery. Was this for real? Or was this a memory? He'd been reliving so many lately that he wasn't quite sure anymore. Maybe they were all mixing together into a new reality.

# *Chapter Twenty-seven*

**S**eetha sat on the foot of Sam's bed while she slept. She had been at the behavioral unit since nine o'clock that morning and Sam had briefly dozed off. Seetha couldn't help noticing how frail and unkempt her once-beautiful daughter was now. How far she had fallen!

Tears ran down her cheeks. She thought about her career and medical research in general. Scientific research held both promise and peril for humanity, and she was looking at an example of peril. Research run wild, and there was nobody to blame but herself. She made a promise to herself that if she ever made it through this mess, she would give up sleep and memory research and concentrate on teaching in the biology department.

Just then, Sam roused, mumbling and waving her arms around. Seetha could tell from the faraway look in her eyes that she was dreaming, or perhaps reliving one of her many fear memories, thanks to Rodney.

Seetha grabbed at her arms, trying to calm her down. "Shh, it's all right, sweetheart. I'm here. It's just a bad dream. Shh."

Sam stopped flailing around and sat straight up, looking out the window into the yard surrounding the hospital. The weird faraway look remained in her eyes. She looked like some freakish daughter of Frankenstein coming to life.

Seetha attempted to both wake her and hug her at the same time. She didn't want to scare her.

"It's him, Mom!" she moaned, pointing out the window. "He's

been here."

Seetha looked out the window. It was mid-day. The room was located on the first floor so Sam might have seen a person outside. That was certainly possible. But why would she be dreaming about it?

Maybe this was only a fear memory, like the time after she had been injected at the lab. On that night, Sam had insisted Rodney was present in the room.

The door flew open and a nurse ran in. Seetha wondered how in the world they knew she was having a nightmare. "Stand back, Ms. Mathis. I know what's going on here. We've seen it before."

Sam started waving her arms around wildly again and looking outside as if a demon were coming straight for her. Her eyes were large ovals. The nurse grabbed both shoulders and began shaking her, slowly at first, then more vigorously. "Sam, wake up. Come out of it. It's a dream. Come on, wake up!"

She reached in her pocket for an ammonia ampoule and waved it under Sam's nose. She moaned and continued waving her arms toward the right side of the bed. The nurse was unfazed, continuing to shake her and speak boldly right in her face.

Sam got wilder, now yelling loudly, "You can't do that!" and waving her hands high and to the right side, as if fighting off an attacker. Then her right hand started a pinching motion using her thumb and pointer finger.

The nurse never missed a beat, remaining forceful, wrestling Sam's arms back down and speaking boldly. Seetha was in shock watching the physical encounter which wasn't much different from a schoolyard fight.

In a minute, Sam collapsed back on the pillow, sound asleep. The nurse remained hovering over her for a short time, as if expecting a repeat of the outburst.

When nothing happened and it seemed as if Sam was indeed asleep, the nurse motioned with her head toward the hall. Seetha followed.

Once outside, the nurse gave a medical analysis. "As best we can tell, Ms. Mathis, your daughter has a recurring bad dream which is very predictable in its presentation and course. If left alone, it repeats the pattern and continues for a long time—"

"You mean you've let her struggle and be terrified like that for *a long time*?"

The nurse seemed a little embarrassed. "Well, yes, but not intentionally. In the beginning, we didn't know what was going on or what to do. We called in one of our doctors to evaluate her during one such episode. Now, we think we've got it figured out."

"How do you know it's a bad dream?"

"That's what Dr. Sinkot thinks it is, or possibly—"

She stopped short.

"Or what?"

"Well, we don't know for sure."

"I'll ask you again, *or what*?"

"It could be a traumatic memory. She may be acting out a traumatic memory."

"You mean the pinching and fighting behaviors? What evidence do you have?"

The nurse paused. "You would have to ask Dr. Sinkot about that. I'm just telling you he mentioned it as one possibility."

"Why did Sam tell me, 'It's him?' Who's she talking about?"

The nurse shook her head. "We're not sure. We believe it's a delusion."

Long uncomfortable pause.

"During one such episode, she did scream out a name."

"What name?" Seetha trembled, knowing what was coming.

"Rodney."

"Oh my God! I knew it." Everything in her told her to run and hide. Maybe grab Sam and move across country. Then, a more sensible portion of her consciousness took over. She would fight this. She would exercise her will in the midst of an emotional storm.

*****

A week later, Seetha frantically cleaned and straightened up the apartment getting everything ready for Sam's homecoming. She was brimming with excitement and wanted to make it warm and welcoming. Dr. Sinkot had said Sam was making sufficient progress now to go home, at least part-time. The nightmares had ceased and Seetha had finally decided that Sam's claim to having seen Rodney in the hospital yard was only a delusion. Nothing more than a ghost from her tormented past.

The plan for Sam's treatment was for her to stay at home with Seetha at nights and return to the behavioral unit during the daytime for the remainder of the summer. Dr. Sinkot was hoping she could continue to improve throughout the summer, even starting school again, though it might require special education for a semester or so.

Seetha toyed with the idea of inviting John Fox to help her pick up Sam and celebrate her homecoming. She told herself it was a crazy idea, but the man *had* been calling and coming around a lot lately and had shown considerable interest in Sam and her situation. Pleasant feelings arose within her as she recalled the usually rough and gruff man coming to the hospital to check on her and insisting that she go home and get something to eat. He had been so kind that day.

She dialed Fox's number.

"Fox speaking."

"John, this is Seetha. . . ."

His tone softened. "Oh, hi there Seetha. How are things going? How's Sam? I'm sorry I haven't been by there this week to see her."

Seetha was taken aback. "You've been going to visit Sam?"

"Uh, well, I guess I thought you knew."

Of course she wouldn't know. Half the time Sam wouldn't talk. *She didn't tell me.*

"I hope you don't mind me seeing her. I tried to be brief and non-intrusive each time."

"Of course not. I appreciate your concern. I just didn't know." Seetha paced the floor, mustering courage to ask the question. "By the way, speaking of Sam, that's why I called. I was wondering if you would like to help me pick her up for her homecoming today. She's getting out."

"That's great news. I'd love to. Is it just a weekend at home?"

Seetha explained the new arrangement about nights at home and weekdays at the hospital for treatment and rehabilitation.

"I've got a better idea," Fox offered.

"Okay, what's that?"

"Let me go with you to pick her up, and eventually take you guys home, but in the meantime, let me take you two on a picnic. I'll take care of everything."

Seetha was thrilled. *Just like a real family.* "We'd love that."

"Okay, tell me when to pick you up."

"How about one hour?"

"Okay, see you then."


Even though they had been dating for several weeks, Seetha saw a completely different side of Detective Fox that day. He graciously helped check Sam out of the hospital and took them both to the Grove on campus where he spread a large quilt out over the lush green grass so they could relax under one of the many hundred-year-old oaks in the Grove. The warm, mid-May sun filtered through the dense foliage above.

Sam seemed content, even smiling a good bit and allowing Seetha to hold her and caress her face. Fox sat nearby on the quilt, but Seetha noticed him edging toward her every now and then.

Soon Fox unpacked a wonderful lunch of fried chicken and several side items.

"Here, I brought us a little something to eat."

"You didn't cook this," Seetha kidded when she bit into a chicken leg. "It tastes like Kentucky Fried Chicken."

Fox grinned. "Never said I did."

"But you transferred it from the KFC container to make it appear you did."

"I guess I was hoping you wouldn't figure out my secret. I don't cook. Not a lick."

Seetha leaned over and entwined her arm into his. "Doesn't matter. It's the thought that counts." She looked him in the eye, resisting the urge to kiss him. "This was sooo sweet of you, John. Thank you."

Fox blew out a long breath as if relieved to hear that. "No problem. I know things have been tough for you lately and I just wanted to make you and Sam feel special."

She glanced down at Sam who was snuggled under her right arm now. "You definitely did that."

Fox leaned back on his elbows. "This is the life. I haven't done anything like this in a long time."

"How long?"

"Oh, I don't know, maybe fifteen years."

Seetha poked him with her elbow. "And who was she?"

Fox seemed momentarily embarrassed. "My ex-wife."

"Sorry."

"It's okay. Didn't work out. I guess I wasn't her type."

"Children?"

"No. We never got that far."

"You said she wasn't your type. What was her type, if I might ask?"

"Fancy, or sophisticated, I guess. A socialite. I'm pretty plain."

"I like your type. A lot, actually," Seetha said, stroking his right arm.

"I'm delighted to know that you do." He smiled.

After eating, Sam was soon sacked out on the quilt, while Seetha and Fox talked and visited.

He nodded over toward the sleeping Sam. "You think that's from the medication?"

"Definitely. She's never slept this much, but Dr. Sinkot says they can begin weaning her off some of the meds soon."

"I hope so."

"I do too."

An uneasy silence followed that statement. Seetha suddenly felt a tugging in her heart, more like a deep yearning, to tell Fox what she had done. Everything. It was risky. He might disapprove of her actions so much that he moved on to someone else. Or worse, launch some kind of criminal investigation.

"What're you thinking?" he asked.

"Not much. Just thinking."

"Deep stuff?"

"You have no idea how deep."

"Tell me. I want to know. I *really* want to know you and Sam more, and that involves sharing deeply-felt issues."

She stood up, careful not to awaken Sam. She probably wouldn't have this kind of opportunity again. "Come over here to the bench. I don't want Sam to hear this."

Fox followed her to a nearby bench where they sat down.

Seetha swiped dark hair out of her eyes. A warm southerly breeze had kicked up.

"John, what I'm about to tell you may jeopardize my job, career, and our relationship." She stopped short. "Are you absolutely sure you want me to continue?"

He shifted his weight as if trying to keep from slipping into cop mode. He reached out and grabbed her hand. "Of course. If you and I are to have any kind of relationship, then it must be built on mutual trust."

"Okay, well, here goes." She sighed, trying to exhale several month's worth of anxiety and stress. "As you may already know, my post-doc, Dex, has been conducting research on sleep and memory. Some of it, and I have to admit that I knew, involved animals and was illegal."

"Yes, I've suspected that due to my investigations into the death of —" Fox cut himself off. "Sorry, I promise not to be a cop. I'm here as a friend only. Please continue."

"There's more. *Much* more."

Then she started from the beginning, telling him about her marriage to Rodney and his abusive tendencies to both her and Sam. She reiterated to Fox that during the marriage she had no idea Rodney was sexually abusing Sam. And she said she still wasn't sure if it were true or not. She told him she only recently learned about that possibility from Dr. Sinkot. Then she proceeded to tell Fox about Dex helping her with her own traumatic memories by using pre-recorded audio recordings played during her sleep.

He listened carefully, not saying a word, but she knew he was analyzing every word like a mechanic listening to a car engine.

She proceeded to tell him that she was so desperate to get help for Sam that she lost all sense of right and wrong, even begging Dex to give her an experimental treatment to remove traumatic memories from Sam.

"And he did it?" Fox's voice rose. She noticed the muscles in his arm tightening. The cop was coming out again.

"Yes, well, he told me exactly what to do and I did it." Tears streamed down her cheeks. "I can't believe I gave my own daughter a shot of God-knows-what and then made her watch a video of brain scans converted into a pattern of lights and colors, all supposedly to heal a traumatic memory."

Fox jumped up. "You mean he made you watch a video with some sort of brain scan patterns on it and it affected Sam this way?" He pointed over at the sleeping teen.

Seetha was terrified. Fox appeared upset. But the cat was out of the bag now. "Yes, and the next day is when she regressed."

He swirled and sat back down. "My God, Seetha."

"There's more. During the treatment, something very strange, almost mystical, happened." She paused. "One of Sam's traumatic memories jumped from her to me."

Fox's blank look unsettled her even more. "What? How do you know that?"

"I know it sounds crazy, but when I was hugging her my head tingled, and I distinctly experienced *her* memory. It was Rodney screaming at her. Something about how he couldn't allow her to tell anyone."

"Couldn't allow her to tell anyone *what*?"

Seetha shook her head. "I suppose the abuse."

"Does that mean he threatened to kill her if she did?"

Seetha paused, allowing the weight of that statement to settle deep into her soul. Could it be?

In a moment, Fox raked his hair back with both hands. "It all makes sense now. All these crimes lately. Dex has been doing it. He's been behind them all."

She didn't know exactly what he meant by that, but continued her confession. She had already incriminated herself anyway. What the hell?

"So, you see, John, I essentially did this to my child. My dear child." Her voice cracked. Tears flowed. "I'm a terrible person."

Fox swept her into his arms. "No, you're not a terrible person. Anybody could see that you just desperately wanted to help your daughter. Dex took advantage of that. It's his fault."

She shook her head vigorously. "No, I knew what I was doing. I'm responsible. I knew better."

Fox held her close and stroked her hair with his right hand. "It's okay. Everything's gonna be okay. I promise."

Seetha broke into an uncontrollable, loud sob.

Fox didn't seem bothered by the crying. He held even more tightly and whispered comfort and encouragement into her ear.

"Please don't worry. If she doesn't get better, I'll help you find the best medical care and rehabilitation available. I've got an uncle who's a retired pediatrician down at the medical school in Jackson. He'll know where to refer us."

Seetha liked hearing him use the term "us." She snuggled even closer to his chest. It was difficult at first, but she allowed herself to relax in his arms.

After about fifteen minutes, Seetha sat up, hair sticking out in all directions like she'd stuck her finger into an electrical outlet. She wiped her eyes. "I've got to ask this. Be honest. Don't you think less of me now than when we first came out here today?"

He smiled. "Not one bit. Everybody makes mistakes. Sure, it was a terrible mistake, but you had Sam's best interest at heart."

Months of heaviness suddenly evaporated. Her heart pounded, this time with joy. If Fox didn't condemn her, maybe she could forgive herself.

Someday.

She pushed back a wind-blown clump of hair from her face. "What did you mean earlier when you said something about all the crimes lately and Dex being involved?"

Fox quickly gave her the thumbnail version of Heather McHann and the DeeVo's gas station incident and then Bonamo's outlandish claim that Dex had planted in his head a "memory" or urge to murder Frankie Peterson. By the time he finished, Seetha was pale. She had no idea Dex had done all that.

"You think it's true?"

"What? That Dex did the secret memory treatments, or that Heather broke into DeeVo's, or that Bonamo killed the Peterson boy?"

Seetha shook her head. This was crazy. "I'm not sure."

Fox was fully in police mode by now. "I'm convinced that Dex may have indeed prompted his girlfriend to break into DeeVo's. She said he asked her to watch a video the night before the incident, and several times since the event she's been found asleep on top of buildings trying to get in. Each time, she says the same thing—that she's waiting, 'until the gas attendant is gone.' Something or somebody put that idea in her head. That's not natural."

"My God." She tried again to control her hair against the breeze.

"And last time it happened, she said she couldn't keep from watching the video. It had to be that video."

Seetha inhaled. "He's using the memory research for his own selfish purposes." Her voice trailed off as she thought about the situation. Of course, she knew about Heather's urges from the time she had come to see her at the clinic, but Fox's assessment now made perfect sense. The video not only prompted her to do the specific behavior, it also had some sort of feedback loop that made her want to watch it again. Then, a different, even worse, possibility entered her mind. Maybe the memory itself Dex had implanted in Heather was causing her to watch the thing over and over in order to survive and perpetuate. The viral memory itself was doing something more than what even Dex had intended.

That was over-the-top spooky.

Fox broke her reverie. "Seems that he was using the research for his own purposes. Now, as for the Bonamo thing, I'm not so sure. Dex didn't know Hope Williams or the Peterson boy. What possible motive could he have for prompting Bonamo to kill someone? Bonamo's smart enough to confuse the issue and try to shift the blame on someone else."

"Why haven't you arrested them?"

Fox stood up, pacing in front of the bench. "Maybe you haven't heard. We did arrest Bonamo several days ago and charged him with murder, but his family down in New Orleans immediately sent a group of slick lawyers up here for the initial hearing and got him out on bail. There'll be a second hearing and a trial, all right, but who knows when the trial might be . . . maybe several months."

Fox looked off in the distance. "That boy and his family are trouble, Seetha." He looked back at her. "This is a selfish thing to say, and probably unethical, but I want you to stay out of that situation completely. Don't you dare become a witness for either side in that trial, no matter who asks you. I'm convinced that his family is associated with the Mafia."

"What about Dex? Are you going to arrest him?"

Fox sat back down on the bench. "I haven't got my strategy figured out just yet, but for now, let's say I'm watching him closely. We certainly could get him in trouble with the university for his unapproved research, but we'd have a hard time convincing a jury that he did anything criminal, other than possibly influencing Heather McHann to break into DeeVo's. Right now, the Bonamo link is weak. It could all be a smoke screen by Bonamo."

# Chapter Twenty-eight

*D*ex threw clothes into his suitcases. He had heard about the Bonamo arrest and was glad he wasn't at the apartment when it had happened. He had to get moved out of the apartment as soon as possible. Bonamo unnerved him. The man was definitely shady, even evil. Dex also had heard about the Bonamo family hiring a passel of lawyers to get him out on bail. That was worrisome. If they could spring Bonamo that fast, there was no telling what else they could do.

Although the cops had never asked him about it, Dex knew Bonamo's defense would be that Dex prompted the murder through some sort of memory treatment. After all, he had a digital recording of Dex "encouraging" him to watch the video of brain scans. That was bad. Really bad.

He considered his predicament. Things were unraveling. Heather was apparently in an unstoppable cycle of climbing on top of buildings all over town and "waiting for the gas attendant to leave." Secondly, the treatment of Samantha Mathis had been ruinous and it was only a matter of time before Seetha spilled her guts to a psychiatrist or the police. She too, would probably say that he made her do it. Lastly, the thing with Bonamo. He would surely play the digital recording to the cops soon, if not already.

*Then why haven't the cops arrested me?*

A scary thought entered his head. Maybe they already knew about the digital recording. Perhaps even Heather had confessed more than he knew and maybe they were just watching him to see what he would do next.

Dex slammed the apartment door and fumbled with the two big suitcases. He looked up and down the parking lot for any signs of a cop car or Bonamo. He didn't want to meet either. He had to get away. But where?

He drove around Oxford for twenty minutes, trying to figure out what to do. If he left town, that would be a sure sign of guilt and the cops would issue an all-points-bulletin on him. He could go to a hotel and check in under a false name, but that too would imply wrongdoing. He had to keep it legal. Reasonable.

Heather was his only alternative. Maybe she would let him sleep on the couch. They were still talking somewhat, but there had definitely been a coldness between them lately. She obviously knew that the anger management "treatment" and the DeeVo's incident were related and now she didn't trust him. Nonetheless, he might convince her to allow him to stay there. He could say he was fearful of Bonamo.

He made his way across town to Heather's apartment and found a parking spot.

On the way up the sidewalk, he rehearsed the exact wording of his plea. This was going to be touchy, to say the least.

He knocked and she opened the door cautiously. "Yes?"

"It's me, Dex. Can we talk?"

She flung the door open then. Irritation marked her face. "What're you doing here? I've told you we aren't together anymore."

He couldn't help noticing how sullen she looked. "This isn't about us as a couple," he pleaded. "It's about helping a friend."

She sighed and nodded him inside.

He took a seat on the edge of the couch in her living room. This had to be good. "Heather, I'm convinced that Vince is after me. I think my life is in danger."

"Danger from what?"

"His family is Mafia. I've told you all that before. Don't you remember?"

"Why would he want to harm you?" She cocked an eyebrow.

"Because he thinks I ratted on him about the Frankie Peterson murder."

Heather displayed a blank look. "I don't follow."

"You know he's a suspect in the murder of his ex-girlfriend's boyfriend. It's been all in the news."

She nodded.

"He thinks I ratted on him, I tell you. He's gonna try to kill me."

Heather's face became even paler. "Are you sure?"

"Absolutely."

"Then why not go to the police? Tell them, not me."

"I have. They don't believe me."

A long pause ensued. "What does all this have to do with me? To be honest, I can't take anymore of your crap."

"I need to stay here a few nights . . ."

She threw up her hands. "Whoa, you're not dragging me into all this mess. After what you did to me."

"What do you mean? I haven't harmed you in any way."

"Don't go there, Dex." She stuck her palms out. "We've been through this a thousand times. Somehow, some way, you put into my head an urge to break into DeeVo's, and you know it. And you have no idea the grief those thoughts have caused me."

He shook his head. "Nope. Absolutely not true. Or if it did happen, it was an accidental mix-up from the brain scans or recordings I used in your anger management treatment." He stopped short. "You've got to believe me."

"I don't know." She wavered.

He knew she would cave in. Heather had a good Christian upbringing and was genuinely kind-hearted, to a fault. "Please."

She stood up. "Five nights. That's all. You can have the couch." She eased into his face. "But if I get one hint of anything dangerous or illegal going on between you and Bonamo, you're outta here immediately. I want nothing to do with that."

He jumped up as if to hug her, then backed off. He had a difficult time controlling his excitement. "Sure. No. No way. There's nothing dangerous going on . . . at least on my part. I'm just trying to stay away from the guy, that's all."

The next evening Dex worked late at the lab again. He looked around at the now orderly countertops and was pleased with his progress so far. All traces of the illegal research in the lab were gone. There was some of the herpes virus vector material left, but he had approval for that. The rest of the questionable stuff, the secret logbooks and a few key portable memory devices, were safely stashed in a hidden sewn-in pocket deep inside his backpack. His plan was to commit to memory the key elements of the logbooks and eventually destroy them as well. The memory devices contained a few brain scans of Seetha Mathis' fear memories for future analysis. They were recordings of fear memories and not at all involved in his "prompting" experiments, so he was fairly sure they couldn't incriminate him. After all, Dr. Mathis had agreed to participate in the recordings. That might have been unethical, but not illegal. And as for his most titillating theory of all, that traumatic memories might actually lead to mental illness in persons with malfunctioning brain immune systems, well, he had never written that down explicitly anywhere. Yes, he had hinted at it some in encoded writings in his secret logbook, but that was all. Most of those theories and experimental results were in his head and would stay that way forever.

He scanned the room: the lab was ready for inspection by any authority. "Bring it on, I'm not scared." He strutted.

Dex walked over to his desk and pulled the secret logbooks out of his backpack. He wanted to re-check what was in the injection he had concocted for Samantha Mathis. What an interesting reaction had occurred! It had knocked the girl clear back to childhood.

It took him a few minutes to decode what he had written about the drug concoction. "Hmm. That might be useful," he mumbled. "If I could just figure out a way to give that same shot to Bonamo!"

He carefully re-read his notes about the injection ingredients. They could be duplicated, all right, but how would he manage to give a grown man a shot without him knowing it?

He started to work, mixing the contents for the injection. He would have to worry about how to administer the thing later.

One thing was for sure. If he could somehow inject Bonamo with the concoction, troubles with the guy would be over. The ever-threatening Bonamo monster would be nothing but a babbling kindergartener.

Two days later Dex formulated a plan to inject Bonamo with the mind-erasing chemicals. He would hide in the biology department when the indoor potted plants were serviced and ambush Bonamo then. Dex had called the Environmental Services Department on campus pretending to be an assistant to the department head and asking them to send someone soon to service the plants. He had made up a story about there being lots of tiny insects all over the potted plants inside the building. When asked about possible times and dates, they had said it would be either Tuesday or Wednesday night before they could service the plants.

Dex would need to be up there both nights to make sure he encountered Bonamo.

Tuesday evening, beginning at five-thirty, he perched by a large set of windows on the fourth floor overlooking the parking lot of the biology building. He would simply have to watch and wait. From living with Bonamo for two years, he knew the Environmental Services Department worked on the indoor plants on campus after hours, but usually no later than ten o'clock.

Nothing happened for three and a half hours and he soon grew tired of watching students meander by, often in pairs, holding hands or snuggling. He reminded himself of why he didn't have time for all that. Other than perhaps an *appearance* of it.

About nine o'clock the Environmental Services van swept into the parking lot and two men popped out. One of them unlocked the biology building door while the other dug sprayers and other small equipment out of the van.

Dex became nervous, even more so than before. Jumping out and injecting Bonamo was one thing, but with the extra man working the plants, how could he get away with it?

When the men disappeared into the building, Dex made his way ever so slowly down the stairs, holding a biohazard bag half-full of discarded glassware, syringes, and broken microscope slides. He guessed Bonamo would begin work on the main floor since that was where most of the potted plants were placed. He reviewed the plan of attack over and over in his mind. He would speak to Bonamo, pretend to walk past him, and trip, shoving the bag of sharps against Bonamo's body. But actually, during the fake fall, he would be holding a spring-loaded syringe under the bag and would shoot Bonamo with its contents. If Bonamo didn't beat the snot out of him right then and there, the plan just might work.

If the other guy was present when it all went down, then so be it. Dex would do his best to make it look like an accident.

He walked out of the stairwell, entering the hallway of the main floor. Dex anxiously gripped the spring-loaded syringe with one hand and the sack of sharps in the other. He would need to hold the two closely together the minute he saw Bonamo. He had to make it look like he was merely carrying a biohazard bag to the hazardous waste container.

Bonamo's deep voice echoed off the empty building's walls as Dex approached another shorter, wider hall, which marked the main building entrance. It sounded as if he was telling the other plant technician how to spray the plants.

Dex gripped the bag and syringe tightly and rounded the corner, headed down the hall.

Bonamo swirled to face him. Shock briefly appeared on his face. "What are you doing up here?" he glared.

Dex never slowed down, as if deliberately headed somewhere. "Hey Vince. Just cleaning up the lab."

Bonamo gave him a look that would scare Satan himself, but Dex tried to remain confident and look ahead, as if walking past him down the hall.

When he got alongside Bonamo, he faked tripping and then lunged to the side toward him, thrusting the bag and the loaded syringe into his chest. The syringe shot its contents somewhere in Bonamo's upper stomach area. In all the commotion Dex deftly stuffed the used syringe in his back pocket.

Bomamo jumped back. "Hey, watch it creep! What the hell are you doing?" He grabbed his stomach. "I think something in that sack poked me." When he saw the "biohazard" label on the sack he blew up.

"There had better not be anything infectious in that bag, you bastard," he screamed. He grabbed Dex and pulled him near his face. "If there is, I'll kill you. I swear, I'll . . ."

When Bonamo noticed the other plant service technician watching his tirade, he released Dex and suddenly began to act civil. It was a clear case of Dr. Jekyll and Mr. Hyde.

"Uh, what I mean is, can you reassure me that the contents of that bag aren't infectious? Should I go to the doctor?"

"I'm terribly sorry," Dex said. "I tripped or something." He held up the biohazard bag. "No, don't be misled by the label. Everybody uses these same bags and we put all our sharps in them, like broken glass, microscope slides, and stuff like that. There's nothing infectious here."

"You sure about that?" Bonamo rubbed his belly.

"Of course." Dex put on his best face. "We do *memory* research, not disease research. I promise."

Bonamo glanced over toward the other plant guy, then back at Dex. "Well, if you're sure."

"I've got to go," Dex said, eager to get away from the Mafia king. "Again, I'm terribly sorry." He pointed down the hall. "I've got to get this down to the waste container and finish up."

Bonamo looked him over like a judge examining a criminal. He rubbed his belly again. "Okay, Dex." He looked back toward the other plant guy again, as if to make sure he heard it. "Good to see you."

# Chapter Twenty-nine

$\mathcal{D}$ex tried to act normal over the next forty-eight hours, hoping to hear that Bonamo had been hospitalized for a sudden regression back to childhood, but yet afraid to ask anybody. He just tried to go about his business at work and lay low. Fortunately, Heather was still allowing him to stay at her apartment so he didn't have to physically face the monster.

When he could stand the suspense no longer, he searched around Oxford for a pay phone where he could make an anonymous call to Bonamo. If he was mentally competent enough to answer a phone call, then the injection had failed. Dex recalled how the Mathis kid had been totally incapacitated within forty-eight hours of the shot.

He found a phone in the poorest section of town outside a Laundromat located next to a BBQ stand in the parking lot of an abandoned gas station. His heart pounded as he placed coins in the ancient-looking device and dialed the number. Ring one; ring two; ring three . . .

Suddenly a voice came on the line. It was clearly Bonamo's. "Hello?"

He certainly sounded normal. Dex's hopes faded like an early morning mist hitting bright sunlight. His attempt to take Bonamo out of the picture obviously hadn't worked. He started to hang up, then decided against it.

*It's a pay phone; there's no way he can know who's calling.*

"Hello?" the voice thundered this time. "Who the hell is this? This

*Jerome & Rosella Goddard*

had better not be some kind of crank call."

Dex slammed the receiver back in its cradle. Same old Bonamo.

Back to the drawing board, except this time, the drawing board was limited. The vast majority of Dex's research supplies, equipment, and notes had been destroyed.

Dex knew he was on borrowed time. The memory erasure injection had failed to work on Bonamo, perhaps due to the lack of a steroid being concurrently in his blood stream. His preliminary animal work and Seetha's own testimony had indicated that steroids helped in the memory treatment process. No matter, now he was in trouble. If Bonamo didn't come after him soon, then Detective Fox surely would. Either way, he needed to get out of town, and fast. He figured maybe he could make a new start somewhere, though probably not as a researcher. He would need to disappear among the masses for a while until all this blew over.

Since he wouldn't be having laboratory facilities at his disposal for quite some time, he needed to do one or two more tiny experiments with the portable memory devices he had hidden in his backpack. For one thing, he wanted to re-watch one of Seetha Mathis' fear memories and use the lab equipment to "cut" the brain scans a little tighter to eliminate pieces of other memories connected to it. He recalled how jumbled the last one had been, being a collection of several memories and not one "clean" one.

Tuesday night after Heather had gone to bed, Dex headed back to the lab with his backpack containing his logbooks and the Seetha Mathis memory recordings. He figured he wouldn't need but about an hour to do the procedure.

Once inside the lab, Dex lay down in one of the recliners used for sleep research, placed the memory stick in a notebook computer, and began watching the memory-based brain firing patterns. He was determined to try to correlate the patterns with the onset of each particular memory. That way, he could "cut" them using the complex electronic equipment in Seetha's lab.

The flashes of light and color patterns danced on the screen like wispy fairies. Soon Dex was enveloped in a thousand sensations; he was re-living the memory. Yellow iridescent light swirled in his periphery, but the center of his field of view remained clear. A dark shadow passed over him. The darkness was like an opaque wall that shut off most of the light in the room. His chest suddenly pulled hard for air, and he felt like he was wrapped up in a blanket, just like in the experiments previously. Dex fought to control the panic rising within him. He had done this before and knew that nothing would *really* happen to him, no matter what he felt like. Then there was motion. Something or somebody was moving toward him. His heart began to race and a sense of impending doom swept over him, just like in times before. He felt terror again. Not just terror — *intense terror.* Just like last time.

The movement came closer — a dark form coming toward him. But unlike the other times, the dark form was not coming from the right side. It was headed straight for him. It was a person! Dex struggled to see who it was, though his vision was still blurred. All he could tell was that it was a man. Had Bonamo followed him to the lab? He hadn't heard the door open.

"Hey! Who are you?"

The man punched him squarely in the nose with such force that Dex fell from the chair to his hands and knees. He covered his head with his hands. His nose hurt intensely and red, slushy blood poured out of it.

Again, Dex felt a flood of uncontrollable fear and terror, unlike anything he had ever experienced before. He rubbed his eyes, trying desperately to look up and see his attacker. The man kicked him in the stomach, bowling him over. He could barely breathe.

"I told you that if you *ever* pulled a stunt like that again, I'd kill you. Are you hard-headed or something?" The attacker placed an exclamation point at the end of that statement with another swift kick to the gut.

Dex flipped backward onto the floor, looking upward, unable to breathe or think. His mind seized with raw fear. The man loomed over him, staring angrily. "I should have finished you off the first time." Dex could now make out the face of his attacker—Bonamo!

Then Bonamo walked around behind him, pulled Dex's head upward by the hair, and slit his throat with a thin, shiny knife.

The Seetha Mathis memory was no longer playing itself out in his mind. This was real. He could see real blood spilling all over the lab floor. *His blood.* Lights in the room began to fade.

Ever darker. Dark.

*****

Fox called Seetha at six-o'clock the next morning with the news, asking her to come to the lab as soon as possible. She couldn't believe it. Dex had been murdered.

While trying to drive through town to the university, she fought back tears. Even though she and Dex weren't close, she still felt an incredible sense of sadness. What a terrible loss! Of course it was Bonamo, or one of his people, who had done this. John Fox had indicated as much to her earlier.

She raked her hair back from her eyes, trying to "will" herself into being strong. Where would all this end? She thought of her daughter back home in bed. Selfish as it was, she carefully reviewed her role in the unethical research over the last few months, trying to see if there was anything that would make her a target by the Bonamos. She certainly hoped not.

Seetha hugged Fox tightly when they met just inside the door of the laboratory.

"I can't believe it, John."

"You don't have to go in there, you know," he said.

"No, I want to help. What do you need me to do?"

"We need technical help. We found a backpack and a couple of personal items, but you know this lab better than we do. Could you just look around at all the research equipment and tell me anything that's new, missing, or out of place?" He paused. "You don't have to examine the body. We'll take care of that. I covered it with a sheet until someone from the crime lab gets here."

"Okay, I think I can do that." Seetha slowly headed for the door to the room where Dex lay dead. Even though everything inside her was screaming "no," she forced herself to go in anyway.

She gasped upon entering. Right there in the middle of the floor, a blue sheet marked the stiff body of her once-brilliant post-doc. One of his arms seemed to be poking upward as if still fighting off the attacker. A pool of blood as big as a pizza pan, now brownish in color, encircled his head. She was glad she wouldn't have to see any more than that.

Seetha checked the equipment and supplies scattered around on the lab countertops, looking for anything out of place or different. Nothing seemed new or awry, but when moved a notebook computer, she noticed it contained a memory stick in its USB port.

She removed it and turned it over in her hand. Scribbled in tiny words on one side of the yellow plastic device was, "27 Feb 2009, S.M., 6 minutes."

"This is one of mine," she said, her cheeks flushing with embarrassment. "One of those Dex made when I was hooked up to the brain scan machine. He must have been up here last night watching that."

Once back outside in the main room, Seetha showed Fox the memory device and awkwardly explained to him that at one time Dex had made a few brain scans of her fear memories.

"He must have been up here reviewing it. There's nothing in there to indicate he was doing anything else."

"No other items that could be Dex's?"

She shook her head.

Fox looked at the memory stick in her hand.

"Oh, there's nothing illegal about this," she explained, red-faced, like a kid caught stealing cookies out of a candy jar. "Unethical, maybe. Illegal, no."

"You think it has anything to do with Bonamo?" Fox glanced back down at the memory device. "Is there anything on here he wouldn't like or want made public?"

"No. Absolutely not. It's nothing but brain scans of me re-calling times when I was afraid." She waved him back inside the room. "Follow me, I'll show you."

She inserted the device and presently squiggly lines appeared on the screen, followed by patterns of light and color. "That's all there is on the thing," she said, pointing. "Brain scans, or at least that's what it should be. I'm not sure about all the colors and lights. Anyway, what could this possibly have to do with Bonamo?"

Fox watched the screen closely. When Seetha saw him doing that, she immediately shut the machine off. "You shouldn't be watching that."

"Why? It's just a bunch of gobbly-gook."

"It can make you re-live that memory."

"Oh yeah, that's right. The memory re-enactment thing. Hard to believe those little lines and dots could affect a person so profoundly."

Seetha ejected the device. "Yes, well, believe me, this stuff produces all kinds of negative and unintended consequences."

# Chapter Thirty

*O*nly a handful of people attended the memorial service for Gregory "Dex" Poindexter, accurately reflecting his isolation from other humans. Seetha was there, of course, along with Heather, Frances, and a few of the faculty from the biology department.

Fox accompanied Seetha for moral support. After the service, he stood with her in the foyer of the funeral home, speaking to a few of the attendees. Dr. Jackson, the biology department chairman, was one of them.

"Dr. Mathis, I'm sorry about Dex." Jackson looked and acted the part of a politician.

She shook his hand. "Thank you."

"You know we need to talk about this next week," he said.

"Yes, sir."

"There'll likely be an internal investigation." Jackson looked at Detective Fox. "Along with the criminal investigation, of course. We've got to make sure everything is on the up-and-up. All of your records and laboratory inspections for the last six months must be up-to-date and available for review." He paused a long time. His eyes conveyed tons of non-verbal information. "Are we together on this?"

Seetha didn't like all the political innuendo but knew she needed to comply anyway. "Yes, sir."

When he started walking away, Seetha followed, stopping him by the door. She lowered her voice so that Fox wouldn't hear. "Sir, do you think I'll be asked to resign?"

Dr. Jackson bit his lip. "No, I don't think so. From what I've been able to piece together, *everything*, and I want you to read between the lines here, Seetha, *everything* that has been done in your lab and at the biology department over the past few months was entirely and completely a result of the illegal activities of Gregory Poindexter. The boy was obviously mentally ill."

Dr. Jackson then smiled and walked out the door.

Seetha blew out a long breath. *That's his out. Dex is the scapegoat. It'll all be buried with him.*

\*\*\*\*\*

Fox put on his reading glasses and leaned back in his chair, thinking about this most recent murder case. A thorough examination of Dex's backpack had revealed a secret pocket with two logbooks and a few portable memory devices, all of which would need to be analyzed by an expert. A cursory glance at them showed that the books may have been written in code, or at least, in a way that perhaps only Dex could understand.

As for Dex's autopsy and toxicology report, it was now in his hand. He was excited, hoping the results would help solidify the case against Vince Bonamo. Other preliminary aspects of the investigation had proven helpful. A struggle had apparently ensued prior to the murder as evidenced by broken glass, items found askew in the room, and some human hair lying around the body. There was no sign of forced entry at the sleep lab, so presumably, Dex had known his killer and allowed him inside, or maybe Bonamo had stolen or copied Dex's key to the lab since they were roommates. Lastly, no fingerprints of anyone other than sleep lab personnel had been found in the room.

He studied the report. The tox portion was unremarkable, with no evidence of drugs, alcohol, or toxic chemicals in Dex's body at the time of his death. However, the other section was interesting. Dex had bled to death from a long, clean cut to the throat. The assailant had obviously used a long, sharp knife. Contributing factors included blunt trauma to the head, which may have immobilized him first before the throat being slit. In addition, there was evidence of inflammation and hair loss on the back of his head.

The hair . . .

Fox drummed his right thumb on the desk, wondering how that had happened. Maybe it occurred as a result of the struggle or when the attacker jerked his head back to slit his throat.

*****

Bonamo's preliminary court appearance occurred ten days after his arrest. Actually this was his second court appearance and was an adversarial proceeding, including the prosecutor and Bonamo's attorneys. The hearing, requested by the Bonamo family, was their effort to test the existence of probable cause by allowing introduction of preliminary evidence, examination and cross-examination of a few witnesses, and limited disclosure of information. Fox made a point to attend, mainly to see who would show up from the Bonamo family in New Orleans and what their initial arguments would be. He wanted to learn everything he could about the Bonamos. They would stop at nothing to free their son.

The scene inside the hundred-year-old Oxford courthouse looked like something from a Perry Mason television show. The twelve-foot ceiling in the room and hard plaster walls allowed human voices to bounce around like ghosts at Halloween. Four ceiling fans slowly stirred the thick and lazy summer air.

Three attorneys from the Bonamo clan stood beside him dressed in what appeared to be thousand-dollar suits, making them stand out like tulips in the arctic tundra. Bonamo stood statue-like, never uttering a word except when specifically asked something by the judge.

One or two different occasions during the proceedings, the trio from New Orleans requested permission to approach the bench and speak privately with the judge. Fox figured that might be an effort to intimidate him or hint at the possibility of a bribe if he went easy on young Bonamo. Fortunately, the judge seemed indifferent to their efforts.

When the proceeding ended, Fox was about to leave when he noticed a flash of motion down by Bonamo and the boys. One of the attorneys standing beside Bonamo suddenly jumped back, grabbing the back of his head.

"What the hell are you doing!" he shouted.

Bonamo straightened back up but remained expressionless.

The judge was halfway to the door when it happened, and turned to see what was going on. "Is there something else, gentlemen?"

One of the other attorneys positioned himself between the judge and the altercation. "No sir. Just a little misunderstanding."

Fox was stunned. What had just happened? If he didn't know better, he would swear Bonamo had pulled the hair of the attorney standing beside him.

Pulling hair? During a court appearance? What a nutty stunt!

Fox watched the Bonamo party leave the courtroom. He rubbed his face. Maybe Bonamo was going to act crazy and plead insanity.

But pulling hair? Then he remembered the autopsy report. Dex's attacker had apparently pulled his hair.

Odd. Very odd.

# Chapter Thirty-one

*A*fter dinner on Tuesday, Seetha made her way back to the lab. She needed to work late, a direct result of Dex's unethical research and the resulting investigation. Dr. Jackson had given her a huge stack of paperwork to fill out from the Internal Audit and Animal Use committees. Fortunately Ms. O'Brien had agreed to let Sam stay at her house until Seetha got home.

She had been working on the pile of forms for days and was almost finished. The investigators' questions centered around what Seetha knew about the unapproved research and when. Each question seemed to ask the same thing except from a different angle. Filling out the paperwork had been a painstaking task. She tried her best to be totally honest with her answers on the paperwork, knowing full well it might lead to negative consequences for her career. No matter. She'd had enough dishonesty and unethical behavior to last a lifetime. After all, she had to live with herself and coming clean was part of that. This was a catharsis, and it felt good.

Seetha made her way into the parking lot. It was empty except for her car at the end of a line of puky-green biology department vans. The thick, humid late June air felt like a blanket against her skin. A warm southerly breeze caused the shrubbery along the side of the parking lot to dance rhythmically, making their shadows wiggle along the pavement like tongues of fire. A chill played up and down her spine even though it wasn't the slightest bit cool.

She tried to reassure herself that she had nothing to fear. It was just her emotions running wild again. Everything was all right now that Dex was dead and Bonamo had been arrested. Sure, he was out on bail now, but there was no link between her and Dex other than their workplace. Bonamo wouldn't have any reason to harm her, nor would he likely commit another crime now that he was in trouble with the law. She glanced at the shadows along the ground with increasing uneasiness. Then why was she so uneasy?

*It's just my imagination.*

Her phone rang. It was Fox. What timing.

"Hey dear, just checking on you. Is everything all right?"

"Oh yeah, I've got to work awhile to get all this mess filled out. I'll be glad when it's over."

"Me too. Maybe then we can spend more time together. Hey, do you need me to come up there to keep you company or walk you out to your car when you get through?"

"No, that's not necessary." Seetha neared the front door. "I'm pretty sure the campus security guys are around here, you know."

"Yeah sure," Fox said. "Probably watching a baseball game over at the guardhouse and eating doughnuts."

She giggled, knowing that was likely true.

"I think I might come up there anyway."

"Thanks, I appreciate the thought, but no, I need to work."

"Then why don't you just call me when you're done and I'll meet you at the door."

"No, that's really not necessary."

"What time do you think you'll be done?"

"Oh, I don't know. I've got to pick up Sam at ten, so it'll have to be before then."

"I worry about you. I may come on up there . . ."

"No, don't. I'd hate for you to have to do that."

*Jerome & Rosella Goddard*

"Will you at least call me when you get home?"

"Sure."

"Okay then, love you."

"Love you too."

After hanging up, Seetha stopped mid-stride, teetering on one leg and fishing in her purse for her keys. Just then, she noticed that the door was propped open with a rug.

She bent and examined the rug, which was pulled half-way out from the inside holding the front door open about five inches. Her hands were suddenly cold and clammy. Maybe the cleaning folks did this by accident . . .

She looked around, then carefully opened the door, flipping on the fluorescent lights in the foyer. She looked down the hall, "Hello? Anybody here?" then felt silly for saying it. Of course, no one was there. The place was quieter than a funeral home on an off-night.

Her shoes clicked noisily as she walked down the hall toward her office. Open but dark rooms off to the side contained all sorts of round and angular shadows. Her heart raced. *What's wrong with me? There's nothing in here.*

She stopped at the entrance to the third door down the hall. All the blood suddenly seemed to drain out of her head, making her feel faint. Rose petals dotted the floor, leading into the dark room.

"Oh, my God, Sam has relapsed." Her lips formed the words slowly, barely above a whisper. Then logic took hold. Sam was at Ms. O'Brien's. Or was she?

Seetha stood still, like a deer spotted by a hunter. She couldn't decide whether to bolt and run or stay and investigate.

Movement. Something moved inside the dark room. It was a shadow that moved, perhaps a hulk of a form in a chair.

Seetha's heart thudded deafeningly as she stared intently at the shadows. There was definitely the dark outline of a man sitting in a chair in the office. His arms were folded across his chest like he was judge, jury, and executioner. Was this Sam's fear memory playing in her head again? The dark form appeared stern and demanding. Words popped into Seetha's head. Was the man speaking, or was this all inside her head?

"I can't let you tell them," the man said. "I *won't* let you tell them." *Maybe I'm going crazy. The memories are loose again.*

Fox was the only one she trusted enough to reveal this kind of thing to. She reached for her phone, but the dark form shot from the chair and grabbed her. This was no dream. She tried to scream, but he quickly clamped his hand over her mouth. "Hey, bitch! Remember me?" His face was so close to her ear she could feel his hot breath.

Even though she could only see his steely forearm around her neck, she instantly knew who it was. *Rodney!*

The room was spinning; her heart pounded; she felt faint. Everything inside her was screaming, "run," but he held her too tightly. This was it. He had come back to kill her!

"You think you and Sam can get me out of your life that easily?" he growled. "I told you I was going to get you, just like I told her. I told her she mustn't tell anyone."

*Tell anyone what?* Seetha's mind whirled.

He wrenched her neck tighter. "I'm going to kill you first, then go get her."

Just then, a blur burst through the front door running down the hall straight toward Rodney. The blur wasn't half the size of Rodney, but lit in to him anyway.

Rodney released Seetha temporarily to fight his attacker. In that split second, she didn't know whether to run or stay. What was going on? Who had come to rescue her?

The scene reminded Seetha of Barney Fife fighting Godzilla. Rodney had a knife in his left hand and swung it wildly at the attacker, but the little guy dodged and darted, fighting back, and screaming, "You better not hurt her!"

"Oh my God." Seetha recognized the voice. It was Robbie Obergon!

Rodney would make mincemeat of the kid.

Her urge to run was in combat with her urge to stay and help. She sprinted a few paces down the hall toward the propped open front door, then started screaming at the top of her lungs. "Help! Help!" Maybe campus security was nearby. "Somebody help me! In here! Help!"

Finally, Rodney connected a right fist to Robbie's little head. The poor guy folded like a limp washrag onto the floor.

Rodney turned toward her. The white fluorescent lights of the hallway revealed the rage in his eyes.

She screamed and took off as fast as she could toward the door, but he caught and tackled her. The tile floor skinned both her knees and palms as she skidded across it. Rodney pounced on her back, then jerked her head upward with seeming delight. He held her head back momentarily, poised to either stab her in the neck or cut her throat.

Seetha knew she was about to die. She desperately tried to scream but nothing came out except a little squeak. Her perception of time changed. Everything was in slow motion except her mind. So this is how her life would end. How tragic. Everything that had happened over the last few months was for naught.

The shiny knife inched toward her throat.

Boom! A gunshot shattered the front door glass and Rodney collapsed onto her back as if suddenly trying to kiss her neck. But no kiss followed. He twitched a few times, then went limp, his heavy body weighing her down. Glass was scattered on the floor around her like fresh snow. She felt something warm and wet on her back—blood.

"Seetha, Seetha," a familiar voice shouted from outside, coming closer. It was Fox!

Seetha awkwardly rolled Rodney's body off her back and rose to her knees. She trembled and suddenly felt the need to go to the bathroom. Fox checked Rodney to make sure he was dead, then swept her up into his arms.

"It's all right. I'm here. It's over now."

Seetha was in a daze. All she could do was say the same thing over and over. "Oh my God, Oh my God, Oh my God. Robbie! He punched Robbie!"

"Robbie who?"

"Robbie Obergon. He tried to save me." She broke free from Fox and half-ran, half-stumbled back down the hall where the young boy lay. She found him unconscious, his face bloody and swollen.

"Call an ambulance," she hollered back to Fox.

Seetha sat down in the hall beside Robbie and gingerly lifted his head into her lap. "Robbie! Are you all right?"

His eyes opened, though the left one was barely visible due to swelling. Blood was caked around his nose and she feared it was broken.

Seetha's heart was filled with compassion for her secret admirer. Sure, the boy had a crush on her and in many ways had intruded in her life. But he only wanted to protect her. In some weird and twisted way, to him, she must have been the "unobtainable" whom he almost worshipped, was even willing to give his life for.

"Dr. Mathis!" he said as plainly as a beat-up kid could say. "Are you all right? What happened to that guy?"

She didn't know how much to tell him. "He's gone. Everything's fine now. Just try to relax. An ambulance is on its way."

"He tried to hurt you! I couldn't let him do that."

"Shh. Don't get upset. It's okay. He's gone. You protected me." Seetha

kissed him on the forehead then pulled his head close to her chest. "Thank you, Robbie."

Robbie relaxed in her arms. He forced a smile through swollen lips.

As soon as the EMTs arrived and attended to Robbie, Seetha again snuggled into Fox's chest. Her knees wobbled. The reality of what had just happened was sinking in.

She nuzzled her chin upward to be able to speak. "You remember, John, me telling you about the memory that jumped from Sam's head into mine during Dex' treatment?"

"Yes," Fox soothed.

"It was from a time Rodney had threatened her."

"Uh, huh."

"It's clear to me now. And it may be the key to her treatment and recovery. Rodney threatened to kill her if she told anyone of the abuse. And God knows what all else he threatened her with. Now, maybe if I can help Sam work through this key issue, she'll get better."

He pulled her out to arm's length. "Are you sure? I mean, shouldn't we leave that to Dr. Sinkot?"

"Yes, of course, we'll work with him on this." She smiled. "I just mean that this one piece of information may really be the root of many of her problems. She's felt a huge weight all these years. Guilt and shame for what all happened, plus fear and dread that if she told anybody, all her loved ones would die. Even her."

Fox pulled her in again. "Don't be afraid. It's going to be all right. I'll do whatever I can to help you and Sam."

Seetha reached up and kissed him. "I believe you."

## Chapter Thirty-two

*T*hree months later, on a Wednesday at lunch, Seetha sat in her office taking a break from the steady stream of sleep disorder patients. She popped the top on a Diet Coke and leaned back in her chair, reflecting on recent developments in her life over the last few months. Things were definitely getting better. The mental and emotional fog she had been encased in for so long was finally beginning to dissipate. She smiled when thinking how Samantha had recovered to a pre-Dex treatment "normal" and was continuing to make progress under Dr. Sinkot's care and some really cutting-edge anti-psychotic drugs. Additional treatment at another facility, as suggested by John Fox, had not been necessary thus far. Sure, Sam still struggled with bouts of disorganized thinking and urges to act out deviant behavior, but at least now she understood the underlying root causes of those urges. Now that Fox was around, the three of them were bonding into a wonderful family unit, something Sam had always said she wanted.

As for her future, Seetha was expecting Jonathon Fox to propose before long. At least, that's what they had been discussing lately. She couldn't have dreamed of finding a better man, and for her, marriage to him couldn't come soon enough. Sam had already given her approval.

Seetha looked out the doorway across the hall to Dex's former office. Traumatic memory research was over for good in her lab. After Heather McHann had sought help at the local hospital for her compulsions, the whole thing unraveled concerning Dex's manipulation through so-called memory "treatments." Based on Heather's comments

*Jerome & Rosella Goddard*

to her doctors and the police, they had confirmed that Dex implanted the urges through a video which she supposedly had already destroyed. Seetha made a mental note to call Heather herself and ask one more time if the infected video had indeed been destroyed.

Seetha took another drink from the Diet Coke, reflecting on the now-defunct research. Not that legitimate memory treatments weren't still needed in many ways. Even in her own life. Traumatic memories from her dad and Rodney still broke out inside her from time to time like a raging inferno, but recent events had changed their "status" in her life. She had finally come to realize that they couldn't kill her and would eventually pass. Sure, memories could temporarily terrorize her, even immobilize her, but they couldn't destroy her. Maybe sheer willpower could enable her to ride them out.

She thought about the research and animal rooms down the hall where Dex had been brutally murdered. Bonamo had been convicted of the crime and was now serving a life sentence in the state penitentiary. Thus far, no amount of Mafia bullying had mitigated his situation. Of course, that could change. The New Orleans Crime Syndicate might get him out tomorrow. During the investigation and trial, Fox had determined that Bonamo only intended to use Dex's research as a cover to kill Frankie Peterson, Hope's boyfriend. He apparently never intended to kill Dex until later, after the incident where Dex injected him with the memory treatment virus. According to Bonamo's own testimony after the trial, that event had made him furious and he just decided to "smoke" him. As for animal research, the internal investigation into Dex's unethical research had led to stricter controls on animal procurement and experimentation at the university, although Seetha's job had been spared. She didn't care one way or another. As soon as she could, she would leave the sleep disorders unit to become a full-time lecturer in the biology department. For her, teaching was a much safer, less stressful endeavor.

Robbie Obergon had fully recovered from his fight with Rodney and was now back in school and work as a student worker. In one of her visits with him at the hospital after Rodney's attack, he humbly admitted following her, both on campus and, at times, in a car. He also confessed that he had read her computer and hard-copy files on her desk at night on several occasions. According to him, he had only wanted to "know her" better. Seetha expressed her deepest gratitude to him and his family for saving her life. The poor boy was still in love with her, but apparently harmless. Harmless to her, anyway, but woe be on anyone who tried to harm her!

At one-thirty Dr. Sinkot called and Seetha smiled upon hearing his voice knowing she had come full circle concerning her assessment of the psychiatrist. She was now convinced he was actually a wonderful, compassionate physician who had his patient's interest at heart all the time. She realized that her earlier disagreements with him had been more about her instability than his professional qualifications.

"Hello, Dr. Sinkot, how are things going today over at the behavioral unit?"

"Fine, thank you. Busy as ever. I'll be glad when we can add additional staff and take some the load off me. Lots of trauma and broken families these days."

"I'm sure."

"I called to check on Sam."

"She's better. *Really* better. That new medicine you gave her seems to really help with the disorganized thought patterns. There's a new clarity about her."

"Glad to hear that. Is she still making progress in her speaking ability?"

"Yes, quite well. Not completely back to normal, but definitely making progress."

"Good. Very good. Well, I just wanted to check in. She's scheduled for an appointment next Friday, but I want you to call me right away if she starts showing any signs of regression."

"Yes. Sure, I will." Seetha swiped hair from her eyes. "I want you to know I really appreciate you calling and checking on Sam regularly."

"No problem. It's my job."

Seetha had a thought. "Dr. Sinkot, may I ask you a question?"

"Sure."

"I'm sure you've heard about all this stuff with Dex here at the university. I know you at least know about his attempted treatments on Sam because I told you about them awhile back. But I also mean his other, very complicated research into traumatic memory spread, treatment, and control."

"Yes, I've heard bits and pieces of his work from a variety of sources. Such a tragedy. He was apparently a brilliant researcher."

"Yes he was. Well, I wanted to get your opinion. Do you think scientists will ever be able to heal or remove traumatic memories from people?"

Long pause. "Don't know. I hope so, because I'll tell you one thing, they're serious business."

"You sound as if you've had personal experience."

"No. None personally."

"Then how would you know about how devastating the fear memories can be?"

"Secondary traumatic stress reactions. S-T-S-R."

"What's that?"

"Well, when we therapists are exposed to these stories of intense trauma and emotional pain, *we* sometimes have a difficult time getting the images of their trauma out of our minds. You wouldn't believe it.

Sometimes the accounts are so gross and perverted and unbelievably cruel . . . in some ways we re-live their terror and it affects us like PTSD, perhaps though, not quite as bad as the original trauma . . . though sometimes I wonder."

Seetha didn't have a clue how to respond to this new theory. She had no idea that therapists *listening* to patients re-counting their traumas could themselves become affected emotionally." She blinked. *Infected.*

*The memories infect their therapists.*

"Uh, wow. Is anything published on this phenomenon?"

"Yes, there's a real good book on treating traumatic memories by a man named John Wilson who provides great data supporting STSR, even though I personally don't need any supporting evidence. I've experienced it myself."

"Tell me more, I mean, if you don't mind."

"I can't reveal my own patient's stories, but I'll tell you this one amazing fact — in that book by Wilson, they did a survey and found that 64% of therapists listening to their patient's accounts of intense trauma actually had intrusive *re-living* of their patient's traumas."

Seetha fell silent.

"Weird, huh?"

"Unbelievable. Absolutely unbelievable."

"I guess it's just an occupational hazard." Sinkot seemed to be ready to move on.

Seetha's mind was whirling so fast trying to process this new information in light of Dex's research that she could barely continue the conversation anyway. "Okay, well, thanks so much for those comments. I need to think on it some more. But, like I said earlier, I'm very grateful that you call weekly checking on Sam. It means a lot to me and her both."

"Okay well, we'll be looking forward to seeing you next Friday."

"Yes, for sure, we'll be there."

"Goodbye."

*****

The biology department's philosophy club met that afternoon at three-o'clock. Seetha was eager to attend because this time she had a question, and her conversation with Dr. Sinkot had only reinforced that burning interest in getting the group's opinion. She wanted to let them analyze the subject of traumatic memories. Maybe their discussion would lend insights into what had happened over the past few months and why.

About ten people were in attendance. Duke Livermore, Meha Wu, several other graduate students, and of course, Jeremy Allen, the red-headed Einstein.

Things progressed slowly at first, with various physics questions being addressed such as the Big Bang and the expansion of space. Seetha zoned out, sipping on another Diet Coke; she wasn't all that interested in those things. Jeremy took the lead in answering most of the questions. She recalled Duke telling her how deep a thinker he was.

Seetha waited patiently for the right moment to ask her question. When the physics and math questions died down, she figured it was time for a biology question.

"I have a biology question."

"Okay, great," Jeremy said. "Biology is good. Let's hear it."

All eyes in the room trained on her. She suddenly had second thoughts. Maybe she shouldn't ask it after all. Word about her treating Sam with an experimental drug had surely gotten around by now. She looked at Duke, who smiled and nodded as if encouraging her to go ahead.

It was now or never. She stood up. Standing wasn't necessary for a philosophy club question, but Seetha figured it might help her get it out. "Well, as you guys know, we had an incident lately where a researcher in my lab was conducting experiments on both animals and humans concerning traumatic or fear memories. And you also probably know that he was murdered as a result of his entanglement with a Mafia family in New Orleans."

She shifted her weight and took a drink of her Diet Coke. "But there's more. Uh, something you may not know about the incident. I have to be honest with you, due to personal problems from my past, I became involved in the unethical research and did some things I'm now very ashamed of. Things went from bad to worse during a time span of about four months last spring and summer and several people were harmed by the research, including my own daughter."

She wiped her sweaty palms. "Anyway, that's not the point. I actually have a question for the group."

They looked at her with anticipation. Not one person appeared shocked at her previous comments. Of course, they knew about what had happened. Small town; small university. Everybody knew everything.

"I want to know your thoughts on traumatic memories and how they seem to get worse in a person's mind, even multiplying and spreading."

You could have heard a pin drop in the room.

She then went into lecture mode, carefully laying out the background science about memories, how they are made, and lastly traumatic memories and how they can torment people and even prompt them to "act out" the specific memory or action.

"That was one topic of my post-doc's illegal research. He explored why and how these memories do this. How they become animate and spread themselves in a human population."

She paused, searching for the right words. "His findings were bizarre. As best we can tell from piecing together some of his notes from a logbook—the ones he didn't destroy or encode—he reported that these memories are like viruses multiplying and infecting new people. He even suggested traumatic memories may be *alive* and have personhood."

She inhaled deeply and made her final point. "Lastly, from bits and pieces of conversations I had with him prior to his death, I think he theorized that the human brain may have some unknown ability to isolate and control traumatic memories, and people with a malfunctioning brain immune system go crazy because it lets the memories multiply unimpeded. I guess you could call them *viral* memories."

She paused again to let that sink in. "That's my question for you today. Are memories in fact alive, able to multiply, and do they take on 'personhood'? If so, how can it be? Wouldn't that totally shake up the foundation of all of biology? How can entities other than things with proteins, or cells and protoplasm be alive?"

Seetha sat back down. Duke gave her a wink of approval. Jeremy rubbed his hands together. "This is really cool stuff. What do you think folks? Let's talk about it."

A girl named Kaitlyn took the lead. "They're not really alive. It just seems that way. When the person dies, his or her memories die. They can't exist outside of a human."

Seetha shuddered, but didn't say a word, recalling the time she had "sensed" Sam's traumatic memories from five feet away. *So they can't live outside of a human, huh?*

"The post-doc's analogy with viruses is perfect," someone else offered. "Viruses can't live outside of a human or other host very long either, yet they're considered alive."

"I think memories *can* spread themselves," Meha Wu injected.

"And that's a characteristic of life, the ability to reproduce. Dr. Mathis just said that these memories can make other people do the same action, which essentially spreads that memory, keeping it alive."

"But there are traumatic memories that *don't* replicate," Duke countered. "Like certain fear memories. If you have a memory of a terrible fire, for example, and you were really scared, how could that repeat itself? The memory can't make a fire happen again. Or a tornado strike again."

"Some memories cause urges in people to act them out and some don't, I guess," Seetha said. "I know it doesn't make sense."

A tall, thin graduate student named William flung up his head and glared around at them all. "Hey, this reminds me of our discussion of demons a while back. A long time ago, people thought everything was a demon. Now we know better. There are scientific explanations for almost every phenomenon." He paused like a preacher waiting for just the right moment to say the main point in a sermon. "However, like I've said before, there *really might be* such things as demons. Remember, that psychiatrist, Dr. Prescott, said they might be real, and he's a highly educated and respected scientist."

Jeremy Allen eyes lit up. "Hey, that's *very* interesting. Back a long time ago, they thought that mysterious urges and promptings were demons. Maybe they were right."

Everybody looked at him. He turned his palms upward. "Maybe the only difference between a traumatic memory and a demon is its name or label."

Seetha was stunned. Little Einstein was right. No matter what people call them, memories are alive and can infect other people. Just as Dr. Sinkot had described therapists re-living their patient's traumatic memories. They had become infected.

Seetha sat back in the chair to let that thought sink in. Memories are alive. They have been from the beginning of humanity and will continue to be until the end of time.

*****

The next morning, Seetha was at the sleep clinic when a familiar face showed up. It was A.D., the lady with the beehive hairdo who had been a patient at the clinic several months earlier and who had later brought her grandson to the clinic. This time, she had two teenaged boys with her.

Tonya, the receptionist greeted them. "Hey, Miss A.D. Great to see you again. What can we do for you today?"

Seetha heard the conversation and walked toward them. A.D. was animated. "Oh, it's not for me this time." She stepped back and waved for the two boys to step forward. "Come on, boys, these people can help you."

"Hi, A.D.," Seetha extended a hand. A.D. sidestepped the hand and hugged her. "Why, hello, doctor." She nodded toward the tallest of the two boys. "You remember, Stephen, don't you?"

"Yes, of course." She shook his hand. "So nice to see you again."

"And this is Roger, his twin," A.D. continued.

She greeted him as well. "Nice to meet you, Roger. I didn't know Stephen had a twin."

The boys smiled, but Seetha noticed what appeared to be fear in their eyes.

A.D. started up again. "I've been telling Roger how much you and Dr. Poindexter helped me and Stephen with our traumatic memories, so I was hoping you could help him. Actually, both boys are suffering from it now."

Seetha wondered what might be bothering the teens, but that could wait a moment. What was especially disturbing was to hear her say

Dex had "helped her and Stephen." As best she could recall, A.D. had come in only a few times for treatment sessions with her or Nurse Frances. And Stephen had come in only once.

"Miss A.D., are you sure Dex worked with you and Stephen?"

"Oh, yes, he met with me several times in the evening and Stephen once or twice." She looked at Stephen momentarily, then smiled widely. "I think his treatments helped us more than anything. At least for me, with my terrible memories of that tornado last year." A questioning look appeared on her face. "Wasn't he just doing what you told him to? I mean, you're his boss."

Seetha rubbed her eyes. She didn't know how much to pursue the matter. Some things might be better left alone. "Did he by any chance hook one or both of you up to a machine or show you a video with squiggly lines or bright flashes of light?"

"Why, yes, he sure did."

"Did he ever give you an injection?" Seetha's fears were steadily increasing.

"Oh no, he asked one time, but I wouldn't let him do that." A.D. turned to Stephen. "Did he give you a shot?"

Stephen shook his head

A.D. paused as if trying to read Seetha's face. "Was that bad that we watched those squiggly line things?"

"No, not necessarily." She didn't know what else to say. Seetha sighed. Oh well, maybe it didn't matter. "Miss A.D., the main thing is that you're feeling better." She reached for the elderly lady's arm. "Did you hear about the terrible tragedy we had here concerning Dr. Poindexter?"

"Yes, I know about the murder. I read the paper, you know. Such a shame."

"Well, it certainly was a shame and a senseless waste of human life. Dex was smart and, uh . . . he certainly discovered some interesting things about sleep and memory."

A.D. lit up, looking back at the boys. "And that's why we're here again.

Seetha had no idea what to say next. "Uh, I guess we could talk informally for a few minutes and then plot a course of treatment if necessary." She pointed toward one of the side rooms. "Let's go in there."

Once inside the patient treatment room, A.D. immediately described the problem. "Roger and Stephen are having a hard time sleeping," she said. "They share a room upstairs and keep waking up throughout the night. And now that school's started again, it's beginning to affect their grades. That's why I brought them to you."

Seetha's mind whirled while A.D. talked, thinking of all the possibilities: teenaged boys, puberty, too much caffeine. One wakes up, then wakes the other one up, etc.

"What kind of dreams?" Seetha asked. "And which boy has them?"

"Oh, you don't understand." A.D. threw up her arms. "Nightmares. They both have nightmares."

That got Seetha's attention. "Both of you?" She alternated looking at the boys.

"Yes, ma'am," Stephen remarked.

"What sort of nightmares? Like some horror movie you guys just watched?"

Stephen shook his head. "No. Weird dreams, all different, but actually similar." Stephen glanced over at Roger. "It's like an unstoppable force pushing us along toward a disaster, but it always starts out with a terrible storm out on some river. One we've never even been on."

"Whoa." Seetha raised her hand, stopping him. "Let me clarify something before we go any further. "Which one of you has the recurring dream? Or, who has the dreams most often? And, I'm assuming, you then wake up your brother to tell him about it."

"No, Dr. Mathis," A.D. interrupted, that's what we're trying to tell you. They *both* have the dream at the *same time* and both wake up as a result of it."

Seetha's heart stood still. This had Dex written all over it. "The *same* dream? At the *same* time?"

They all three nodded.

Her mind raced, and she couldn't help thinking about this situation in terms of Dex's research. Both boys were probably infected with a traumatic memory. Perhaps it had infected Stephen during his treatments by Dex months ago and had now jumped to the other boy.

She tried to remain calm and not show her concern. "Okay, let's talk about it. So, I guess, the first thing I need to know is, have either one of you ever had a traumatic experience like a near-drowning event, car accident, or crime? Maybe this dream is a result of that."

"No," Stephen said. "Nothing like that."

"They've lived a fairly sheltered life," A.D. threw in.

Seetha was at a loss for words. What was she going to tell them? There was nothing she could do. She didn't understand the mysterious world Dex had uncovered. Worse yet, what was the prognosis? If Dex's theory was true, these boys were infected with viral memories that could spread to others. Not only that, but if either one of them had any defect in his brain immunity, then he would be vulnerable to serious mental illness, because the memories would multiply inside his head like some ungodly fungus or bacteria. She had seen that first-hand with her daughter Sam.

She leaned back in her chair and blew out a long breath. What on earth had Dex done? She had been content to let all that research die with him. But no, the memories were now loose. The toothpaste was out of its tube and she could think of no way to put it back.

Just then a thought hit her. This situation with the boys was one way Dex's infective memories had been released into the human population. Were there others? What about Heather? What if Heather had not destroyed the video Dex gave her?

Seetha asked Tonya to help A.D. and the boys fill out the necessary paperwork for a medical consult. Perhaps a clinical neuroscientist would be needed to evaluate the boys. One thing was for sure — this was way above her head. She wanted nothing to do with it.

She excused herself to go make the call to Heather. She had to find out the status of that infected video. Her pulse quickened, fearing the worst.

Heather picked up the call on the second ring. "Hello."

"Heather, this is Seetha Mathis."

"Oh hi, Dr. Mathis," she said.

"I know we haven't spoken much since Dex's death. I just wanted to check on you, and also discuss a particular matter with you."

"I'm fine. Actually getting better, I think. Thanks for asking."

"Are you still receiving treatment for the sleep-walking urges?"

"Yes, like I said, I think I'm better now. At least I *feel* better."

"Uh, well, it's probably none of my business, but I wanted to ask about the video Dex gave you, you know, the one we think originally implanted the sleep walking urges in you."

"How did you know about that?"

"Detective Fox." Seetha switched the phone to her other ear. "He also questioned me about incidents surrounding Dex's research and death, you know."

"Did he tell you it was an anger management video?"

"No, I don't think I knew the exact nature of the video."

"Well, it was, and I had a love-hate relationship with it ever since Dex gave it to me."

Seetha sensed something much worse was coming. "A love-hate relationship? What do you mean by that?"

"At first it scared me. I mean, wanting to watch the video all the time. I've always been a little OCD, but that compulsion scared me. But now, well, watching it helps me. It helps me tremendously by causing me to feel better about myself and to quit being so angry at the world. It sorta soothes my soul, so-to-speak."

"Do you watch it? Still?" Seetha trembled waiting for the answer.

"No, well, yes, I do, actually."

"So it's not destroyed. I was under the impression that your therapist and Detective Fox had both instructed you to destroy the thing."

Heather's voice suddenly became different, higher. "Why would I destroy something I love? Watching that video gives me great comfort and inner calm."

Seetha was dumbfounded, not knowing what to say next.

Heather continued, "In fact, guess what? I just recently did an experiment with the video to see if others are helped by it as much as I am."

*My God, where is this going?* "What did you do, Heather?" She tried to remain calm and not sound threatening. "What did you do with the video?"

"I put it out on YouTube in the self-help category."

Seetha collapsed back into her chair. The viral memories were for sure loose now.

"And guess what, Dr. Mathis?"

*Do I really want to hear this?* "What?"

"I just checked the website and it has received over a million hits. The little counter is spinning like a top. I guess others like it as much as I do."

About the Authors

Jerome Goddard grew up in Booneville, Mississippi and attended college at the University of Mississippi (B.A. and M.S.) and Mississippi State University (Ph.D.). He is currently an Extension Professor of Medical and Veterinary Entomology at Mississippi State University.

Rosella Goddard is from Iuka, Mississippi and has a B.A.E. from the University of Mississippi. She homeschooled their two sons and served over 25 years as a youth minister and Scoutmaster for Troop 99 in the Boy Scouts.

Jerome and Rosella reside in Starkville, Mississippi. They have two sons, Jerome II and Joseph, and daughters-in-law Lindsey and Lauren.